# The Kismet Pension

Melanie Gilbert

Copyright © 2025 by Melanie Ann Gilbert

Published by the author

ISBN 978-625-95881-8-6

Visit the author's website at
www.melanieanngilbert.com

All rights reserved.

All rights reserved. No part of this book may be reproduced or distributed in any form without prior written permission from the author, with the exception of non-commercial uses permitted by copyright law.

The story, all names, characters, and incidents portrayed in this production are fictitious. No identification with actual persons (living or deceased), places, buildings, and products is intended or should be inferred.

Cover design by Nskvsky

# A note about titles in Turkish

In Turkish culture, titles are very important.

Unless you know them well, a man's Christian name is usually followed by the word Bey (pronounced 'bay'). The equivalent for a woman is Hanum.

Children speaking to elders will always refer to them as Abi (big brother), Abla (big sister), Auntie, Uncle, Grandmother or Granddad (Dede), depending on how old they are. This includes everyone, not just actual relatives.

These terms will also be used by an adult speaking to someone older to whom they are close.

# 1

Fatma hurried along the lane, her plastic shoes splashing in the puddles left by the night's storm and spattering mud onto her baggy trousers. A shy sun was peering through the clouds and she was warm in the three layers of wool she was wearing. She was also puffing with the effort; she had never been slim and her comfortable size was not suited to rushing. But when Nazla had called and begged her to come over she sounded so miserable that Fatma had stopped only to tie her headscarf more firmly and pull on another cardigan before leaving the house. The month of March was, after all, the month of woes when the weather could change in the time it took to hang out the washing.

She passed through the open gate into the field that Nazla and her husband Osman referred to as The Orchard. Fatma herself had never thought it deserving of the title. While it certainly contained an abundance of fruit trees – apple, pear, pomegranate, quince, peach and even almond – these had been planted higgledy-piggledy and at various times. The result was a study in disorderliness. The almond trees had already exploded into a froth of pink blossom and an excited army of bees was going from flower to flower collecting pollen. Fatma pulled her headscarf up to cover all but her eyes and hastened through the field to the house behind.

At the side door a pair of lurid pink sports shoes told her Derya had already arrived. She kicked off her own shoes and entered the kitchen where she was welcomed by the rich aroma of deep-roasted coffee and the sight of Derya watching over the pot on the stove to make sure its contents did not boil. The three women had been friends since school and more than thirty years of shared history meant they were quite at home in each other's kitchens. What shocked Fatma was seeing Nazla sitting at the table with her head in her hands. Nazla had always been striking with her pale skin, thick chestnut hair and grey eyes. Now, her eyes were red and her cheeks shiny with tears.

'Nazla dear, whatever has happened?'

Nazla looked up and the sight of her friend prompted fresh sobs. 'Oh Fatma, I don't know what to do.' She took a deep breath and sniffed. 'You'll think me so stupid!'

Derya placed a tiny, beautifully decorated cup in front of Nazla. 'There, Nazla, drink that and you'll feel better.'

Nazla gave a weak smile.

'First, do tell us what is troubling you,' said Fatma, trying not to show her impatience. Had it been Derya sitting crying she would not have been so concerned, for Derya was prone to being emotional and even melodramatic. Nazla, on the other hand, was usually level-headed and sensible.

'We're going to be homeless!' she said now with a wail.

Fatma frowned. 'But *this* is your house, Nazla. How can you be homeless?'

Nazla took a deep breath. 'This house was Hasan Uncle's. He gave it to Osman when we got married.'

Fatma nodded; everyone knew that. Osman's uncle had built the house hoping to spend his retirement in the village where he grew up but after a lifetime devoted to teaching in the most prestigious schools in the capital he missed the bustle and excitement of the city. When he returned there the house was left at the mercy of winter storms and infestations of mice until Osman and Nazla fixed it up and moved in.

'So the house is yours,' said Fatma.

Nazla took a sip of coffee. She licked the shadow of foam that clung to her lip and sighed. 'Only in word. Hasan Uncle never got round to putting it in our name. I tried to get Osman to push him but whenever I mentioned it, he said there was no hurry. I think he was embarrassed to beg.'

Fatma snorted. How typical of a man, she thought, to put things off until later! Then something more pertinent occurred to her. 'But Hasan Uncle died last year, didn't he?'

'Yes, may he rest in peace! His wife called to give us the news and said she knew he had meant to give us the house. She said she'd see to it that it was officially transferred into Osman's name.'

Fatma waited. She still could not see why Nazla was so upset. 'That's good then, isn't it?'

Nazla lifted her chin and clicked her tongue to indicate it was not. 'The deed still hasn't been changed and that good lady died on Sunday, God rest her soul.' Tears spilled down her cheeks again. 'And now we're going to lose the house!'

Derya rushed over and put an arm around Nazla, making shushing noises to comfort her. Her own eyes were shiny with tears and she had tied the corners of her headscarf in a knot above her forehead so the ends flapped in consternation.

Fatma took another sip of the coffee and considered the situation. It was not good, but she thought there were still ways to redeem it.

'Who told you about her passing?'

'Her son called last night.'

'And did this man say anything about the house?'

Nazla shook her head and dabbed at her face with a paper napkin. 'And Osman said it would have been disrespectful to ask.'

'Maybe he doesn't know the house exists!' said Derya.

Fatma snorted again. 'If not, he's bound to come across the deed amongst his mother's papers. And if he doesn't, do you suggest Nazla just carries on living here hoping that someone doesn't turn up next year or in ten years' time to claim the house?' She frowned at the ridiculous suggestion and Derya went back to comforting Nazla. 'But if he's a decent person and you tell him what Hasan Uncle planned to do, he'll have to transfer the deed.'

'Do you think so?' Nazla looked hopefully at Fatma.

'Of course. It's not as though he's losing anything that was his! And a small house with a few donum of land in a village like Ortakoy is unlikely to interest someone from the city. What would he do with it?'

All three were silent as they contemplated this. Nazla took another sip of coffee. 'What if he expects us to pay something for it?' She looked round the room as though assessing its worth. 'The money Osman earns driving tourists around in the summer is barely enough to keep us and the bank would never give us a loan.'

'Didn't you say that the lady Hasan Uncle married was a wealthy widow? If so, her son will have inherited plenty and have no need of your money.'

'That's true.'

'Nazla dear, I understand your worries but you'll have to wait a decent amount of time, then Osman can call this man and explain the situation. I'm sure he'll be reasonable about it and if he isn't you'll have us and the whole village ready to take your side. He won't be allowed to sell your home!'

Nazla gave Fatma a weak smile and busied herself collecting the empty coffee cups and taking them to the sink. Usually when they finished their coffee they would turn the cups over for Derya to read their fortunes in the coffee grounds. Today it seemed nobody wanted to look into the future.

Nazla made a pot of tea and they talked of less distressing things like Derya's daughter Zeynep who was training to be a hairdresser and the wedding that was to take place in the village that weekend. Then Nazla's three daughters came home from school. Eda, the eldest, was quiet and well-mannered but the two younger ones burst into the kitchen like whirlwinds, arguing over whose fault it was that one of them had mud on her uniform. Fatma decided it was time to leave.

'Make sure you talk to Osman,' she urged Nazla from the door. 'He needs to get this sorted.' She managed to avoid adding that if he had sorted things earlier, they would not now be in the situation they were.

Fatma walked back along the lane at a more leisurely pace. Down in the valley a flock of seagulls was following a tractor as it ploughed the heavy soil ready for planting while other fields were already green with new growth. The mountains opposite still sported a cap of snow, unlike the slopes above the village which were kept warmer by air blowing off the sea. The view was constantly changing but reassuringly familiar. Fatma had known it her whole life and could not imagine living anywhere else. She felt thankful that unlike Nazla her own situation was straight-forward and her ownership of the little house her father had built and the guest house that stood beside it was undisputed.

She was almost home when she came across a girl dragging a goat whose belly was so round it was almost touching the ground. The girl's hair was as red as the anemones that were blooming on the verge.

'Hello, Leyla! When do you think she's going to have her baby?'

'Soon, Fatma Auntie. She can hardly walk.' The goat gave a plaintive bleat as though to confirm this.

'Why aren't you at school, child?'

'My mother's ill so I stayed at home to care for her.' Fatma knew that the girl's mother was more likely to be suffering the effects of one of her father's pummellings than any real illness. It was a well-known secret that Ibrahim the blacksmith drank too much and beat his wife but there was little anyone could do for the woman unless she chose to report her husband. Instead, they all kept an eye on Leyla and tried to make the child's life a little easier.

'Come by sometime and I'll give you some eggs. Our hens are laying more than we can eat!' Fatma said.

There were certainly some drawbacks to living in the village: the way people clung so obstinately to the past, for example, and the way they all felt the need to discuss your business. But the villagers also looked after their own and Fatma was sure they would support Osman and Nazla if necessary.

*

As he stepped out of the lift and crossed the fifth-floor landing to the apartment Harun thought he could smell his mother's perfume. He stood in front of the door and heard her voice exclaiming with delight at seeing him. He knew, though, that they were just memories triggered by the millions of times these things had happened in the past.

He unlocked the door and stepped into the entrance hall where it was instantly apparent that things had changed. The apartment had been shut up since the day he had come round and found his mother sitting in her favourite chair, dressed and coiffed but departed from this life. It had only been three days but the air was dense and stale and the place felt empty and a little uncared for.

He went into the living room and walked over to the picture window that offered the most magnificent view of Istanbul and the great Bosphorus waterway that split the city in two. His mother and father had moved into this apartment shortly after they married. When his father died, his mother refused to move somewhere smaller and much later when she married Hasan she insisted he move into her home. All because of this view.

Harun watched a ferry heading from the Asian shore toward the European, a pleasure boat taking visitors out to the islands. Once, he had loved gazing on it almost as much as his mother, but he was feeling morose. It had been a shock to lose her. She was seventy-seven years old but she had appeared healthy and there were no signs that her heart was planning to give out, or if there were she had not mentioned them. He had always been close to her, choosing to live just a few streets away so he could see her regularly. He missed her already and felt a sort of rootlessness now that the last link to his childhood was gone. There was a cousin of his father's in America who had visited once when he was young but apart from that he had no family except his wife and son.

He turned to his mother's antique writing desk that sat where she could enjoy the view. The papers in it were neatly arranged in files with stickers labelling their contents and he quickly found what he needed to register her death. He also found a file that said 'deeds' and took it to look at later. Closing the drawers, he took a last look at the view, admiring the way the sun had broken through the clouds to make a patina of light and shadow on the water. Then he left the apartment.

He walked along the streets where as a boy he had played, conjuring stories and games from their outlandish names: Grandad Galip Street, Captain Tom Tom Street, Throat Cutter Street. Now, he just tried to avoid the oily puddles and hoped he would get to the registry office before it was too busy. It was a vain hope. As he got near to the grand old building – the same one where his mother had married Hasan eight years before – he saw there were already crowds of people at the entrance. Inside, the queue for the Office of Births and Deaths came out of the door and down the corridor.

He joined the end of it and shuffled along with the others. Some had the crazed, sleep-deprived look of new parents, others looked like him – weighed down by the pain of loss. They were all resigned to the wait. It was a familiar part of life in a country that loved bureaucracy and was only warily beginning to embrace computers.

Finally it was Harun's turn and he handed over his mother's identity card and the doctor's confirmation of death. The young woman, her face impassive, peered at the screen; for her it was one passing in a long list she would log that day. He wanted to say, 'That was my mother! She was an amazing woman!' but he guessed she would just smile as though he were a little deranged and hurry to get him out of the office as soon as possible. He didn't blame her; spending all day registering deaths must make you a little immune to it.

He left the office and walked down the hill and across the Galata Bridge. He sighed at the sight of rubbish bobbing on the murky surface of the Golden Horn. Ahead he could see the minarets of Suleymaniye Mosque and the entrance to Sirkeci Station, once the final destination of the Orient Express. The history of the city had always fascinated him but today even that had lost its charm.

He turned into the Grand Bazaar and walked along the first street. It was early and the narrow lanes were not crowded yet. A number of shop owners offered their condolences as he passed. His own shop was several streets in, an average-sized unit for the Bazaar which meant tiny by normal retail standards, crammed with antique silver and brass and some reproductions for the tourists. His assistant, Talat, was behind the counter.

'Harun Bey! I wasn't expecting you today.'

'I hadn't planned to come in but I'm tired of sitting at home.'

'I'm sorry about your mother. She was a great lady.' The young man had already expressed his sympathies over the telephone when Harun had called him to ask him to take care of the shop and again when he had visited the house one evening with that express purpose.

'Thank you. Yes, she was. I'm grateful to you for looking after the place.' A quick glance around assured him that the shelves were free of dust, everything was well displayed and Talat was in the process of cataloguing some new arrivals he had bought at an auction the week before. 'I can see you have done a good job!'

The young man smiled broadly. When Harun took him on, Talat had been an awkward teenager and the other shop-owners had laughed and said he would never make a good salesman. But six years later Talat was a serious, hard-working young man capable of managing the shop alone but who didn't shirk the more mundane duties like dusting and stock-taking. By contrast the cocky young men hired by the other businesses rarely lasted a year before they thought themselves worthy of a more prestigious job or a higher salary, or before the boss fired them for one or other misdemeanour.

Harun examined the new pieces – a large brass samovar and an ornate mirror – and they discussed which customers might be interested in buying them. Although the shop was small they sold to people all over the country and even some collectors abroad. The internet had allowed the business to expand in a way he could not have imagined when he first opened it. But today, even the prospect of a profitable sale and a happy customer could not lift his mood.

He left Talat and wove his way through the narrow alleys, now thronged with tourists, to his favourite restaurant. He ordered Sultan's delight – a dish of lamb on a bed of pureed eggplant – and a sweet Turkish coffee. While he waited, he picked up a magazine left by a previous diner and flicked through it. The headline 'The best medicine for melancholy' caught his eye.

His own ennui could not be attributed solely to the loss of his mother since it had started several months before. His wife, Zuhal, had noticed and thought it so out-of-character that she suggested he see someone – a doctor or a counsellor. Harun was a modern man who tried hard to read Zuhal's moods and show empathy for others, but he was not good at talking about his own feelings and had not followed her advice. Now, though, the article in the magazine caught his attention and he started to read. By the time his food arrived, he was so engrossed that he propped the magazine against the salt cellar and continued reading as he ate. It was not what he had expected.

# 2

The swallows always arrived before the tourists. The year the Kismet Pension was built they gathered under the eaves and made their nests before the walls were even whitewashed and they had returned every year since. They were back again and fixing up their nests with mud from a puddle by the chicken coop. Fatma watched them swooping down and waiting their turn to scoop up the dirt, then fluttering up and clinging to the wall to carry out their home repairs. She was pleased to see them. In her mind they had become a sort of omen: if the birds returned the guests would too.

The Kismet Pension was the first and only guest house in Ortakoy and Fatma was its proud owner. Her pride was quite justifiable, given the amount of opposition she had faced to build it. When she first had the idea even she was not sure if it would work. Tourism was taking off down in the town but the village was a little far out, the ruins still largely unexplored, and the road to the beach was not for the faint-hearted. But she had had a hunch and Fatma had always been one to follow her instincts.

Earlier, when she left school she had scandalised her mother by refusing to stay at home and learn the secrets of running a house and taking care of a family, choosing instead to help her father on the farm. It was not unusual for women to work in the fields but usually their role was confined to planting and picking, monotonous work for which they had more patience and dexterity than men. But Fatma's progressive father, the esteemed Suleyman Bey, happily taught his daughter everything about farming, from when to plant and how to care for each crop to how to apply for a grant from the Ministry of Agriculture.

She learned so well that when her beloved Baba died, she easily took on the task of running the farm alone. By that time she was married but her husband Mehmet, who had grown up in the town, had little interest in farming, or indeed in anything that resembled hard work. Fatma managed admirably by herself but without her father's gentle presence she soon became disillusioned with farming and came up with the idea for the Kismet.

She knew from the start that her mother would be one of her toughest adversaries since the project would require them to sell the land down in the valley and Melahat, like most villagers, equated land with wealth. Fatma planned her campaign carefully. First she dropped hints about how tired she was and how worried about the falling returns in farming. Then she started to idly speculate about the future of her children, Ahmet and Melek, a calculated move as Melahat loved her grandchildren. Fatma told her mother about the farmers who were trying to diversify by planting pomegranate trees which took seven years or more to give a good crop, and the pioneer who had set up an ostrich farm, only to see the birds all die of a mystery illness.

When she finally laid out her plan, her mother had indeed tried to veto any sale of land but Fatma reminded her that she had put up little objection to her sister, Hilal, selling her share of the land when she got married. Powerless in the face of Fatma's arguments her mother had given in, though she had shown her disapproval by going to stay with Hilal in town for the whole time the guest house was being built.

Fatma's husband, Mehmet, had been easier to win over. Once she had reassured him that his role in the new venture would be mainly collecting guests from the bus station in town and driving those brave enough to face the journey down to the beach, he readily accepted it.

There had been others who objected to her plan, villagers who Fatma recognised as falling into two groups: those who thought a woman should know her place and not upset the traditional order of things and those who were just plain jealous. Fortunately, during her foray into farming she had got used to disapproval and learned to give little thought to what people said about her.

The Kismet Pension had now opened its doors to guests for eight summers. It was rarely full but the procession of visitors was steady enough for it to be counted a success. For those touring the country, it offered a handy place to rest between visits to better-known sites; others came to escape the English breakfast and pie and chips commercialism of the local resort; and in spring and autumn the pension provided a suitable base for the botanists who tramped the mountain paths in their stout shoes and shower-proof jackets hoping to find a new species of orchid.

Now, watching the swallows fixing their nests, Fatma thought of the work that needed to be done to get the pension ready for another season. Together with Derya, who as well as being her friend also helped out at the pension, she would clean up the dust and cobwebs that had gathered over the winter. The linen and curtains would all need washing and the rugs beating out. Mehmet and Ahmet would be called upon to unstick windows swollen by the rains and fix any leaking taps. But this year there was a much larger problem to be tackled: that of the large muddy hole at the back of the pension.

The previous summer when the heat was driving people to sit under the air conditioning in their rooms or escape for the day to the beach, Fatma had come up with idea of building a swimming pool at the pension. She had spent several months considering it, before, convinced that it would attract more customers and perhaps even persuade those who came to stay longer, she had broached the subject with her family.

She had not expected the improvement to be totally without trouble. Her mother objected on the grounds that a swimming pool would encourage debauchery and bring damnation on them all – possibilities that

Fatma was happy to dismiss.

Ismail, the builder she had used to build the pension and to whom she had returned to discuss the feasibility of adding a swimming pool, raised the more practical problem of getting a digger into the back garden. His solution was to dig the ground by hand, though he had warned that it would take longer. Even so, the current rate of progress was making Fatma nervous. The problem was that the two men Ismail sent had turned up with their meagre possessions in a couple of plastic bags and taken up residence in one of the rooms, then spent most of their time drinking tea and chatting.

Fatma left the swallows to their work and went round to take another look. The men were once more sitting on upturned buckets with the teapot boiling on a small gas burner beside them.

'How's the work coming on?' she asked.

The taller man, who did most of the talking, sucked his teeth. 'It's tricky, Fatma Abla.' Abla – big sister – was meant to show respect and yet this man managed to make it sound mocking.

'I only asked for a small pool,' said Fatma. 'You have built one before, I suppose?' She glared at the other man who was less self-assured.

He looked into his glass of tea and left his friend to answer.

'Of course. We've done hundreds.'

'Then what is the problem?'

'This digging by hand takes time. And the ground is soft. The sides need to be straight so we can put up shuttering but they keep crumbling. It's wet too.

I think water is leaking in from the ditch there.' He pointed to the small stream that ran down the side of the pension.

'You might make better progress if you spent more time working and less time drinking tea,' said Fatma.

The man held up his glass and inspected it. 'If there is tea, there is hope!' he said, quoting a popular saying. 'You wouldn't deny us tea, would you, Abla?' He grinned showing his teeth, which were stained dark brown.

'It's fine to take a break and drink tea when you've done some work but you only just finished breakfast! I'm going to speak to Ismail – he's an old friend of mine, you know.' It was true she and Ismail had been at the village school together, which was why she had gone to him in the first place. 'I'm going to tell him I'm not happy with the work and ask him to send some other workers.'

The man with the bad teeth shrugged. The other one put down his glass and stood up. Fatma turned and stomped back towards the little house beside the pension, irritated by the men's laziness and frustrated by a feeling of powerlessness. She was not confident that speaking with Ismail would bring results. He had bigger and more important jobs on the go and probably could not spare any other workers. It had even occurred to her that he might have sent these two because they were so inept as to be useless elsewhere.

Somehow she had to find a way to get the work done. The way it looked at the moment, the pool would certainly not attract any guests and could even put off any who were thinking of staying.

\*

When Harun arrived home he found his wife Zuhal in the kitchen making helva. The sweet smell tickled his nostrils.

'I'm going to take this round to all the neighbours,' she said. It was a tradition when someone died – something sweet to make up for the sorrow. 'Was it difficult, my love, going back to the apartment?'

'It was strange,' he said, 'but it feels good to have taken the first step in sorting things out.' Actually he was feeling more positive than he had for some time.

The article he had read in the lokanta had not been suggesting drugs or even counselling for melancholy; the 'medicine' of the title was a visit to a retreat where burned-out city dwellers could reconnect with nature and enjoy activities such as hiking, bird-watching and yoga. Harun was not keen on joining groups and even shunned guided tours of ancient sites in favour of exploring alone and letting his imagination conjure up its own images, but he liked the idea of getting away from the complications of modern life. They usually took their summer holiday at one of the fashionable resorts where the well-off sipped cocktails and watched for celebrities in beach clubs with specially-imported sand. This year, he thought, they should go somewhere quiet and unsophisticated where they could enjoy simpler pleasures.

Zuhal gave him a glass of tea and a dish of helva and picked up a tray bearing more plates. 'I'll start dinner when I come back,' she said. 'Help yourself to more tea.'

Harun nodded and smiled. He was lost in thought,

wondering if he could persuade her to try camping.

He took his plate and glass and sat at the dining table with the file his mother had marked 'deeds'. He opened it and saw the top page was the deed to the apartment overlooking the Bosphorus, which had been changed into his mother's name after his father's death and would now be changed into his. He didn't plan to sell the apartment. It was worth a lot of money and should be passed on to his son, Barish. He thought they might take out the better antiques and rent it, perhaps to a foreigner working in one of the nearby embassies.

Beneath the apartment's title deed was another property deed. It was in the name of Hasan Chelik and was for a piece of land almost four donum in size, situated in the village of Ortakoy. Harun examined the deed but apart from parcel and plot numbers it gave no further information. The next page was a revision of the deed which showed that a house had been built on the land.

He remembered Hasan talking of his village and his early childhood there before he left to continue his studies in the city. He had told Harun how he tried to fit back into the village when he retired but was lonely. Harun had assumed the old man had given his property there to relatives but he saw this was not the case. He had still owned the land when he died and since his possessions had passed to his wife and hers would now pass to Harun, he found himself the owner of land and a house in a place he had never visited. He felt a flutter of excitement.

He knew the village was on the Mediterranean

coast. As a student, he and a friend had taken a road trip through that area and he recalled pine-clad mountains, turquoise bays and the overpowering smells of oleander and jasmine. He opened his laptop and searched for Ortakoy. It was a common name and the result brought up villages and towns all over the country. He narrowed his search to the Mediterranean region and found Hasan's Ortakoy on a map, close to the sea and not far from one of the towns that he knew had embraced the tourist industry enthusiastically. There was not much information about the place but a page written by an American amateur historian mentioned the ruins there and a yachting site suggested the secluded Cold Water Bay just below the village as a perfect overnight stop for sailors. There was a picture of a shingle beach fringed with olive and pine trees and water so clear you could see the stones on the bottom.

When Zuhal returned after almost an hour Harun was feverishly checking things on the computer. The glass of tea and helva sat untouched on the table.

'You look a little flushed, my love, what's the matter?' She felt his brow. 'Do you have a temperature?'

'No, Zuhal, I'm not ill but you might think me a little deranged. I've had an idea, something quite radical, but I haven't felt this enthusiastic about anything in a long while. I hardly dare talk about it in case it isn't possible.'

Zuhal waited. 'So are you going to tell me about it?'

'I am – of course, I am. I'm just thinking where to

start. Have you heard of ecotourism and retreats?'

'Yes. Oya was invited to give yoga classes at a retreat last summer. She didn't go but the place looked amazing. I can ask her the name of it if you want to try one.'

'I don't want to go to a retreat; I want to open one!' Harun laughed at his wife's look of confusion. 'Hasan Uncle owned a plot in the village and that land now belongs to us. It's close to one of the resorts there and the scenery is stunning. How would you like to paint these landscapes?' He turned his laptop to reveal the picture of the bay.

Zuhal was an artist and her paintings were filled with bold colours. 'It's beautiful, but I still don't understand quite what you have in mind.'

Harun held up the magazine, open to the feature on the retreat. 'This article describes these places that offer trekking, yoga, craft activities, things like that. People fed up with the city go there to de-stress and recharge their batteries. It says it's the latest boom in tourism.'

'And you want to set up a retreat on Hasan Uncle's land?'

'If it's suitable, yes. Goodness knows there are enough people in this city who need something to lift their spirits. I should know, I'm one of them!'

'And what experience do you have of the hospitality industry?'

'My dear, hospitality is in our blood! You know the saying "A guest comes with ten blessings, eats one and leaves nine"?'

'Yes, and there is another one that goes "The

master of the house is the servant of the guest"!' said Zuhal. 'It's not an easy business, you know.'

'I know that but I already work with people in the shop.'

'And talking of the shop, what do you plan to do with that while you go swanning off to the other end of the country?'

'Talat will take care of it. He's ready for a bit more of a challenge and I've taught him well, Zuhal.' He picked up a piece of helva, round and smooth like a pebble, and put it in his mouth.

'And are you planning on opening your retreat this year? It's already April and the tourist season starts in a few weeks.'

'That is a good point. And it's why I've been looking at these!' He clicked a button on the computer and a new page came up. It showed pictures of wooden cabins with small front porches and shingled roofs. 'They're pre-built, put together on site in a day and you don't need planning permission.'

'That's clever but will they be comfortable? These people might want to get back to nature but they don't want to sleep in a hut.'

'The chalets have electricity and running water. They can be fitted with air conditioning and insect screens and with your talent for decorating, my darling, I'm sure you can make them charming and cosy.' Harun knew the opportunity to use her skill for interior design would appeal to his wife.

'So you have it all thought out!' Zuhal shook her head but Harun could see his enthusiasm was beginning to infect her.

'In theory but the important thing is to see the land as soon as possible so we know whether or not it's suitable. Which is why I thought I'd fly down there tomorrow.'

'Tomorrow? But I have lessons tomorrow!' Zuhal taught art at a nearby college.

'I guessed you might. That's why I thought I'd go down by myself and check it out. If it looks promising you and Barish can fly down at the weekend and see what you think. I don't know about you, my dear, but I have a really good feeling about this!'

# 3

Harun parked the rental car at the side of the road and looked around. The narrow lane widened here to make a sort of square flanked on one side by a shop and a coffee house. On the other side were houses in the typical village style: squat, flat-roofed with small windows and white-washed walls. They sat in gardens, most of which had a vegetable patch and a few chickens scratching round.

Two old men sitting at a table outside the coffee house were watching Harun with interest. He got out of the car, shut the door and pressed the button to lock it. There was a loud thwack as the doors locked and he felt clumsy and inept, sure that nobody round here locked their car. He pressed the key fob again and the noise was accompanied by the lights flashing as the car unlocked. He smiled apologetically at the two old men, one of whom pushed a hand under his woollen hat and started scratching his head.

Feeling awkward and not wanting to attract too much attention he headed for the shop. The space in front of the door was filled with boxes of vegetables, shovels, rolls of plastic sheeting and bags of logs.

Inside it was gloomy and it took his eyes a moment to adjust but when they did he saw the shelves were crammed with things – tins and packets of foodstuff, toiletries, candles, socks; he even saw some children's toys. He took a bottle of soda from one of the fridges and put it on the counter. The man standing behind it had bright blue eyes and a thatch of white hair.

'Good day, Sir. Do you need anything else?'

'Yes, I wonder if you could help me. Do you know where Osman Chelik lives? I was hoping to speak to him.'

The man smiled. 'Round here everyone knows everyone! Where are you from?' He moved a box of batteries and a pile of letters to reveal a telephone on the counter.

'I'm from Istanbul. I flew down this morning. I've come to—' He stopped. He'd been about to tell the man about inheriting the land and his plans for it but a voice in his head told him to be cautious. Aside from what the locals might think, even with a paper from the land registry office in town showing the location of the plot he had been unable to find it and still did not know if it was suitable. 'I'm hoping to speak to Osman about his uncle, Hasan.'

The shop owner had already dialled a number and Harun heard it ring a few times and then stop as someone answered it.

'Osman, my friend, there's a gentleman in the shop who'd like to speak to you.' There was a muffled response that Harun couldn't make out, then the man with the blue eyes asked, 'Who shall I tell him is looking for him?'

'Harun Karajan, Kadriye's son.'

The shopkeeper passed on the information, then nodded and murmured something Harun didn't catch before ending the call.

'Osman will be here soon. He asked if you would wait in the coffee house just along the street.' The man pointed unnecessarily. Harun thanked him, paid for the bottle of soda and went next door.

Inside the coffee house the air was thick with steam and cigarette smoke. As he had expected the place went quiet when he entered, cups stopped half-way to mouths, backgammon chips paused mid-move. He gave his most amiable smile and focused on the man standing by the stove drying cups with a cloth.

'A sweet coffee please. I'll sit outside.' He stepped back out, relieved to escape the heavy air and the scrutiny. It felt strange to be an outsider. In Istanbul he was well-known in the Grand Bazaar and at the auction houses he frequented. He and Zuhal even tended to visit the same two or three restaurants where they were on first name terms with the owners. His coffee arrived and he inhaled the spicy aroma; at least that was familiar.

As he waited for Osman, he tried not to get too excited. He had not seen the land but the village was even better than he could have hoped. Barely half an hour's drive from town, it still managed to seem cut off from the bustle of modern life, as witnessed by all the men sitting round drinking coffee in the middle of the day. The view across the valley and of the mountains opposite was breathtaking and there was a smell that pervaded the place, a combination of pine resin, wild herbs and the smell of the earth itself that made his lungs expand.

'Harun Bey, I think,' said a man, waking him from his reverie.

'Osman, brother.' He jumped up and shook the man's hand. 'We're almost related. Your uncle was a special man and brought my mother a lot of happiness. Us too – we were very fond of him.'

Osman nodded. His face was soft and pink and unlike most of the men Harun had seen inside he did not have a moustache. 'Hasan Uncle was a very fine man. I'm sorry not to have met your mother and I'm sorry for your loss. Bashiniz sa-olsun,' he said. May your wound be healed.

Harun felt the now-familiar stab of pain at the reminder that his mother was gone. It was not as sharp as it had been though. 'Thank you. To tell you the truth, I think she lost her passion for life when Hasan Uncle died. That's what my wife said and I realised she was right. Women have more of a sense for this sort of thing, don't you think?'

'You are right, Harun Bey.' Osman was still standing, fiddling with the edge of the old wool jacket he was wearing.

'Please sit down, my friend. I apologise for not calling to let you know I was coming but it was a spur of the moment decision, a whim, you might say.'

'You are welcome here any time,' said Osman sitting down. The proprietor came out and placed a cup of coffee and a glass of water in front of him, though Harun had not seen Osman order anything.

'That's good to know, especially as I might be spending more time here. I have a plan, you see, for the land that belonged to Hasan Uncle.'

Osman visibly flinched. He was twisting the button of his jacket which was hanging by a couple of threads. 'So... your mother didn't speak to you about the land?'

'No, she never mentioned it! I only found out about it yesterday when I was going through her papers. I happened to have just read something about people wanting to spend time away from the city and the pressures of modern life and how there are special retreats springing up to cater for them—'

'You see the thing is, Harun Bey, that plot is my home. Hasan Uncle gave it to me when I got married but we never got round to changing the name on the deeds and when your mother – God rest her soul – called to tell me of his death she said she would see it was done.' The last thread snapped and the button came off. Osman looked at it miserably and slipped it into his pocket.

Harun felt his bubble of excitement burst. Everything had seemed so perfect, as though the universe were pushing him in this direction. Now it seemed the path had come to a dead end. But looking at Osman and seeing the misery in the man's eyes he realised his disappointment was churlish. 'Oh, I'm so sorry. I had no idea. How stupid of me! Have no fear, my friend, I will make sure that Hasan Uncle's wishes are carried out.'

Osman looked at him uncertainly. 'Do you mean that?'

'Of course! The land should be yours. Mine was just a silly idea that I dreamed up and I can always look for another place to do it. Now I'm here, we can go to the land registry office in town and change the name on the title deed.' Harun remembered the thrill he had felt earlier in the day when he visited that place and gave the clerk the details of 'his' land.

Osman took a sip of his coffee and licked the froth from his lips.

'We can go this afternoon if you like.'

'No, it can wait. We must go home and tell my wife. She's been beside herself with worry since we heard of your mother's passing. We didn't know that you would be such a gentleman. We thought we might lose our home!'

Harun felt his spirits lifting at the knowledge that he was doing the right thing. It was true, he could look for another place to build a retreat and what was moving your plans when compared to the threat of losing your home?

'Where are you staying? You must stay with us. You can get to know the village a bit better. And if you want to look for another piece of land…'

'I have a hotel booked in town. I left my things there earlier.'

'I won't hear of it! My wife will be disappointed if you don't stay with us!' Osman had finished his coffee and was on his feet. 'Come on. Let's go and see her now!'

'But we haven't paid the bill.'

Osman made a noise that sounded like Pfff. 'I have a tab with Ali. I'll pay him later.'

They both got in Harun's rental car and on Osman's direction he turned it around and headed back to the mosque and onto the road that he had driven up and down before.

'Pull over here!' Osman ordered, pointing to a gate that was half-open, hanging crookedly.

He got out of the car and headed into the field. Harun took in the view before following him up the path between the fruit trees, trying not to think what a perfect spot this would have made for a retreat.

'This is the orchard. See? We have apple trees, pomegranates, apricots, peaches, almonds, those are the ones with the blossom on,' he said excitedly, pointing at the various trees. At the back of the field, they followed the path between two poplars and came out in front of a pretty, two-storey house.

Osman started shouting, 'Nazla! Nazla! Look who I've brought.'

He went round the side of the house, pushed open the door and went in. Harun waited. He thought Osman's wife might need a moment to understand that he had not come to turf her out of the house. He looked at the orchard and the pine-covered slopes above it. An idea was starting to form in his mind.

\*

It was with some difficulty – and the promise that he would be back to stay the following day – that Harun managed to persuade Osman to let him return to the hotel for the evening. He was touched by their hospitality but was emotionally drained and wanted only to speak to Zuhal on the phone and then sit quietly in the bar with a whisky or two to consider everything that had happened.

'What's the village like?' was Zuhal's first question when she answered the phone.

'It's perfect!' said Harun.

'And Hasan Granddad's plot?'

'It's an orchard with a fantastic view.'

'That sounds promising!'

'Unfortunately, his nephew lives there with his family and Hasan promised the plot to them years ago.'

'Oh dear. Are you very disappointed, my love?'

Harun roared with laughter. 'Not at all, because we've come to a wonderful agreement. Osman's going to have the back field and the house and I'm going to build on the orchard and give him a job as manager!'

\*

Fatma tasted a spoonful of the soup she was stirring and tried to decide if it needed more salt. She sighed. She knew that no matter how much care she took over the meal her sister would find fault in it. It was Hilal's way. Even on the telephone that morning she had managed to make Fatma feel bad.

'Selam, Fatma Abla. Mother says it's so long since you called her there must be something wrong and she wants to come and check on you all.'

'But I called her two days ago!' Fatma was annoyed with herself for letting Hilal rile her. Their mother divided her time between Hilal's house in town and the village and Fatma knew the real reason she wanted to come back now was to attend the upcoming wedding celebrations.

'Well anyway, I've said we'll drive her up to you tomorrow evening, though it means we'll have to get lame Selim to watch the shop.' Hilal's husband, Jemal, had run a small shop selling cigarettes, sweets and drinks. Hilal had shown little interest in the shop until Jemal was knocked off his scooter late one night returning from a rather dubious bar and left her a widow, a role she embraced enthusiastically. She reinvented Jemal as a loving husband and father and took over the running of his shop with their son, Mesut.

'It'll be lovely to see you,' Fatma had said, though now as she added a pinch of salt to the soup she wished she could have sent Mehmet down to collect her mother and avoided all this fuss. Her dear father, God bless his soul, had told her that Hilal's constant criticism stemmed from her own insecurity but it was still hard to swallow, especially since as the younger sister she should have shown Fatma more respect.

Melek came into the kitchen. 'When are Hilal Auntie and Grandma coming?'

'She said they'd be here about six.' Fatma took out plates and cutlery and put them on the table. 'I hope your father isn't late. I reminded him this morning but you know what he's like when he gets involved in a game.'

Mehmet spent most afternoons and some evenings in the coffee house, playing backgammon and putting the world to rights with his friends.

Fatma shook her head. 'And I asked your brother

to go round and chivvy along those idiots working on the pool but I expect he's just joined them in drinking tea and idling.'

Melek set the table and cut bread. Fatma took a large jar from under the sink and spooned pickles into a bowl. She had just taken the rice off the cooker and covered the pan with a muslin cloth when they heard the sound of a car outside. Fatma watched from the door as Melek ran out and helped her grandmother heave herself out of the passenger seat. The old lady was short and round and Melek had to bend to kiss her cheek.

'Hello my lamb, have you grown since I left?' It was barely a month since Melahat had left the village but she said this every time she returned.

'Hello Grandma. Welcome.' Melek turned to her aunt who had emerged from the back seat of the car. Hilal was only slightly taller than their mother and slightly rounder too.

'Hello Auntie Hilal. You are well come!'

'Hosh bulduk. We found it well,' replied Hilal in the traditional way. Mesut got out of the driver's seat, gave Melek's cheek a quick pinch and went off to find Ahmet.

Fatma hugged her mother and sister and followed them through to the kitchen. Melahat had lived in the house all her married life and Hilal had grown up there and they treated it proprietarily.

'Well sister, how have you been?' asked Fatma, readying herself for a list of complaints.

'Ay! How can I tell you? So much has been happening, you can't imagine.' Hilal never missed a chance to point out how exciting the town was in comparison to the village.

'Everyone's upset about the changes to the bus station.'

Their shop was tucked into the back of the bus station and most of its customers came from there. The old terminal had recently been knocked down and a smart new one was being built in its place but until it was ready the long-distance buses were all stopping at a petrol station on the edge of town.

'We're all losing business. Mesut brought it up at a meeting today but the head of the Chamber of Commerce said the only thing to do is wait. And I don't feel well at all. I think it's my heart – it feels as if someone is squeezing it, though it could be my lungs because I have trouble breathing when I stand up. The new doctor says if I lose some weight I'll feel better but when I try to diet I feel weak so I persuaded him to give me more of those tablets. They help a little…'

'We could all do with losing some weight, Hilal,' said Fatma, 'but it's not easy, I know. It's all the bread we eat.' She could have added 'and in your case the chocolates and candy'; Hilal had always had a sweet tooth and the shop provided her with an endless supply of sugary treats. Fatma knew better, though, than to antagonize her sister.

Mehmet came in, bringing with him cool air and a strong smell of cigarette smoke that made Fatma wrinkle her nose.

'Greetings Melahat Mother! Welcome Hilal,' he said, laying a hand on his sister-in-law's shoulder. Mehmet had always had a knack for charming

Fatma's mother and sister and both women smiled warmly at him.

'The food's ready,' said Fatma. 'Shall we eat straight away?'

As they ate Mehmet filled Melahat in on the village gossip and Hilal quizzed Melek about her grades at school.

'Of course,' Fatma heard her say, 'Mesut would have gone to high school if his father, may he rest in peace, had not been taken from us.' Mesut himself was busy wiping a piece of bread round his bowl having finished a second serving of soup and did not appear to hear his mother's dubious claim.

Hilal suggested that the dry beans might have needed a little more cooking and that the meat was a little on the tough side but she managed to eat a large plate of it nonetheless. When they had all finished, Mehmet and the boys trailed off to the sitting room calling 'Health to your hand!' in thanks for the food, and Melek cleared the table, washed the dishes and went to her room to do homework.

Fatma put the teapot on the stove to boil. She was just thinking that her sister was in a better mood than usual when Hilal gave a dramatic gasp and said, 'Dear Abla, are you very upset about Osman's orchard?'

Fatma felt a pang of guilt. She had been busy with Derya getting the pension ready and had not seen Nazla since the day they had gone for coffee and learned of their friend's predicament. She was surprised that Hilal should know about it and unsure why she thought Fatma would be so upset.

'Well of course it's awful. I saw Nazla last week

and she's afraid they might lose the house. I told her it won't come to that.' There was a glint in Hilal's eye that made Fatma uncomfortable. 'Why? What have you heard?'

Melahat sucked her teeth and Hilal arched her eyebrows. 'So you haven't heard the latest? I'm surprised Nazla hasn't told you.' Hilal waited while Fatma poured water onto the tea and left the pot to simmer. 'Osman and Nazla aren't losing the house. The man from Istanbul, the new owner, is signing the house and the back field over to them. But he's planning to build some sort of guest house in the orchard. You're going to have competition!' Hilal took a lump of sugar from the bowl on the table and popped it in her mouth.

Fatma felt a flutter of fear. She busied herself setting out glasses and pouring the tea. Surely if this were true Nazla would have told her. Hilal's sources were, she reminded herself, notoriously unreliable.

'Who did you hear this from?'

'Mother heard it from Nurdan Auntie when she called to tell her she was coming here for the wedding.' Nurdan was Melahat's friend and Osman's aunt. 'Osman told her when he went round to fix a leaking tap.'

Fatma felt a tightness in her chest. 'He can make all the plans he wants,' she said, doing her best to keep her voice steady, 'but he'll never get permission to build on the orchard. And even if he did, does he think it's so easy to find guests in Ortakoy?' She set the glasses on the table.

'I don't know about any of that,' sniffed Hilal,

dropping three sugar cubes into her tea and stirring vigorously so the spoon rang against the glass. 'But you'll be able to ask him yourself. Apparently his wife and son are coming down at the weekend and they'll all be at the wedding!'

Fatma took the opportunity to steer the conversation to the much-anticipated nuptials of the village headman's daughter to the son of the shopkeeper. She pushed Hilal's news to the back of her mind until the visitors had driven off and she had settled her mother in her room. Then she sat at the kitchen table with a last glass of tea and considered the situation.

What she had said about the difficulty of getting planning permission was true, on top of which it was harder and more costly to build out here as everything had to be brought from town. This man would surely see how ridiculous his plan was when he looked into it properly and there was no point getting upset about something that would so clearly never happen.

What she could not dismiss, though, was the feeling that Nazla had betrayed her. Fatma had promised to support her friend when she had been afraid they would lose the house; why had Nazla not even bothered telling her about the latest developments?

# 4

In the past, village weddings sometimes lasted a whole week. These days they were more modest affairs but they still required much organisation and considerable expense. The wedding taking place that weekend in Ortakoy had needed more planning than most because with both families being prominent in the community, the guests would expect a good celebration.

The bride's father was Galip, the elected village chief responsible for sorting out minor disputes and representing the village at higher levels. The groom's father was Atilla, the owner of the village store. Their children had known each other all their lives, living as they did right across from one another. They had taken little notice of each other until they left school and Ayhan started helping his father in the shop. Then, Idil suddenly started finding excuses to go there.

The families did nothing to discourage the liaison and by the time a delegation of Ayhan's parents, an older uncle, the hopeful groom and his brother visited Idil's parents to ask for their daughter's hand, it was just a formality. Still, they observed the usual custom of taking chocolates and sweet pastries while the bride-to-be played her part by serving coffee to her future in-laws.

As the groom's father, Atilla was keen to fulfil his duty of providing the couple with a house. He had always planned that his sons would marry and move into apartments above the family home. The problem was that he had not yet got round to building the upper floors and as he was reluctant to take a bank loan, the building could only progress as fast as he could earn money. Finally, after two years, it was finished and the marriage could go ahead.

The night before the wedding the women of the village gathered for the henna night. The bride's hand was daubed with henna and a gold coin placed in her palm while her friends danced around her holding candles, all of which was supposed to bring good fortune to the marriage. There was a lot of laughter as some of the older women told stories of their own weddings and even their wedding nights. There were also the customary tears from Idil, and her mother.

Melek had taken part enthusiastically; her best friend, Selma, was the bride's younger sister. Melahat had sat with her old friend Nurdan catching up on gossip and nodding approvingly at the proceedings. Fatma had cried off with a headache.

Now it was the wedding lunch. Metal tables and chairs had been set up on the field next to the bride's home and a mobile chef with a tall toque and a bad temper had cooked cauldrons of chicken stew and keshkek – a creamed wheat dish popular on these occasions. The whole village had turned out to help celebrate or, as some more sceptical people might say, to take advantage of the opportunity for free food.

Melek and Selma had been running around for more than two hours carrying plates of food and clearing tables. The tide of villagers had finally subsided and the girls collected the last dishes, piled them next to the plastic tub where the chef's assistant was washing them and escaped up the narrow path at the back of Selma's house. In more troubled times, political rebels had taken this path up to the caves where they could hide from enemies. Now it was used only by shepherds and the occasional lovers on a secret tryst.

Melek ducked through a semi-circular tunnel to come out on the middle tier of the amphitheatre and set off up the worn steps. Selma, who was not blessed with such long legs, followed behind. At the top, they sat on the ancient, lichen-covered stones squinting in the bright sun as they looked over the valley with its scattering of villages and line of willows where the river wound through. Sounds drifted up to them: a couple of dogs having a barking contest, a tractor labouring across a field, the call to prayer ringing out from the minaret.

'Thank goodness that's over. Some people are so rude!' said Selma.

'Greedy too,' said Melek. 'Idris the taxi driver ate two plates of keshkek and then asked for another one to take away!'

'And I'm sick of people telling me it'll be my turn next. I'm not in a hurry to get married like Idil.'

'Ugh, me neither. Why would you choose to spend the rest of your life with one person?' Melek wrinkled her nose at the idea.

'I don't know. I asked Idil but she said she just knew she and Ayhan were meant to be together.'

Neither of the girls had any experience of relationships. The boys they knew in the village all seemed dull and awkward while those at school were mostly loud and brash. One boy had shown an interest in Melek at the start of the year but when she ignored his advances he quickly turned his attentions to another girl.

'Grandma told me yesterday that for a while she was afraid Mum would never get married. She said all the men were scared of her!'

'Your dad wasn't though. Where did they meet?'

'At a wedding.'

The two girls giggled.

'Was it love at first sight?' asked Selma in a silly, melodramatic voice.

Melek snorted. 'I don't know. Grandma said he drove up from town to see her every Sunday after they met.' She tried to imagine her parents courting but it was hard. These days their relationship consisted mainly of her mother getting exasperated and her passive father trying to placate her.

Both girls were quiet, contemplating the large issues of love and marriage. A flock of goldfinches landed on the thistles that covered the slope above the theatre and bobbed up and down, pecking at the purple flowers. When Selma started speaking again the birds flew off twittering indignantly.

'Well, I'm not getting married until I'm at least twenty-five. I want to finish university first and get a job and live on my own for a while.'

'What about me? Can't I live with you?'

'Of course you can, Meli. We can share a flat in the city and cook dinner together after work and meet friends at the weekend.'

'Wouldn't that be wonderful?' Melek picked up a pebble and tossed it down the steps. It bounced off a row of seats and sent a lizard scuttling into a crack in the stones. 'My mother thinks I'm going to stay in the village and run the pension. She doesn't even know I want to go to university.'

'Fatma Auntie will understand if you talk to her.'

'Do you think so?' Melek did not look convinced.

'She doesn't exactly follow traditions herself.'

'No, Mum does exactly what she wants. The trouble is she expects the rest of us to do exactly what she wants too.' Melek threw another stone. This one bounced twice and landed on the dry earth of the arena, sending up a little puff of dust.

Selma nudged her friend teasingly. 'Well, you're definitely going to leave the village. Don't you remember what the fortune teller said?'

One lunchtime the two girls had been sitting on the sea front eating sticky dough balls when a gypsy woman came along and offered to tell their fortunes. At first they declined but curiosity got the better of them. The woman took out a drawstring bag, emptied a pile of beads, shells and bones into Melek's palm and told her to throw them on the table. She examined the charms, pushed a couple around and said, 'You're going to travel. You'll have a good job, be an important lady. Rich too!'

When Selma took her turn, the gypsy looked thoughtful. 'You'll have a long life and a husband who loves you. And I see lots of children!'

Now Melek gave her friend a playful punch on the arm. 'I thought you didn't believe her predictions!'

Selma, who besides Idil had younger twin brothers, was adamant that she would have only one child. She'd been horrified by the gypsy's prophecy.

'She definitely got that thing about children wrong!'

'Maybe they're not all yours,' Melek said. 'Perhaps she meant you're going to be a teacher!'

Selma tugged at a piece of grass that was growing out of a crack in the stone. 'Maybe. I wouldn't mind that. But she said you're going to have an important job and I don't think she meant running the Kismet Pension!'

\*

The field where the lunch had taken place now looked quite different. The tables had mostly gone, along with the bad-tempered chef, his assistant and all his pots and pans. The one remaining table had been decorated with swags of satin and artificial flowers and the chairs had been set out in lines facing an empty space that would act as a dance floor. In the corner a rough stage had been fashioned from pallets and chipboard and lights strung on cables cast a soft, yellow glow in the gathering dusk.

Inside the house, the bride had been getting ready

for several hours. Her friend had come to do her hair and Melek and Selma had helped her get dressed and do her make up. When her mother came and fixed a heavy gold bracelet round Idil's wrist – a last present from her family – the two women both started to cry.

The living room was clogged up with an assortment of relatives who had come for the wedding and were using the occasion to catch up on the latest births, deaths and illnesses in the family. One of Selma's brothers, carried away with the excitement and pretending to be his favourite superhero, had jumped off the settee and hit his head on the coffee table, producing an egg-sized swelling to which Selma was applying ice.

Melek escaped outside and breathed in the fresh air and faint smell of woodsmoke. The sky was dark blue with streaks of orange where the sun had set. The musicians were warming up and the first few guests were starting to take seats. The groom's younger brother was standing with his father, looking awkward in his suit and tie.

'Hi Arif. You look smart!' Melek said encouragingly.

'Thanks, Melek Abla. You look lovely too.'

Even in the yellow light of the electric bulbs, Melek saw him blush. 'Is Ayhan nervous?'

'I shouldn't think so. I've never seen him nervous about anything and he loves being the centre of attention.'

Melek smiled, thinking how different the brothers were. Ayhan was confident and did indeed thrive on attention while Arif was shy and awkward, more so since he had hit adolescence and been plagued by spots.

She saw her own brother arriving. Ahmet was wearing jeans and a shirt and had gelled his dark hair into spikes in an attempt to look like one of the latest pop stars. Her mother was just behind him wearing her best skirt and for once without a headscarf. Her thick, black hair was clipped up at the back and she had even put in some gold earrings.

Melek heard a commotion at the gate and turned to see the bride and groom trying to enter the field. Their path was blocked by Idil's brothers who were taking advantage of an old custom and demanding payment to let the couple through. Idil was giving them an earful but Ayhan pulled some notes from his pocket and handed them over and the boys stood aside.

The couple proceeded slowly, partly due to the number of people they had to stop and greet and also because the bride's full, hooped skirt obscured the rough ground and required her to tread carefully. They reached the bridal table and were about to sit down when the organ player called them up for the first dance. Melek watched as Ayhan took hold of Idil and the couple started swaying gently to the music. There was clapping and a few of the young men whistled and Ayhan pulled his bride as close as her stiff skirt would allow.

Melek was trying to imagine her mother and father at their wedding when she noticed that many of the guests had turned from the dance floor and were looking towards the lane. A man in a checked shirt and smart leather jacket, with thick hair swept back from his face and a well-trimmed beard, was standing at the edge of the field. Next to him was a woman wearing a clinging dress and a shawl that she had wrapped casually round her shoulders. Her hair was a riot of curls and an assortment of beads and bangles glittered round her neck and wrists.

The first song ended and the band launched into one of the most popular songs in their repertoire, causing a rush for the dance floor. Selma caught Melek's hand and dragged her onto the dance floor, dodging her brothers who were playing chase and a couple of matronly ladies who were shaking their ample backsides. As Melek danced her attention was drawn back to the strangers. The man had gone to sit where her father and some of his friends were drinking raki. She was surprised to see the glamorous woman sitting with Nazla and her mother.

'Who are those people?' she asked Selma, shouting over the music.

Selma shrugged. 'I don't know but they arrived with Osman Uncle so they're probably the new owners of his land. The man came to see my Dad—' Her words were cut off by a shout from one of the groom's friends who began hurling himself round the dance floor, clicking a pair of wooden spoons in each hand.

Melek and Selma danced to another song, then the zurna and davul started up and the dancers formed a circle and Melek, whose eyes were scratchy from all the dust hovering in the air, moved away. Curious, she threaded her way through the groups of guests to where her mother was sitting.

'Hello Nazla Auntie. How are you?' Melek snuck a glance at the woman and saw an unfamiliar boy sitting beside her looking bored.

'I'm well thank you, Melek,' said her mother's friend a little stiffly. 'Zuhal Hanum, this is Fatma's daughter, Melek. Melek, this is Zuhal Hanum. She's visiting from Istanbul.'

'It's lovely to meet you, Melek,' said the woman. Her bangles jingled as she held out her hand. 'And this is my son Barish,' she said, turning slightly to indicate the boy. 'Perhaps you could take him off for a while; I'm sure he'd much rather spend time with you than with us!'

Melek froze. The boy raised his eyebrows and looked annoyed and she wished she had stayed on the dance floor with Selma. Then his face split into a smile, showing perfect white teeth and the smallest dimple in his chin and Melek's stomach flipped.

'Hi Melek! Please ignore my mother, she likes to embarrass me.'

'It's fine.' Melek tried to hide her discomposure with a shrug.

'We can go over there and get a drink if you like.'

The boy stood and squeezed his way out of the row of chairs and Melek followed him to a table set out with bottles of water, cartons of juice and plastic cups of cola. She took a juice, then, afraid she might look like a little child sipping from the straw, swapped it for water. Barish took a cup of cola, drank it down and put the empty cup in the bin under the table. They moved to one side and watched the dancers for a minute.

'So you live in the village?'

'Yes. How long are you here for?'

'I fly back tomorrow but if my dad has his way, we might be spending the summer here.'

Melek felt a flutter in her chest. 'Wh-what's it like, living in Istanbul?'

'It's good most of the time.' He put his head on one side and his thick hair fell across his forehead. 'There's a lot of stuff going on, you don't really get bored. The crowds can be a pain at times though. Like in the Covered Market where my dad's shop is – you have to fight your way through the people some days.'

A group of young men were dancing energetically and one of them stumbled back and bumped into Melek. Barish took a step towards her as though to catch her. Melek felt her cheeks blush.

'Aren't you going to introduce us?' She looked up to see Selma standing in front of them giving her a meaningful look.

'Barish, this is my best friend, Selma. It's her sister's wedding. Selma, this is Barish. He lives in Istanbul.'

'Really? You're so lucky! Melek and I were just saying how we can't wait until we can get away from the village!'

'Is it that awful?'

'It's just boring sometimes. And some of the people are nosy and like to gossip.' Melek pinched the back of her friend's arm. 'Ow!' Selma rubbed the spot and muttered something about mosquitoes.

'There are good things too,' said Melek.

'Like?' Barish looked straight at her and she felt her cheeks burning again.

'It's safe, there's never any crime. The mountains are beautiful – and the beach. Have you seen the beach?

'Not yet. Dad said he'd take us down there tomorrow. Will I be able to swim?'

The girls both laughed. 'Only if you're brave!' said Melek.

'The sea's freezing at this time of year!' added Selma. 'My mother's calling me, I have to go. See you later, Barish!'

Melek told Barish about the amphitheatre and how she liked to sit at the top and imagine who had sat there before her and what spectacle they had seen. She asked him about the palaces in Istanbul and he told her how his step-grandfather Hasan had taken him all over the city and made its history come alive. They talked about school, their best and worst teachers, which singers they liked, what films they had seen.

The six-storey cake was carried out precariously and placed on a table in front of the bride and groom. Ayhan had to pay another bribe before the baker's assistant would give him a knife to cut it with. Then it was the gifting ceremony and Melek took the gold sovereign her mother had bought for the couple and joined the queue. It moved agonisingly slowly as each person stopped to congratulate the bride and groom, exchange handshakes and kisses, sometimes even pose for photographs. Finally, it was her turn and she added the gold token to all the others hanging round the bride's neck, kissed both parties and hurried back to the drinks table. She felt a rush of excitement to see Barish waiting there for her.

The music got louder and the dancing wilder. On the edge of the field someone fired a rifle into the air 'Pow! Pow! Pow! Pow!' and a man threw piles of dollar bills into the air for the musicians, who scuttled between the dancers collecting them.

Barish laughed. 'Weddings are much more fun here than in Istanbul!'

Then Ahmet came to say they were leaving and Melek tried to sound casual as she said, 'I might see you again in the summer, Barish.'

'I hope so,' he said, giving her a broad smile that made her heart thump as she went to say goodbye to Selma and the other members of the wedding party.

At home she was getting a glass of milk when her mother accosted her.

'What do you think of their crazy plan, then?'

'Mmm?'

'That boy you were talking to – didn't he tell you what his father wants to do?'

'He said they might spend the summer here.' Melek felt her cheeks glowing at the memory.

'His father is the new owner of Osman's orchard and he's got some ridiculous idea of building something called a "retreat" on it!'

'What?'

'Mad, isn't it?' her mother said, as though Melek had agreed with her. She slammed the tea caddy down on the marble counter and banged the lid onto the teapot. 'But don't worry. I've invited them here for tea tomorrow afternoon and I'm going to make him see how impossible it is. He'll be off back to Istanbul and never want to hear the name Ortakoy again by the time I've finished with him.'

Melek shut the fridge door and went to her room without any milk. She got into bed and tried to sleep but her mind was racing. Just the thought of Barish made her feel hot and flustered but then her mother's words would echo in her head. She loved her mother but sometimes she wished she would be a little less opinionated.

# 5

Harun woke with a raging thirst and a sour taste in his mouth. He liked raki but he had struggled to keep up with some of the village men, particularly Mehmet. The man was good company and was obviously popular but something about him had struck Harun as strange. In a place where women were still not treated as equals, when Osman introduced Mehmet as the owner of the Kismet Pension he had laughed heartily and said his wife was the owner, not him.

Harun had noticed the guest house as he first drove into the village and thought it would be both useful and politic to speak to the owners: useful because they might be able to give him advice and politic because he wanted to assure them that he would not steal their guests. He was pleased to discover the owner – or at least the husband of the owner – was such an amiable character. And it seemed he would have a chance to talk to the wife as she had invited them all to the pension that afternoon.

The sun was slicing through the thin curtains of Osman's younger daughters' bedroom where he and Zuhal were sleeping in twin beds with pink satin covers. Zuhal's bed was already empty, the cover pulled up neatly and he could hear her voice coming from downstairs, mingling with the clink of plates and pans as someone prepared breakfast. His stomach groaned with hunger.

Downstairs he found Nazla frying eggs in a kitchen steamy with the smell of olive oil and simmering tea.

'Good morning, Harun Bey. I hope you slept well.' Osman's wife was always polite but he still sensed a reserve in her.

'Splendidly, thank you.'

'Could the large amount of raki you consumed last night have had anything to do with that?' asked Zuhal, giving his shoulder a squeeze as he sat down at the table.

'A little, maybe. But also the village air and the wonderful hospitality. It makes such a change from the city!'

Osman came into the kitchen, his fleshy face still creased from the pillow, and Nazla called the girls, who were in the living room watching television. Zuhal roused Barish from bed and they all sat down to breakfast. As well as the eggs there was a crumbly cheese called 'chukelek', fat green olives that Nazla said came from the trees round the house and tomatoes sliced and dribbled with olive oil and thyme. There was a spicy pepper and walnut paste and jam made with fruit from the orchard. To mop it all up there was crusty bread bought that morning from the village shop and flat bread which Nazla made herself that tasted of the smoke and the outdoors and to wash it down numerous glasses of tea from the pot that was kept boiling on the stove so that the air in the kitchen was damp and the windows steamed up. It was the sort of breakfast Harun imagined serving to his guests: simple and healthy, using local products and bursting with flavour.

As they ate, they discussed the wedding. Nazla said how lovely the bride had looked and Zuhal exclaimed at how much gold had been pinned on the couple. The two younger girls complained that the bride's brothers had pulled their ponytails. Barish was quiet and ate little. Used to sleeping late at the weekend, when the girls left the table he excused himself and went back to snooze on the sofa that had been pulled out for him to sleep on.

Harun ate until his stomach felt heavy and the sour taste had quite gone from his mouth, then accepted another glass of tea from Nazla and went outside. He stood by the two poplar trees looking at the orchard and the patches of green fields visible in the valley below. He heard a noise and turned to see Osman joining him.

'It's a great view, isn't it?'

'Amazing. Everything about this place is wonderful, better than I could ever have imagined.'

'Are you going to go ahead with your plans?'

'Oh yes! Finding the land, seeing the village, eating a breakfast like we just enjoyed – it all makes me more determined. Are you sure you're alright with us dividing the plot like this?'

When Harun had seen the plot he had inherited, he had realised it consisted of two parcels – the orchard in front and the land with the house at the back. As Nazla cried with relief at the news that they weren't going to lose their home, he had quizzed Osman and found out that the orchard earned him very little money which was why he worked as a driver for one of the tour companies in the summer.

When he heard that, the solution seemed simple to Harun. He would sign the back field and the house over to Osman, keep the orchard and build his retreat on it and give Osman a job that didn't take him away from home all summer and a decent wage. Osman had accepted the offer enthusiastically but Harun sensed that his wife still had doubts.

'Osman, brother, are you sure you're alright with me keeping the orchard? Nazla seems a little unhappy about something.'

'Harun Bey, I'm delighted with our agreement and Nazla will be too once everything is settled. She's a little more…wary than I am.'

'I'll have to cut down some of the trees, you know.'

'Of course. There isn't much order to the place I'm afraid…'

'Much better! This has an organic feel to it. Now, I'm thinking of ten bungalows and a communal area for eating and drinking somewhere in the middle.'

Harun finished his tea, put the glass on an old tree stump and headed into the orchard with Osman following behind. They spent the next two hours pacing the plot to find the best sites for the chalets and marking them with stones and fallen branches. When they had finished Harun stood by the gate and looked back at the orchard. After the mixed emotions of the last week it suddenly felt as though his plan was going to become a reality.

*

In the kitchen of the Kismet Pension, Fatma was watching Melek fry cheese pastries.

'You're being too rough with them! Take that one out before it unravels and all the cheese comes out!'

Melek scooped the offending pastry out of the oil. 'I am capable of cooking cheese rolls, Mother!'

When she had first heard news of the planned development Fatma had resolved to stay calm and not get upset by something that was so unlikely to happen. She had, however, been only moderately successful in her aim and meeting the man responsible at the wedding, and seeing the way the villagers fussed over him, had only added to her annoyance.

At breakfast that morning she had tried to garner her family's support.

'So Mehmet, did you find out anything about the gentleman you were talking to last night, aside from the fact that he is as fond of raki as you?'

'Harun Bey? His mother was married to Hasan Uncle so he's inherited the orchard. Apparently he's giving the house to Osman.'

'How generous of him!' Fatma had learned this at the wedding from a rather sheepish Nazla.

'What's he like?' asked Melahat, who had eaten so much keshkek at the wedding lunch that she was still too bloated and uncomfortable to attend the evening's celebrations.

'Very decent,' said Mehmet.

'His wife's quite flashy,' said Ahmet.

'Not flashy, stylish,' said Melek.

'It doesn't matter what they're like,' said Fatma testily. 'Did you hear his plans?'

'Not exactly, my dear. We talked more about Istanbul and his shop there.'

'He's planning to build a guest house on the orchard!'

Mehmet looked surprised. Ahmet whistled.

'You didn't know?' Melahat asked them. 'We told Fatma the other day and I knew even before I came back to the village.' She took a noisy sip of tea.

'You're always the first to hear the gossip, Grandma,' said Ahmet and the old lady grinned proudly.

Fatma coughed. 'Well, now we all know. The question is: what are we going to do about it?'

'We can't do anything about it, Mother. It's his land and he's free to do what he wants on it.' Melek's voice was high and indignant.

Fatma tried a different tactic. 'He may be free to do what he wants but don't you think we should warn him of the difficulties he's going to face?' There was silence as they all considered this. 'I think it's our duty, which is why I've invited them round for tea this afternoon. I'll let him know how unpleasant some of the villagers will be when they learn of his plans and how hard it is to find guests out here. I'm sure he'll see reason.'

There had been no reply from the others, who were suddenly very interested in the food in front of them.

Now Fatma left Melek to finish the pastries while

she set the tea to boil. She counted out glasses and plates and put them on a tray for Melek to take out. It was a pleasant spring day and she planned to have the visitors sit outside at the tables used in the summer by the guests. She wished the pool wasn't such an eyesore but there was nothing she could do about it. After banging nails into some boards and fixing them to one side of the hole the workers were having more tea.

At the sound of a car pulling up Fatma went round to the front of the pension.

'Zuhal Hanum, you are welcome! Harun Bey, it is good to meet you!'

'And you, Fatma Hanum. We are happy to come!' The man shook her hand vigorously. His wife surprised Fatma by kissing her on both cheeks. She was jangling with as many bangles and beads as the night before. Their son, the sullen boy who had gone off to talk to Melek, nodded a greeting.

'Hello Osman. Isn't Nazla with you?'

'No, Fatma. She has a lot of ironing.'

Fatma knew that the ironing was an excuse. She had noticed at the wedding how uncomfortable Nazla looked and guessed she was feeling guilty for not having warned her. She led the way to the back of the pension where her mother was already installed at a table drinking tea.

'Harun Bey, this is my mother Melahat. Mother, meet Harun Bey and Zuhal Hanum!'

The visitors greeted the old lady in the proper way, bending to kiss her hand and lifting it to their brow. Melahat beamed at the show of respect.

Mehmet and Ahmet appeared and she introduced them. 'I do apologise for the mess, Harun Bey.' Fatma waved towards the muddy crater. 'We're having a swimming pool built ready for the summer.'

'Excellent. I'm sure your guests will love that. How long have you had the pension, Fatma Hanum?'

'Eight years. The land belonged to my dear father and I had the Kismet built on it. Would you like to see a room?'

'I'd love to!'

Fatma led the visitors through the pension, pleased that she and Derya had cleared the worst of the dust and cobwebs. Upstairs, she opened the door to one of the rooms.

'We're still getting ready for the season, you understand. Some of the walls need whitewashing and we still have to hang the curtains and put the rugs down. There's so much work!'

'I'm sure there is,' said Zuhal. 'It's a charming room, Fatma Hanum.'

Harun stepped onto the balcony. 'Zuhal, come and see this incredible view.' They both stood taking it in for a few minutes.

'You are lucky, Fatma Hanum, to have such a beautiful place!' said Harun.

Fatma smiled, then checked herself. 'Luck had nothing to do with it, Harun Bey. It took hard work and determination to build this place. Shall we go down and have tea?'

When they rejoined the others, Mehmet was talking to Osman and the two boys were sitting together discussing the latest football results. Melek brought out the tea tray but she seemed nervous, dropping a teaspoon on the ground and spilling sugar on the table. Fatma frowned at her daughter, then went back to loading plates with pastries and cakes.

Once everyone had a plate of food and a glass of tea in front of them and the guests had complimented Fatma on the spread, some general conversation was attempted. They discussed the weather and how fortunate it was that it had been mild and dry for the wedding. Then Harun talked about the beach where they had been earlier.

'That road needs some attention! The sea was very calm though, just a few tiny waves at the edge.'

'It's always like that. It's sheltered by the island,' said Mehmet.

'Are you allowed on there?' asked Barish.

'Of course. We climb up to the top sometimes,' said Ahmet. 'It's quite steep though.'

'That view from the bend in the road where you catch the first glimpse of the sea is stunning,' said Zuhal. 'I'm definitely going down to paint it when I come back.'

Fatma took her cue. 'So you are planning to return?'

'Actually,' said Harun, 'I'm not leaving! Zuhal and Barish will go back to Istanbul until term finishes but I'm going to stay here. You may have heard about my plans, Fatma Hanum. I was very pleased when I heard you had invited us here as I was hoping to talk to you!'

'I heard something,' said Fatma, trying to sound

vague. 'But I really didn't know whether to believe it. The village is a terrible place for gossip, you know!'

Ahmet sniggered and looked at his grandmother.

'Ah, but this time the gossip is true! I'm planning to build a retreat, somewhere people can relax and regenerate by doing things like yoga, hiking, painting. I had the idea because I've been feeling a little jaded myself recently and when I saw this spot...well, it's the perfect place to get-away!'

'Yes, I suppose it might seem that way,' said Fatma. 'But you know, Harun Bey, it isn't so great when you get to know it. It's too hot in the summer to even lift a paint brush, let alone go walking or do any of that yoga and the mosquitoes will drive you crazy.'

'I imagine in the summer months we'll have to move the activities to early morning and late afternoon and I'll definitely warn people to bring mosquito repellent.'

'Then there are the villagers. They don't take well to outsiders.'

Harun clapped Osman on the back. 'They've all been very welcoming so far.'

'That's because they think you're just visiting. When they hear you want to move here and set up a business that will bring more strangers to the village they'll act differently, believe me.'

Melek started refilling tea glasses. She rattled spoons and fussed over how strong everyone liked their tea. As Fatma waited she noticed with annoyance that Harun Bey was still smiling broadly.

'It's even hard to find good builders who will come out here,' she continued. 'The ones that will come charge you double for everything. And actually the orchard is classed as agricultural land which means you probably won't get permission to build on it.'

Fatma took a deep breath. She was struggling to keep her voice at a level that suggested she was just a concerned bystander looking out for Harun's interests.

Harun's smile did not waver. 'But I don't need planning permission, Fatma Hanum! I won't be building anything like your lovely guest house here. I'm going to put up wooden chalets.'

'And you think people will pay to stay in a wooden hut?' Fatma's voice was sharp now.

Melek placed a fresh glass of tea in front of her so heavily that some of the contents spilled into the saucer.

'I intend to make them very comfortable,' said Harun. 'City people like the idea of staying somewhere simple. I've even seen one retreat where you stay in a nomad yurt!'

'Allahallah!' said Melahat, who could still remember the days when the yoruk people passed through the village every spring taking their families and flocks up to the high pastures for the summer. 'People pay to stay in a tent and go for walks?'

'Walking – or hiking – will be just one of the things we offer, Melahat Auntie,' said Harun. 'Zuhal will give painting lessons – she's an artist, you know. We'll have yoga – everyone wants to do yoga these days – and maybe some local crafts.'

'What about kilim weaving?' asked Melahat, helping herself to another piece of cake. 'We all did that when I was a girl. My fingers are too stiff now and the young people go and buy their rugs from a shop.'

'That's an excellent idea, Melahat Auntie!' said Harun.

Fatma glared at her mother but the old lady was busy tucking into the slice of cake. 'But Harun Bey, how will you get this place ready in time? The season starts in less than a month.'

'It'll be a push, I know, but that's another good thing about the chalets – they bring them from the factory and put them up in a day. We won't be ready for May but I think we can open in June, don't you, Osman?'

Fatma looked at Osman, who wriggled uncomfortably and started stirring his half-empty glass of tea.

Harun clapped him on the back. 'Osman has kindly agreed to work with us.'

Fatma realised with dismay that there was another reason Nazla was avoiding her. She was also beginning to tire of Harun's relentless optimism. She looked to her family for support but the boys were talking about fishing, Mehmet was telling Zuhal how the swallows had returned to the same nests ever since the pension was built and Melek was noisily gathering empty plates.

'You sound very sure about all this, Harun Bey, but I have to tell you I think you're making a big mistake. All this trouble you're going to go to and for what? It's hard getting people to come to Ortakoy; I should know, I've been trying to do it for years. Most of them prefer the fashionable resorts up the coast and if they do make it this far, they choose somewhere with better roads and more nightlife.'

'The thing is, Fatma Hanum, the people I'm going to be targeting will be glad of the remoteness and the lack of development. They are exactly what make the village perfect for a retreat! My business will be quite different from yours and I want you to know that I will not in any way be invading your space or trying to take your customers.'

Fatma snorted.

'In fact, I think we can help each other. You might have guests who fancy some painting lessons and perhaps my guests could come and use your pool when it's ready.'

This was too much for Fatma. She sat up straighter in her chair and in a voice stiff with contempt said, 'That's very kind of you, Harun Bey, but I have managed quite well on my own up to now and intend to continue in just the same way.'

'Of course, I didn't mean…' For the first time that afternoon Harun's smile faltered.

His wife looked at her watch. 'Harun, we need to get going or Barish and I will miss our flight! Thank you so much for your hospitality, Fatma Hanum. I look forward to seeing more of you when I'm back in the village!'

The visitors got in the car and headed towards the main road to town and Osman scuttled off up the road, obviously relieved to escape the awkwardness of the afternoon.

As soon as he had gone Fatma rounded on her

family. 'Is it too much to expect a little support from you all?'

'I don't know why you are so against the man, my dear. He seems very pleasant to me,' said Mehmet.

'Yes Mum, and Osman Uncle must like him if he's going to work for him,' said Ahmet.

'And didn't you hear what he said, Mother? His place is going to be quite different to the pension,' said Melek.

'He liked my idea of kilim weaving,' said Melahat.

Fatma shook her head. 'You are all so easily taken in. But don't forget what they say: "Every man with a beard is not your grandfather!" People aren't always what they seem and unlike you I don't trust this man at all.'

\*

In the car, Harun was quiet for some time. He too was unhappy with the way the meeting had gone.

Eventually he said, 'When she invited us to tea, I thought she wanted to give me advice about the business.'

'She did,' said Zuhal, 'and her advice is not to do it! Are you going to take it?'

'No!' He banged one hand on the dashboard. 'I suppose Fatma Hanum is just afraid of having competition. I need to prove to her that I'm not a threat.' He smiled at his wife. 'I'm sure I can win her over!'

'Maybe,' said Zuhal, 'but I have a feeling that your usual tactics of flattery and charm aren't going to work on this lady!'

# 6

Fatma believed that in most things women were as capable as – and in many cases more capable than – men. The Kismet pension's very existence as well as its continued success were proof of her own capabilities. If she had relied on Mehmet to provide for the family goodness only knows where they would have been now.

However, it was also necessary to know when to admit defeat. There were men of a certain mentality who refused to listen to a woman and it had become obvious that the men working on the swimming pool fell into that category. She had tried to get them working first by encouragement and later threats, she had left them alone to get on with their work and she had hung around watching them and counting the number of times they stopped for tea; but nothing she did had worked. Reluctantly she decided to hand the problem over and see if the men in the family had any more success.

She accosted them at breakfast. 'Those men have been here nearly two weeks and all they've done is make a big mess and eat and drink at my expense.'

'One of them told me this is their last job of the season,' said Mehmet. 'When they finish here, they'll be off back to their homes and families in the east.'

'So they've started their holiday early. Well, it won't do. I've tried talking to them but they won't listen to me. I want you two,' she looked from Mehmet to Ahmet, 'to start supervising the job.'

'What do we know about building swimming pools?' asked Ahmet, who had been planning to spend the day riding around on his friend Huso's new motorbike looking for girls to impress.

'You don't need to know how to build a pool; you just need to recognize if someone is working or idling – something you should be an expert on!'

'Your mother's right,' said Mehmet, who disliked confrontation anywhere and particularly within his family. 'If we keep an eye on them, the men will have to work harder.'

Buoyed with hope that one of her problems had been solved, Fatma turned her attention to the other thing that was bothering her and called Nazla to invite her round for coffee.

Nazla arrived quickly, still looking nervous. 'I'm sorry I didn't tell you about Harun Bey's plans, Fatma. I was afraid you'd be cross with me.'

'Why would I be cross with you, Nazla? It's not your fault this man inherited the orchard and has got this crazy scheme in his head.'

'And I thought you might not be happy about Osman working for him.' Nazla looked miserable. 'But to tell the truth, I'm not happy about it either.'

'Good. Then you'll be interested in what I have to

say.'

Derya joined them and made coffee, dabbing at her eyes and nose and complaining as she did every year about the mimosa blossom which released cascades of yellow pollen and set off her allergies. Fatma, who never had much patience with minor complaints, soon cut her off.

'So, I wanted to talk to you both about Harun Bey. This man thinks he can just turn up in the village and put his crazy plan in action. I tried to make him see sense but he didn't want to listen. Now it's up to us to stop him. Are you with me?'

Nazla fiddled with her coffee cup. 'I…well…it's a bit difficult, Fatma. He's giving us the house.'

'The house is yours anyway in all but name and if Osman had got things sorted while Hasan Uncle was alive—'

'God bless his soul,' said Derya.

'—the orchard would be yours too and we wouldn't be in this position. You said you're not happy about Osman working there.'

'I'm not. He didn't even ask me before he accepted Harun's offer.'

'I thought you'd be pleased he can give up the driving job and be around more,' said Derya.

Nazla took a sip of coffee.

'What's bothering you, Nazla?' asked Fatma.

'You'll think I'm being silly but I'm worried if he spends his days surrounded by all these smart, city women in their fancy clothes he might stray.'

Fatma turned a snort of laughter into a cough. 'Men *are* easily impressed but do you really think these ladies will look at Osman?'

'It's not that ridiculous, Fatma. Osman isn't bad-looking and women are often attracted to tough men – men who can saw down a tree or fix an engine.'

Fatma thought of the soap operas Nazla loved in which the rich wife often got involved with a handsome, young gardener or chauffeur; she had never seen one where the woman fell for a balding, forty-year-old farmer.

'My cousin's husband worked in a hotel in town and started to stay out late. Then he brought home new clothes and told her he'd bought them with his tips. In the end, he went to live with a much older English lady and he hardly knew a word of English. Do you see why I'm worried?'

'Yes, I see, Nazla dear. And it was wrong of Osman to take the job without consulting you. So will you help me stop this thing?'

'I will but I'll have to keep it a secret from Osman.'

'What about you, Derya?'

Derya fiddled with the knot in her headscarf. 'I-I'm not sure. He seems like a good man.'

'Have you thought what might happen if business declined at the Kismet Pension?' Fatma looked troubled. 'It would be hard, but I'd have to manage without you.'

Derya dabbed at her eyes, which were watering either from the pollen or at the thought of losing her job.

'You see, this affects us all. We need to come up with ways to upset his plans.'

Derya and Nazla gazed into their coffee cups for

inspiration.

'I'll tell you my ideas. First, I think we should check if the ownership is legal. Was the land in Hasan Uncle's name and is Harun Bey entitled to inherit it? Then we can check if he's allowed to open this sort of business on farmland.'

'Perhaps,' said Nazla, 'we could convince him that the land is cursed. It *is* where Osman's grandfather had his accident...'

Fatma thought her friend had been watching too many soap operas. 'Yes, and perhaps we could dress up as ghosts and say it's haunted.'

Nazla frowned. 'Well, I don't know! I've never done this before.'

'None of us has, which is why I think we need to gather more support. "What can one hand offer when two hands can make a sound!", as the saying goes. Talk to your friends and neighbours, tell them what he's planning to do. We'll set up an opposition group. I've read about people forming groups and stopping huge companies and even governments. I'm sure we can find a way to stop Harun Bey and his wooden huts.'

\*

Harun was getting on with his plans. He wished he could have sorted the misunderstanding with Fatma before he started work on the retreat but with the start of the season so close, he could not afford to wait.

After the tea party had ended so uncomfortably he had tried to find out more about her from Osman.

'Is there a particular reason Fatma Hanum is

opposed to me?'

'Fatma is...well, she's different to most of the women in the village,' Osman said. 'She shocked everyone when she left school by working on the farm with her father, the very fine Suleyman Bey.'

'But I've seen a lot of women working in the fields. In fact, I think I've seen more women there than men!'

'Women do a lot of the planting and picking but Fatma actually ran the place with her father until he died, and then she ran it alone.'

'And Mehmet Bey?'

'He was never really interested in the farm. When they were first married he did a little, but he grew up in town and I suppose he just didn't take to farming.'

'But it seems to be her who is in charge at the pension too.'

'It is. It was Fatma's idea to build the Kismet and I suppose they had just got used to her making all the decisions. It doesn't seem to bother Mehmet but there are others who think he should control his wife better!'

Harun was used to assertive women – he was married to one – and he had found them to be generally smarter and more tenacious than men. The task of winning Fatma over would be harder than he had thought but he hoped that when she saw the retreat take shape she might see how different it was to the pension and come round to the idea.

He could have looked on the website to choose the model of chalet and ordered them on the telephone but he was interested to see the factory. He also felt in need of a day away from the village where every time he went out he was accosted by people who wanted to talk to him. Contrary to Fatma's warning, they were still friendly even now they knew his intentions, but being the focus of so much interest was exhausting. He hoped his celebrity status would fade as the locals got used to having him around.

The company was based in a city up the coast and the journey took three hours. Harun spent a couple of hours looking round the factory, drinking tea with the manager and coming to an agreement on price and payment for the ten chalets. Afterwards he found a café on the sea front and ate grilled bass before driving back with the radio in the rental car turned up high, singing along to the songs he knew. He was buzzing with an energy he had not felt for some time.

The next step was to find someone to make the furniture. He knew from Osman that there was a carpenter in the village. He had also learned that this man had taken over his father's workshop and in Harun's experience craftsmen who followed in their father's footsteps were skilled and took pride in their work. He also liked the idea of giving business to a local man. His only concern was whether the carpenter would be able to complete the job in time.

The workshop was tucked down the side of a modest village house and consisted of brick walls and a corrugated metal roof that extended out on one side over an area where planks of wood were stacked. Inside, the floor was swept clean and the large machines were still and silent. They found the carpenter Metin sitting on a plastic stool with a cup of coffee and a newspaper. Osman made the introductions.

'Pleased to meet you, Harun Bey.' Metin put down his newspaper and jumped up. He pulled over another plastic stool and a slightly wobbly wooden chair, which he offered to Harun. 'Please don't think this is the standard of our work. This chair was made by my eleven-year-old son!' he said.

'In that case, I am honoured to sit on it!' said Harun, though he sat a little gingerly.

The carpenter called his wife and asked her to make coffee for them. They talked about the pleasantness of the spring weather and Osman teased Metin about his favourite football team losing at the weekend. Harun was getting used to the fact that village people liked to indulge in small talk before tackling the uglier subject of business.

After Metin's wife had brought coffee and water and a small bowl of Turkish delight, Harun explained his plans and detailed the things he needed the carpenter to make.

'I can make all these things for you, Harun Bey,' said Metin.

Harun hoped the man would not be offended by his next question. 'Can you manage such a large job on your own?'

Metin smiled ruefully. 'I know how the workshop must look to you but there was a time when four of us worked here and the machines were never quiet. We made doors and windows for all the houses around and plenty of furniture too. These days people prefer to get plastic windows and those flimsy fibreboard doors and they buy their furniture from the big shops in town. I'm just glad my father is not here to see it, God rest his soul.' He shook his head sadly. 'But I am still quite capable of completing a job like this. I have an assistant who is off today and I call a friend to help when I need him.'

'The thing is, Metin Usta, we don't have much time. The chalets will be ready in three weeks and I'd like to be open in five, six at the latest.'

'That's possible. I'll need some money in advance to buy that much wood but once we have it we'll work flat out to make sure you have the things in time.'

He took a tattered notebook and pencil from on top of one of the machines and wrote the details of Harun's order and the measurements they settled on for the furniture. They discussed the cost of different woods and what finish would look best. When it was time to agree the price, Osman pushed the carpenter to give Harun Bey a good price and Metin pushed for a little more money up front but eventually they agreed a deal and shook hands. Then Osman and Harun went to the coffee house to celebrate the progress made and Harun lost six games of backgammon in a row to Mehmet, who was the village champion.

# 7

～

Fatma was trying to wake Ahmet. Since she had asked them to oversee the work on the pool her husband and son had spent more time at the pension and there were some small signs of progress. Today though, Ahmet hadn't got up for breakfast and by mid-morning was still sleeping soundly. Once, annoyed by her son's propensity for lying in bed, Fatma had visited a spell-maker in the hope of a cure. But the woman, who had three sons of her own, knew the limit of her powers and recommended a bucket of cold water.

Fatma was just considering this course of action when a howl from the other end of the little house made the sleeper sit up and look at her questioningly.

'I don't know. Get out of bed if you want to see!' She left him and hurried to the kitchen.

The source of the howl, which had now subsided to an agonised groan, was one of the pool workers. The man was sitting at the table holding one wrist with the other hand while Mehmet stood at the sink filling the teapot, which was strange enough in itself.

He looked at Fatma in alarm. 'Birhat fell into the

pool and I think he may have broken his wrist,' he said.

'Let me see,' said Fatma. The man obediently held out his hand, supporting it under the forearm. The injured hand drooped at an unexpected angle.

'Not broken but dislocated,' she said. 'Does it hurt?'

'So much, Fatma Hanum. Big pain.'

'Should we take him to hospital?' asked Mehmet.

'That will mean a long wait. It's market day and the hospital will be full of people who've gone to town for the market and decided to get their ailments checked out while they're there. I have a better idea!' Fatma went out to the hall and made a phone call. When she came back, she turned off the gas under the teapot.

'We can have tea when we come back. We'll only be half an hour or so.'

The injured man looked wary but he followed Fatma out of the door. They all got into Mehmet's little red car and Fatma directed him to take the road to Yeshilkoy.

'Where are we going, my dear?' asked Mehmet.

'To the bonesetter who treated Hamdi's back last year. Derya said he went in doubled over in pain and came out skipping.'

In Yeshilkoy, a village slightly larger than Ortakoy, Fatma directed her husband until they came to a tiny house, the last building on a dead-end street. It was old and shabby and the man who opened the door was much the same.

'Mr Gurbuz! You come highly recommended by

Hamdi Shahin,' said Fatma. 'This man has had a fall. I think he has put his wrist out. Can you fix it?'

The man gave a gummy smile.

'I am Gurbuz the bonesetter, seventy-eight years old and been doing this since I was a boy. I can fix this man's wrist, but it will be painful.'

The injured man pulled his wrist in protectively and made a whimpering sound but he sat on the wooden bench the old man indicated.

The bonesetter took hold of his hand and felt around the wrist, which made him gasp. Then he looked at Mehmet.

'Sit there, next to him and put your arm round him there. Now hold tight!' The old man pulled sharply on the hand. The patient's mouth opened in a howl of surprise and pain and Fatma heard a crunching sound come from the wrist. Then the bonesetter released the hand and its owner twisted it tentatively back and forth and looked up in amazement.

Mehmet, who hated pain, even somebody else's, looked sick as he released his hold on the man.

'There will be a little pain for a few days when you move it but it should be good as new.'

'Thank you, Gurbuz Bey. It's a miracle!' said the worker.

'How much do we owe you?' asked Fatma.

'No charge,' said the bonesetter. 'You can leave me an offering if you wish,' he said, indicating a box on the windowsill. Fatma nudged Mehmet, who dropped a couple of notes into the box and they left, thanking the old man again.

As Fatma had said, they were home barely half

an hour after they had left. The man went round to tell his friend about the miracle and Fatma finished making the tea and even put some flour cookies out for Mehmet to take round to the men.

'What's this for – are you encouraging them to drink tea now?' he teased but Fatma just smiled and shooed him out of the door.

When he brought the tray back later he was shaking his head. 'Well done my dear, you played that well. Birhat's very grateful to you and his friend sends his thanks too. He says to tell you they'll be ready to pour the concrete tomorrow and the pool will be finished in a week.'

\*

The next day Fatma got Mehmet to drive her to town. Her first stop was the land registry office where she requested a land map and noted down the plot and parcel numbers of the orchard and the field behind it. The clerk instructed her to fill out an enquiry slip and go away for a few hours while they processed it. His supercilious manner reminded her of the officials she used to deal with at the Ministry of Agriculture and she used the same way of dealing with him, namely to imagine him asleep in bed wearing stripy pyjamas and snoring like a wild boar.

After handing in the completed slip, she went to visit a lawyer. This lady had managed to secure compensation for Hilal from the lorry driver who had knocked her husband off his scooter, despite the fact that he'd been in no state to ride it.

The receptionist was busy inspecting her bright

pink fingernails. She told Fatma to take a seat while she called her boss, then waved her through to the lady's office.

'Welcome, Fatma Hanum. How are you? Is Hilal Hanum well? And your families?'

'We are all well, thank you Turkan Hanum. And you – are you well?'

'Thanks be to God! What can I do for you?'

'I have a question. If someone owns a piece of land and they die, does it always pass to their wife? This piece of land is in the village and has been in the same family for many generations while this lady lives in Istanbul. Lived, I should say as she's dead now, God rest her soul.'

'I'm afraid the history doesn't make any difference, Fatma Hanum. Unless the land is in trust it will automatically pass to the deceased's wife and children.'

'He didn't have any children but his wife has a son who believes he is the new owner of the land.'

'He will indeed inherit his mother's estate.'

'But ownership of the land had not been transferred from the original owner to his wife.'

'That's just procedure, I'm afraid. Sometimes land goes several generations without being re-registered and we have to deal with twenty people who all have a claim to it. But the rules of inheritance are still the same.'

'The original owner had a nephew who has been using the land for a long time. Isn't there something about continuous usage leading to ownership?'

'Only for Treasury land. Otherwise anyone could

move onto your land when you weren't around and after a while claim ownership.'

'I suppose so,' said Fatma. She was running out of possible legal arguments. 'But the owner had always meant to transfer the land to his nephew. Even his wife knew that had been his intention and she said she would carry it through.'

'I'm sorry Fatma Hanum but if they didn't actually change the name on the deed, then the law doesn't recognise it. Is this a problem for you personally?'

'It's a problem for the village. The new owner of this land is planning to do something dreadful with it!'

'Then maybe you should talk to the planning board and see if he is violating any of their laws. Good luck – and give my greetings to Hilal Hanum!'

The land registry office was closed for lunch so she went to visit an old friend who had an office selling insurance. It was a business that was growing as people bought more expensive cars and possessions and found that praying and trusting in God were not always sufficient to protect them. The office was above a lokanta and Fatma and her friend sat on the small balcony and drank tea amid the smell of cooking that drifted up from below.

Fatma told her friend about the potential threat to the Kismet posed by Harun and his plans. Her friend expressed sympathy and then launched into a long story about how the girl who used to work for her had opened her own office and even stolen a few of her customers by selling cheaper policies. These, her friend explained, did not cover all the possible disasters, and her talk of fires, floods, accidents and earthquakes made Fatma quite anxious.

She made her excuses and left and went to stand at the door to the land registry office until it opened. When it did, she was the first one in and after taking her enquiry slip the snooty clerk handed her a ticket that showed the owner of the two plots was Hasan Chelik.

Undaunted and ignoring her throbbing feet, she followed the signs to the planning office. There she learned that it was not illegal to operate a business on agricultural land and that as long as the building did not have foundations it did not need planning permission. The man said that wooden bungalows such as she described were becoming quite popular and most passed fire department standards as fire retardant; nothing, he said gravely, was completely fireproof. A safety officer would check the place before it opened and if there was any irregularity it would not be issued with an operating licence. This was, however, very unusual, he said, smiling as if he had just given her the news she longed to hear.

Fatma found Mehmet drinking tea in the tea garden next to the car park and they set off for the village. In the car she took off her best shoes, wiggled her toes and rubbed her sore heel. She was disappointed and some people, she thought, might be tempted at this point to give up. But life had taught Fatma that you usually had to fight for the things you wanted. To her, this was just the first round in a campaign that she had no intention of losing.

The next round was drumming up more support

and before she looked further afield she made another attempt to recruit her family. As usual, she chose to confront them when they were sitting eating; the proximity of food seemed to put them in a more receptive mood.

'I spoke with a lawyer today and it seems that Harun Bey *is* now the legal owner of the orchard and can put his bungalows on the land.'

'I think he probably checked those things for himself,' said Ahmet, dipping bread into the chicken stew.

'So do any of you have a suggestion of how we can stop him?' Fatma looked around.

Ahmet took another mouthful of stew. 'We could hire someone to scare him off – a few threats, anonymous letters, that sort of thing.'

Fatma raised her eyebrows. 'We aren't members of the mafia and I don't know about you but I don't know any hitmen.' These ridiculous television shows, she thought, have a lot to answer for. 'What we need is an opposition group. Ahmet, you speak to the young people and see who's prepared to help. Mehmet, you can ask in the coffee house.'

'But Harun Bey comes into the coffee house and everyone likes him there,' objected Mehmet.

'Yes, I'm sure they all want to be friends with the big man from the city but will they be as happy when the place is overrun with his guests trying to get a cappuccino?'

'What are you going to do while we're trying to find you some supporters?' asked Ahmet.

'I'm going to visit Atilla, Communist Ali and

Demir. As fellow business owners they should understand my fears better than anyone. Once we've got enough people, we'll have a meeting and plan our assault.'

'Mother! This is not a war!' said Melek.

'That's what you think!' muttered Fatma, as she stood to clear the plates.

# 8

Eager to get the campaign started, the next morning after clearing the breakfast table Fatma tied a white, muslin scarf over her head, put on her outdoor shoes and left the house. It had rained in the night and everything in the garden was damp and fresh. The sky was pale blue but bruised, grey clouds still hung above the mountains and the pale sun cast their shadows, huge and ominous, on the valley below.

Along the lane the jewel-like anemones that had brightened the grassy verges in previous weeks had now been replaced by scarlet poppies and butter-yellow daisies. Down in the valley, fields of wheat had grown enough to ripple in the breeze. Fatma waved to her mother's friend Nurdan who was sitting on a chair by her front door enjoying the fresh air.

As she approached the orchard, Fatma heard the roar of a chain saw. Her heart thumped as she crept forward to peer round the bushes by the gate. There was no sign of Harun Bey but Osman was standing on a homemade ladder cutting branches off a tree. Judging from the amount of wood that was scattered about the orchard he had been doing it for some time.

He was wearing old trousers that sagged dangerously at the back and a shirt that gaped over his belly. His neck was shiny and his bald head had a dusting of sawdust. The sight reminded Fatma of Nazla's fears and she thought again how unlikely it was that the ladies of Istanbul would find Osman irresistible; then again, you never could tell.

She hurried past the gate before Osman could see her, turned at the junction by the mosque and carried on into the centre of the village. Sitting right in the middle where the road widened into a sort of village square was the general store. It was not a large or fancy establishment but it held an impressive range of products, as well as receiving post for some of the more distant homes and offering a telephone for those without one. The shopkeeper Atilla had been at school with Fatma and Melahat had once entertained hopes they might marry but Atilla had chosen a shy girl from Yeshilkoy as his wife.

'Selam Fatma! How are you today?' Atilla's intense blue eyes might have looked cold on someone else but were softened by his warm smile.

'Good morning, Atilla. I'm very well, thank you. You must be relieved the wedding is over!'

'It *is* nice not to have to worry about it anymore. And the newly-weds are happy, which is what matters!'

'Yes, of course. Bir yastukta kojasunlar!' said Fatma. 'May they grow old sharing a pillow!' She pulled at her cardigan. It was warm in the shop and smelt of the brine in which the olives and cheese were kept. 'I have some worries myself, Atilla – and I was hoping you might be able to help me with them.'

'Of course, Fatma. Tell me what they are and I will do my best.'

He pointed to a small wooden stool but Fatma preferred to remain standing.

'I'm sure you've met the new owner of Osman's orchard and heard his plans for the land.'

Atilla gave a nod.

'Well, you see, I'm quite against these plans! Apart from the fact that they pose a threat to my business, I don't think they're suitable for the village at all. I was hoping you might support me in trying to stop him.'

'Ah, I see,' said Atilla. His smile had faded and he looked a little worried. 'In what way do you think his plans are unsuitable?'

'He wants to make a place where people come and recover from their stressful lives by doing yoga, painting, things like that.'

'That doesn't sound too awful.'

'Do you know what yoga is, Atilla? It involves twisting your body into unnatural positions and chanting. They do it wearing tight-fitting garments; some people even do it naked!' Fatma, who had known little about yoga herself until the previous week, had been finding out all she could.

The village Imam had come into the shop. This holy man was tall and thin and though only in his early thirties he had a dried-out look. He had arrived in the village the previous year when the old Imam had died and he was not popular. Where his predecessor had accepted that aside from holidays only a handful of old men would respond to the call to prayer, the new Imam went round urging people to attend the mosque and berating them for their godless ways. On the Eid festival when attendance had been good, he had talked for so long that the women had begun to wonder where the men had disappeared to and the pastries warming in the ovens were all burned.

Now this man was looking at Fatma with interest.

'And as well as this, these people will be treating our village like a zoo,' she continued, 'wandering around laughing at our old-fashioned ways. And who knows what they might be capable of? You see stories every night on the news of the awful things that happen in the city.'

The Imam had taken a packet of tea and a box of sugar cubes from the shelves. Atilla put them in a bag and took the money before responding to Fatma.

'I'm not sure these people will actually be dangerous but I do sympathise with your situation. I would be upset if a second shop opened in the village. What do you propose doing?'

'I'm not sure yet but if we work together I think we can come up with something.'

The Imam, who had been checking his change, nodded his thanks and ducked out of the door. Atilla fiddled with some coins on the counter.

'I'll help if I can, Fatma. Nothing illegal or dangerous though!' He smiled to show he was joking.

Fatma smiled too. Atilla was influential in the village and his support was valuable. She left the shop and walked next door to the coffee house. There were a few men sitting outside at the tables set under the plane tree but Fatma headed straight into the smoky interior of the cafe. All heads turned to her in surprise. Mehmet was playing backgammon with Derya's husband Hamdi and his hand, which had been about to throw the dice, froze in mid-air when he saw Fatma.

'Trouble with the wife, Mehmet Abi?' whispered Hamdi.

Fatma glared at him. Communist Ali, the proprietor of the coffee house, put down the tray of dirty cups he had been carrying and approached Fatma.

'Can I help you with something, Fatma Hanum?' he asked.

Fatma flushed and took a deep breath. 'I hope so, Ali B-, Ali.' She never knew how to address the coffee house owner. As a title, 'Bey' was surely against his communist principles and she couldn't call him 'Abi' as he was younger than her.

She felt her face flushing. She wished there was less of an audience but asking to talk to Ali alone would only cause intrigue, and besides this way ensured the coffee house clientele all heard her mission, a task she did not trust Mehmet to carry out.

She described again the trouble the retreat would bring, the sort of people it would attract and the ways in which the village would be affected. When she finished, Communist Ali took the towel that was always draped over his shoulder and started to dry cups.

'I'm sorry, Fatma Hanum but I believe in a free country.' Ali had once gone to prison for his beliefs; these days he stayed away from politics, though he had not managed to lose the moniker. 'If this man wants to try a new business on land that is his, I don't think anyone should stop him. The village could do with shaking up a bit anyway. I thought you supported change.'

'Not all change is a good thing!' snapped Fatma. 'What about you, Hamdi, what are your feelings about this man?'

Hamdi looked uncomfortable. He operated a mobile greengrocery and the Kismet Pension was one of his biggest customers in the summer months.

'I've only met Harun Bey briefly,' he said looking at Mehmet who nodded reassuringly.

Fatma clenched her fists in frustration. She had thought it would be easier to get people to join her.

A man stood up at one a table in the corner. 'Fatma Hanum, I'm with you on this!'

She felt a surge of relief and turned to see Chetin Karatash. Chetin was the twin brother of Metin the carpenter. Unlike most twins, these two could not stand each other. The animosity had started very early when their mother, faced with the unexpected dilemma of two babies, had in desperation given one to her mother to care for. She swapped them regularly but even so the boys quickly understood they were rivals for their mother's attention. When they were older, she stopped farming one out and kept both boys with her but the damage had been done.

If she cooked Metin's favourite dish, Chetin would eat extra so there was less for his brother. When Chetin picked a few flowers from the hedgerow for her, Metin cut all the roses in the neighbour's garden.

It was a race to see who would get married first (Metin but only by a few months), who would provide the first grandchild (again Metin), who would have the first son (Chetin).

Their father was the village carpenter and for a short while had entertained the hope that his sons might jointly take over the business. When he realised that would be impossible, he chose the calmer and more dexterous Metin as his successor and found Chetin a job with the forestry department, adding even more to the latter's feelings of injustice.

Both men were short and stocky but Chetin had a way of sticking out his chest and bobbing his head that reminded Fatma of a cockerel. He was doing it now as he stood in front of her in the coffee house.

'We shouldn't allow this man to turn the village into a playground for these la-di-das from Istanbul,' he said.

Fatma looked around for any other support but most of the men had returned to their conversations. Chetin was not a person she usually consorted with but it seemed she would have to take all the help she could get.

'Good. I'm glad somebody is prepared to defend the village.'

Outside the coffee house she consoled herself with the thought that given his ongoing feud with his brother, Chetin was sure to have some good ideas of how to stop the retreat. Her efforts so far had, however, not been hugely successful. The fug of cigarette smoke inside had made her eyes water and she was warm in her two jumpers. She was tempted to go home, but there was one more person she needed to talk to, one she was confident would help.

Demir ran the restaurant at the beach with the help of his wife Dudu and his unreliable son Murat. In summer they slept in a tree house just behind the restaurant which saved them having to make the hair-raising journey down there every day. In winter they lived in a house at the end of the village.

The paperwork for the restaurant was somewhat irregular and Fatma had helped them more than once when the authorities had tried to close it down. She was sure Demir would understand her wish to protect her business and in addition, he owed her several favours.

She found Demir digging in his garden. The oversized flat cap he always wore was pushed up high on his forehead so the early spring sun could get to his face. When he saw Fatma he straightened up and pulled his cap down.

'Fatma Hanum. What a surprise!'

'I'm sorry to disturb you, Demir but there's something I'd like to discuss with you.'

She repeated her concerns for the third time that day, emphasising that Atilla 'and others' had already agreed to join her in opposing the retreat. Demir took little persuading.

'What do you suggest we do, Fatma Hanum?'

'I'll arrange a meeting and we'll discuss ideas. I'm sure together we can come up with a plan.'

Back at the Kismet Pension Fatma felt tired and snappy. She had secured the support of Atilla and Demir and his wife, and the rather dubious backing of Chetin. But her reception at the coffee house had upset her, not least Mehmet's lack of loyalty. She took her frustration out on him.

'How nice it must be to be a man and be allowed to do what you want!'

'What do you mean, my dear?'

'When I was building the Kismet Pension people were quick to voice their complaints but nobody wants to stand up to this man – and he isn't even from the village.'

'My dear, what you need to understand is that it's because of you that they are more accepting. You've shown them that changes in the village can be good.'

'I never said all change was good!' snapped Fatma, before going inside to make a pot of tea.

*

In the little house, Melek was studying. The window was open and she heard her mother complaining about Harun Bey.

Fatma sometimes got worked up about things – Ahmet sleeping late, her father spending too much time in the coffee house – and made terrible threats, only to forget all about them the following day. Melek had been hoping that the same would happen with her opposition to the retreat. After all, her mother was a good person; she would not really do anything to harm someone else's business, would she? And what could she do anyway?

After hearing her rant, Melek realised that her mother was determined to wage some sort of battle and what was more she had been round and tried to get half the village on her side. She thought of Barish – his easy smile, his Istanbul cool – and cringed with shame. How could she look him in the face, knowing what her mother was trying to do?

There was only one person she could talk to about her torment so she set off for the village to see Selma. On the way she scuttled past the orchard with her head down and overtook Leyla leading her goat with two handsome kids skittering circles around them. Normally she would have stopped to chat to the younger girl but today she just gave a quick greeting and hurried on.

Selma was delighted to see her but she could see something was wrong. Melek greeted her friend's mother, then the two girls disappeared into Selma's room to get away from her brothers. The room had previously belonged to Selma and Idil and was much more spacious since the departure of Idil to her new home and the removal of the second bed.

Flopping onto the remaining one, Selma fixed Melek with a mock tragic look. 'What's wrong, Meli, can't stop thinking of dream boy?'

After the wedding, Selma had quizzed Melek about Barish and Melek had told her friend how comfortable she felt with him. She did not tell her how her insides flipped every time she thought of him and how just picturing his smile and the way his hair fell over his brow caused a tingling in strange places.

Now she looked forlorn. 'He's probably forgotten all about me now he's back in the city. I bet he's surrounded by pretty girls…'

'He didn't look as though he would forget you

quickly, Meli. Maybe he's tired of those city girls. And by the way, you're pretty too, and clever and—'

'And my mother has gone completely crazy and is going to do everything she can to ruin his father's plans,' said Melek miserably. She had always been proud of her mother before; now she wondered what it would be like to have a mother like Selma's, who was content to look after the home and family.

'Hmm, that's awkward. But Dad says Barish's father has it all arranged and I don't think even Fatma Auntie can do anything to stop him.'

'That doesn't mean she won't try. And by the time she realises it's useless, Barish won't want anything to do with me.'

'He can't hold you responsible. Parents are always being a pain!'

Melek remembered Barish saying his mother liked to embarrass him but it was hardly on a level with what Fatma was doing. 'But how will I even see him? She won't want me going to the retreat and I can't see her making him welcome at the pension.'

'Then you'll have to meet secretly. It will be so romantic!'

# 9

The newly formed opposition group was meeting at the Kismet Pension and Fatma had been fussing around since breakfast. She had got Ahmet to push three tables together and, hoping for a good turnout, had made tea in the large urn. She felt confident that Nazla, who was well-known and universally liked in the village, would have recruited a good number of people.

She herself had received one unexpected offer of help. The day after her trip to the village there had been a knock on the door of the house and she had opened it to find the Imam standing on the step.

'Selamun Aleykum, Fatma Hanum.'

'Aleykum selam.' Fatma hoped he wasn't going to ask her to persuade Mehmet to visit the mosque more often. She did not think even her powers of persuasion were up to that task.

'I heard you telling Atilla Bey about the new arrival in our village.'

Fatma was puzzled. 'I can't imagine he'll be attending the mosque, Erdem Hoja. He doesn't look like the type to me.'

'Maybe not but at the moment I'm more concerned about his plans and the effect they might have on the village. Allah knows there are few enough devout souls here already.'

'Erdem Hoja, are you saying you want to join our...campaign?'

The Imam coughed. 'I don't wish to get mixed up in anything inappropriate. However, I've thought of something that might help your cause. There are laws banning certain businesses operating in the vicinity of a mosque, particularly if they involve the sale of alcohol.'

'Oh yes?'

'This man's land is not far from my mosque and tomorrow when I am in town for a meeting at the Ministry of Religious Affairs I'm going to find out whether his plans fall foul of this law. I'll let you know, Fatma Hanum.'

He gave a quick nod and without even wishing her good day, went out of the garden and back towards the mosque. Fatma stood on the stop watching the tall, spare figure retreating. Unpopular though he was, the Imam's support would lend their struggle status and she thought it might be a sign that things were turning in their favour.

Nazla arrived first.

'Greetings, Fatma. The pool is beginning to look good.' The erstwhile muddy hole was now lined with bright turquoise tiles and the two men were laying marble slabs round the edge.

'Welcome, Nazla. How are things?'

'Oh, alright. Eda has a bit of a cough. You know

how changeable the weather is at this time of year and children never listen when you tell them to wear more clothes!'

'Grated black turnip mixed with honey is the best cure for a cough,' said Fatma. 'But what about our business – did you find some people who want to help?'

'I tried, Fatma, but most people don't want to get involved.'

'Don't these people realise that they *are* involved? This retreat affects all of us!'

'You're right, of course. I'm sorry.'

Fatma sighed. 'It's not your fault, Nazla. I got the same reaction in the coffee house and Derya hasn't found anyone willing to help.'

'Nurdan Auntie supports us,' said Nazla.

'Nurdan Auntie is seventy-five years old and is always talking about her weak heart.'

'Well, obviously she won't be marching around protesting but she's on our side, which is something. She also says there are bad djinns in the field. She thinks they were responsible for her father's accident and she believes they'll force Harun Bey to abandon his project.'

Fatma ignored this. 'Anyone else?'

'Buket is willing to help.'

Buket was an unfortunate young woman whose parents had arranged for her to marry a distant cousin in Istanbul. The man turned out to be a nasty drunk who knocked her about on a regular basis. After a particularly bad beating that broke her arm, she finally told her mother who got on the bus that night and returned to the village with her daughter and two young grandsons. As a result of her experience, Buket hated anyone from the city.

'I've got the support of Atilla, Demir and Chetin.'

'Chetin Karatash?' Nazla looked horrified. 'Are you sure he can be trusted? What reason does he have for objecting to the retreat? Don't tell me he's looking out for the village, because that man only ever looks out for himself!'

'I don't know why, I only know that we can't afford to be picky. And nasty as he is, Chetin might be useful in our campaign. If you're worried about how it makes us look, you might be pleased to know we have the support of Erdem Hoja!'

Before she could explain, Demir and Dudu arrived and Fatma went to start pouring the tea. Chetin came in strutting as usual, accompanied by a man he introduced as Crazy Kerim. They worked together at the forestry commission and Kerim was keen, Chetin said, to join their struggle. Judging by the nasty scar that ran across his cheek, Fatma suspected Crazy Kerim would happily join any struggle just for the hell of it.

Fatma felt a surge of hope when she saw Mehmet. She had told her family about the meeting and asked them to be there but they had all looked shifty and mumbled about having things to do. Her hope waned when she realised Mehmet was just assisting Melahat who always wanted to be involved if there was a possibility of drama. Once he had settled her in a chair with a glass of tea, he claimed pressing business and disappeared in the little red car.

Derya came out of the laundry room and helped Fatma serve the tea. She sat at the table though Fatma noticed she was fidgeting and looking uncomfortable. Buket arrived, also looking nervous, and the last to come was Atilla, clicking a set of worry beads in one hand.

Fatma started the meeting by telling everyone about her trip to town. She related what she had learned from the lawyer and the land registry and planning offices. Then she explained the Imam's involvement in their cause.

'He's in town finding out today but until we hear back I suggest we come up with some other ideas,' she said.

'Harun Bey is waiting for a digger to come from town,' said Nazla. 'Perhaps we could do something to delay its arrival?'

'Do you know who he's rented it from?' Atilla continued to click the beads as he spoke. 'I know the owner of the biggest company round here. His name's Rushtem.'

'Oh yes! I heard Osman on the phone speaking to a Rushtem Bey.'

'We did our national service together in Kars. Do you know, sometimes in winter when we opened the door to the barracks you couldn't see out for the snow!' Atilla shook his head at the memory.

'Yes, well, as you know this man perhaps you could ask him not to send a machine out here,' said Fatma.

'Rushtem won't like losing business. And there are other companies they could go to.'

'Couldn't he just keep putting it off – making excuses to delay its arrival?'

'Won't this man want to know why?' Nazla asked Atilla.

The beads clicked faster. 'I'll tell him we've heard rumours about Harun Bey and want to check if they're true before he starts this building. Rushtem won't ask too many questions. I can't delay him forever, though.'

'Can anyone else think of something we could do?'

'I have a suggestion, Fatma,' said Chetin. 'Harun Bey has placed a big order for furniture. If something were to go wrong with that, he might reconsider his plans.'

'And what would he do with the ten bungalows he's ordered?' asked Nazla.

'Well, it would slow things down at least.'

'So you propose sabotaging your brother's business?' asked Demir.

Fatma suddenly understood why Chetin had wanted to join them.

He shrugged at Demir. 'Do you have a better suggestion?'

'How were you thinking of doing it?' asked Fatma.

'By burning down the workshop!'

'Are you crazy? Someone could die!' said Atilla, standing as if to leave.

'Nobody's burning anything down!' said Fatma emphatically.

Chetin looked sulky. He stirred the tea Nazla had just poured for him, making the spoon clink aggressively against the glass. 'Then I'll fiddle with his precious machines. They won't check the settings every day and with a bit of luck by the time they realise the length is wrong they'll have cut all the wood too short.'

'How will that stop him?' asked Buket.

'He'll have paid for the wood up front and if he wants his furniture he'll have to pay out again,' said Chetin.

'But everyone says he has plenty of money!' said Buket.

'I think,' said Fatma, 'there isn't one easy way to stop this man. But if we put enough obstacles in his path, he'll eventually get tired and abandon his project. It's just a game to him after all.'

Demir nodded and the peak of his cap bobbed up and down. 'Fatma Hanum is right; it's called a war of attrition. You wear someone down by attacking on many fronts just like our grandfathers did when they fought to defend this country!'

They talked about it a little more. Atilla wasn't happy with the plan but once Chetin had assured him that the mistake would look like just that – an unfortunate error – they agreed that if the Imam did not come back with good news he could go ahead with his plan.

Then Nazla got up to leave as it was almost time for the girls to be getting home from school and the younger two would get up to mischief if left alone. The others chatted over another glass of tea and then they left too. Derya collected the glasses and took them to the kitchen. Fatma poured a last glass of tea for herself and her mother.

'You're very quiet, Mother. Have you nothing to say?'

Melahat waggled her head from side to side in a way that showed regret. 'If I were you, my girl, I'd pray for a miracle. That lot couldn't take a dummy from a baby's mouth!'

\*

That night, Fatma waited for a call from the Imam. The phone rang twice and both times she rushed to answer it but the first time it was Selma calling for Melek and the second was Nurdan Auntie calling to ask Melahat to help her make helva the following day. She had seen her husband in a dream and he had asked for it; Nurdan Auntie's husband had been dead for nearly fifteen years but still his wish was not to be denied.

Fatma was about to go round to the pension the next morning when the telephone rang, its voice shrill in the quiet house. Fatma picked up the receiver and heard the nasal tones of the Imam; she said a quick prayer that it might be good news.

'Fatma Hanum, it seems the law only forbids the sale of alcohol up to 50 metres around the mosque, which is unfortunate since the site of this planned monstrosity is significantly further than that.'

'Well, thank you for checking it, Erdem Hoja.'

He wished Fatma good luck in her mission, adding that God was sure to help her. Fatma replaced the receiver and wished God would come up with something soon; then she felt guilty and whispered a prayer for forgiveness. God had given her brains and determination so she could tackle such problems on her own and so far she had not met a challenge she hadn't managed to overcome.

# 10

All over the country young people were looking forward to Children's Day when they would perform the poems, songs and dance routines they had learned for the occasion and be rewarded with so many sugary treats that they ended up feeling sick. The children of Ortakoy had an added reason to get excited and that was the party held every year at the Kismet Pension to celebrate the holiday.

This year however, Fatma had been so distracted by recent events that she lost track of the date until Derya managed to slip into the conversation the fact that it was already the twentieth of the month.

'The twentieth? Allahallah! Why didn't anyone tell me?' Fatma stood up from the pile of cotton batting with which they were filling cushions. Her cardigan, flowery trousers, even her headscarf were covered in a fuzz of cotton fibres. 'There are three days left until Children's Day and we have a party to organise!'

She hurried off to find Mehmet and Ahmet, who were whitewashing walls in the pension, and gave them each a list of party-related jobs. At least, she thought as she sat down to plan the food, the pension was looking good and the pool would be finished. Not that any mothers would be allowing their children to get in it at this time of year; the weather was still much too cool.

Once the initial panic was over and the essentials had been arranged Fatma realised that the party provided the perfect opportunity to remind people what the Kismet Pension gave to the village. This year's event needed to be better than ever.

'A Hacivat and Karagoz puppet show – that always entertains the children!' said her mother when she asked the family for ideas.

'It may have done fifty years ago, Grandma, but not these days,' said Melek.

'Fireworks are cool!' said Ahmet.

'This is an afternoon party for children!' Fatma shook her head.

'What about a magician, Mum? I saw an advertisement for one who was performing in town,' suggested Melek.

'Mmm, maybe. But he'll probably want a hefty sum to come out here. Don't you have a friend whose son runs a dance troupe?' Fatma asked Mehmet, who had been reading the football pages of the newspaper and trying to stay out of the conversation.

'Yes, my dear.'

'Well, when you see him at the coffee house later, ask him to have a word with his son and see if he can send a group of dancers. Just five or six would be fine. There isn't enough space for too many of them and we don't want them falling in the pool!'

The next day the pool was finally finished. Ismail

arrived with the pump and filter and spent several hours in the cramped engine room fitting them. When he had finished, Ahmet brought over the hosepipe and Fatma, Ismail and the two workers stood reverently to one side and watched as the first splash of water hit the bottom of the pool.

Ismail gave Ahmet a lesson on which valves to open and close and how to clean the pool while Birhat and his friend stuffed their clothes and the contentious teapot into carrier bags. Fatma thanked the men for their work and gave them each a small bonus and a bag of oranges to take to their families. Then they all left for town, the two men to catch a bus that would take them on the twenty-hour journey home. How sad, Fatma thought, having to travel so far to find work. One of them, she knew, had a baby he had not seen.

When they had gone, she joined Derya in the kitchen where they started preparing food for the party. As she worked the sound of the water gushing into the pool gave Fatma a feeling of satisfaction bordering on smugness. By the evening the water level had almost reached the top and Ahmet turned off the hose.

In bed that night Fatma went through a mental list of chores. They had rolled the cheese pastries and picked and stuffed all the tender new leaves from the vine that grew by the front door of the house. They had mixed the meatballs and set the chicken thighs to marinate in yogurt, garlic and lemon juice. Melek had baked biscuits and made several trays of mosaic cake that were chilling in the fridge and there were enough bottles of fizzy drinks and ayran to satisfy the thirst of the whole village. Ahmet was going to wash the floor and set out the tables in the morning and it would take only an hour or so to finish filling the pool. Satisfied there was nothing they had missed she went to sleep confident that the party would be a success.

*

The morning of the party woolly clouds were scudding across the sky. Fatma rose early and fried spicy sausage and eggs, the smell of which drew even Ahmet from his bed. There was no dawdling over breakfast this morning. As they ate, Fatma went through their various tasks for the day and as soon as they had finished she dispatched them to begin the work. She was washing the dishes when Ahmet came rushing back in.

'The pool's gone down!' he said.

Fatma had visions of the garden wall collapsing and the pool heading down the rocky slope below the pension. 'What do you mean "gone down"?'

'Like someone's pulled the plug out. The water's nowhere near where it was last night.'

'You must have turned the wrong valve!'

'I didn't touch anything after Ismail left!'

'I told you building this thing would attract bad djinn!' said Melahat, the only one who had been allowed to sit at the table with a second glass of tea. Fatma was already on her way out of the door.

She hurried through the garden and past the front of the pension, plastic sandals slapping on the path. As she went, she tried to think if anyone else might have played with the valves – not a djinn but someone who wanted to cause mischief, make her look foolish? She dismissed the idea as unlikely, not least because there were few people around who knew anything about swimming pools.

She followed Ahmet to the edge of the pool and looked in. The tiles were bright, the water was rippling in the breeze but there was no ignoring the fact that its surface was a whole three tiles below where it had been the previous evening.

'Do you know what's happened to this?' she asked Mehmet, who was cleaning the barbecue.

'No, my dear. It looks as though we have a leak.'

Fatma frowned. 'You watched those idiots pouring the concrete. Is it possible it's sprung a leak already?' Mehmet returned to sweeping the ashes out of the barbecue and Fatma turned to Ahmet. 'Fill it up again. I'm going to call Ismail.'

Ismail apologised but said he couldn't come to sort out the problem until the following day. It was not ideal but Fatma hoped that if they filled the pool just before the guests arrived, it would look alright for the party.

Next she went to see how Derya was getting on in the kitchen and found her standing over the sink sloshing water into her mouth.

'Whatever is the matter?'

'Pe-pe-pe,' sputtered Derya, waving a hand in front of her mouth and pointing to the worktop. Her face was bright pink and sweat had dampened the hair on her brow.

Fatma frowned and inspected the food on the

worktop. There was a large bowl of shakshuka – a dish of fried aubergine in a pepper, garlic and tomato sauce. Fatma took a spoon of the mixture and went to eat it.

'No!' Derya managed to say. 'Pe-pe-pepper. Hot!'

'Oh nonsense, Derya. You never were any good with spicy food.' Fatma put the spoon in her mouth. The shakshuka was good. The aubergine were young and tender and the sauce was rich with a tinge of heat. The tinge got stronger and became a kick. Then it became a burning sensation that made her tongue feel twice its usual size. She picked up one of the peppers that was sitting on the side and sniffed it. It was long and dark green and looked just like the peppers they always used. She took a tiny bite from the pointy end of the pepper and her mouth exploded.

Dropping the pepper Fatma ran to the sink and Derya moved over to give her access to the tap. As she sluiced water into her mouth the fingers that had held the pepper came in contact with her nose and that started burning too. In the end, she stuck her face under the tap and after a minute sufficient feeling returned to her mouth that she could speak.

'Who would grow such ridiculously hot peppers? You should have tried them before you put them in the pan.'

'I'm sorry, Fatma, but they looked like normal peppers,' Derya sniffed.

'Yes, you're right. Oh well, we can't serve that to children.'

'Shall I ask Hamdi to bring us some more aubergine?'

Fatma looked out at Ahmet who was already setting out the tables. 'No, I think we'll have to do without shakshuka. There's plenty of other food. Just make sure you don't put those things in the salad!'

When the preparations were finished the place looked festive with the pool full, the tables covered with bright cloths and balloons and flags tied round the bar. The clouds were beginning to clump together and the wind was tugging at the table cloths and decorations but Fatma thought it would be night, possibly even the next day, before the rain came.

The guests started to arrive. Nazla came with her boisterous younger daughters and Eda, who had recovered from her cough. Selma brought a half-full bowl of mulberries and her younger brothers whose hands and mouths were stained a dark purple. Hamdi arrived with his and Derya's youngest child, twelve-year-old Aslan, and Buket came with her two boys and her elderly parents. Metin's wife brought their three children and Chetin's wife arrived a little later and stood as far from her sister-in-law as possible; the animosity extended beyond the brothers to their spouses.

Fatma was on her way to the kitchen to fetch the chicken when she saw a figure hovering in the corner shyly. The other children had new clothes for the holiday but Leyla was wearing a home-knitted jumper and baggy trousers that finished just above her bony ankles.

'Hello, Leyla. I'm glad you came.'

The girl pulled at a thread on her jumper. 'Thank you, Fatma Auntie. Melek Abla invited me.'

'Of course she did. Let's go and find her, shall we?' She took the girl's hand and led her over to where Melek was overseeing a game of blind man's bluff.

'Make sure the others don't tease her, will you?' she whispered to her daughter after handing over her small charge.

Even without the shakshuka the spread of food covered three tables. Mehmet spent more than an hour at the barbecue, with Hamdi and Buket's father – the only other men present – chipping in with their advice on where the coals were hottest and which pieces of chicken were cooked. Why was it, Fatma wondered, that men who never went near a kitchen thought themselves experts on cooking over a fire? Perhaps it was something primitive from the days of hunting and cave dwelling. She rewarded their exertions, though, with a tray of cold beers.

The children dived on the food, ate quickly and were soon running round chasing balloons and playing games again. The women took their time, enjoying the food and the chance to gossip. At half past three, only a little after the appointed time, the dancers arrived. Ahmet turned off the music, Melek rounded up the children and got most of them to sit down and Fatma made an announcement.

'Welcome to the Kismet Pension. I hope you're all enjoying the party so far. We've organised some extra entertainment this year. I give you – the Zafer dance troupe!'

The dancers came out in their costumes and took up their places. The music began and they started with the Zeybek, a dance traditional to the region.

The audience clapped along and cheered when the dancers performed more difficult moves. When the Zeybek was finished, the boys disappeared into the pension to change and the girls did a sweet dance that represented a bride getting ready for her wedding day.

The boys returned wearing the long tunics, tight trousers and knee-length boots of Caucasian dancers. The music was faster and the dancing more frenetic with a lot of leaping and spinning. The girls by contrast danced with such tiny steps and fluttering movements they looked as though they were on wheels.

Fatma was beginning to relax and enjoy the show when one of the dancers reached into a bag at his waist and drew out a clutch of knives. She knew these dances sometimes included knife throwing but the dancers in this case were teenagers; surely they would not perform the real stunt? The boy with the knives had already made one of the other dancers lie on the floor with a wooden board held to his chest. Fatma looked around for the group leader but he was by the bar talking to Ahmet and not even watching the performance.

There was a drum roll of suspense. The boy with the knives balanced one upside-down on his chin. Fatma wanted to shout out but was afraid of distracting him and causing him to miss his target. He dipped his head and set the knife spinning towards the board where it buried itself with a dull thud that made Fatma's insides clench. He did a little dance and balanced the next knife, then let it fall and plant itself next to the first. There were cheers and the third knife thumped into the wood.

The boy balanced the fourth knife on his chin. There was a rumble of thunder in the distance. Then, just as he tilted his head to throw the knife, the boy on the floor sneezed causing the board to slip to one side. The boy rolled the other way, the knife hit the floor where he had been a second before. Fatma jumped to her feet. The audience clapped and laughed thinking it was all part of the act.

Then the boy on the floor got up and the knife-thrower threw a punch that sent him sprawling back down with blood pouring from his split lip and left nobody in any doubt about its authenticity. The adults gasped in horror while the children whooped with delight. The dancers gathered round their fallen comrade and their leader dragged the other boy away. Fatma waved at Ahmet to put on some music and followed them to where their minibus was parked at the front of the pension.

'No harm done!' said the leader as he bundled the boy onto the bus. 'I hope you'll recommend us to your friends.'

'I will but can I suggest you stick to the dancing?'

'But the audience loves the knife throwing! It's usually fine but these two had already had a falling out today and Nuri thought Alp sneezed on purpose to put him off.'

'That would be a foolish thing to do when he's aiming a knife at you.'

The man shrugged. 'Boys!' He took his money and left.

*

Melek was serving cake when the first spots of rain started to fall. She wrapped the rest in napkins for the guests to take home and in five minutes the only people left were the family and Derya, all sheltering under the bar. The rain was getting harder – large drops that were soaking the tablecloths and pitting the surface of the pool, which was again three tiles below the top.

'Well, my dear, everyone enjoyed themselves,' said Mehmet.

'I'm not sure that boy did. He could have lost a tooth,' said Melek.

'That was some punch!' said Ahmet with admiration.

'Shall we have some tea, Derya?' asked Fatma. One thing was certain, she thought as she watched her friend scuttle through the rain to the kitchen to put the teapot on: the villagers would not forget this party in a hurry.

*

While his wife and daughter had been attending the party Chetin had been carrying out an important and highly secret mission. He had chosen that afternoon when his brother's wife and children – along with half the village – would be at the Kismet Pension and Metin would be fishing where he was every Sunday without fail. Chetin was wearing a baseball cap for the job but had no need for any further disguise; from a distance people often confused him with his brother anyway.

His plan relied on the fact that Metin kept the key in the same place it had always been – under the block of stone carved with strange hieroglyphs that their father had dug up in the garden. He crouched down and lifted the heavy slab and was relieved to see the key there. He undid the padlock, slid back the metal door and, after a quick look round, went in.

Inside, the smell of freshly-sawn wood brought a lump to Chetin's throat. As a child he had spent much time in here watching his father work, playing with offcuts of wood, vying with his brother for who would sweep the floor. When their father chose Metin to take over the business, he told everyone that he didn't care and that he found carpentry boring but it wasn't true, he just said it to hide his hurt.

He pushed aside the memories and focused on his plan. He went to each machine and adjusted the controls carefully – not so much that it would be noticed immediately but enough that the pieces would no longer fit. In just a few minutes he had finished and was pulling shut the door of the workshop and replacing the key in its place. As he walked back up the path all thought of Harun Bey and his retreat had completely slipped his mind. His only regret was that he wouldn't be there to see his brother's face when he discovered the mistake.

# 11

The Kismet Pension always opened on the first of May. Some years there were no guests for a day or two and Ahmet would grumble about having to sit around waiting but the date had become important to Fatma and, as she pointed out, it was not as if he had anything else to do.

This year she felt a more pressing need to open and attract some visitors. Empty, the place gave off a slightly forlorn air but if Harun Bey saw it full of guests he might realise that Ortakoy already offered people the perfect place to escape and unwind. She also wanted to show him that she was quite capable of finding guests without his help.

In the week after the party she put everybody to work. Mehmet went round with his toolbox carrying out repairs. Ahmet painted the front door blue and varnished all the tables and chairs. She and Derya finished hanging curtains and beating rugs and even planted geraniums in tins that had once contained olives.

Ismail turned up and quickly found that a faulty valve was responsible for the disappearing water.

Once he had replaced it they turned on the hose and filled the pool. Fatma made him stay to lunch to thank him for his help and also to keep him there until they could establish that the leak really was fixed. An hour later, when he had eaten a good meal of chicken shish kebab, chips and shepherd's salad, the water was still lapping over the marble sides of the pool and she felt confident enough to allow him to leave.

\*

On the morning of the first, Mehmet always went down to the bus station in town to tout for business. When a bus came in, he hovered near the door holding a board with pictures of the Kismet and calling, 'nice, clean pension, very cheap price!' If anyone showed interest, they would haggle a bit over the price, then Mehmet would load passengers and luggage into the small, red car and drive them to Ortakoy.

He did this happily for a few days, spending the time in between arrivals catching up with the men who worked for the bus companies and enjoying having some different opponents to beat at backgammon. After that he always tired of going to town and gave the board to one of the taxi drivers so he could find them guests.

This year Fatma made him leave the village at six o'clock to be at the bus station in time for the arrival of the overnight buses. She had given a sign advertising the pension to Hilal to display in the shop and another to the pump attendant at the petrol station on the main road, to whom she offered a small commission on any guests he sent. She had also found a piece of board that had once been the back of a wardrobe, painted it black and chalked 'Open – rooms available' in Turkish and English. She took this out to the front of the pension and propped it against an old tyre in such a way that anyone passing along the lane would be sure to see it.

She went inside and checked that all the room keys were hanging ready behind the tiny reception desk. She opened the large book in which she recorded guests' details, turned to a new page and wrote the year at the top and the date underneath. In a drawer she found some brochures for activities and trips offered by the tour agencies in town and fanned them attractively on the desk. With nothing else to do but wait she went back to the house.

Her mother was watching television in the small sitting room. A presenter wearing too much make-up and a strapless dress better suited to a grand soiree than a morning chat show was sympathising with a woman whose husband had run off with a Russian dancer leaving her with two young children.

'Can you believe this?' asked Melahat indignantly. 'Such dreadful stories these days.'

'There have always been dreadful stories, you just get to hear about them more these days,' said Fatma. 'Would you like a coffee, Mother?'

'Mm, make it sweet. My blood sugar level must be low – I feel quite dizzy.'

In the kitchen, Fatma spooned coffee into the long-handled coffee pot and dropped in four lumps of sugar. She usually took hers only moderately sweet but it was too much trouble to make each cup separately. She would make up for the extra sugar by foregoing the pistachio-flavoured lokum she usually ate with her coffee.

'Nurdan says there's a lot of work going on in the orchard,' Melahat said as Fatma set the tray on the table. 'Has that rogue Chetin carried out his plan yet?'

'I think he tried,' said Fatma vaguely. Chetin had called to tell her he had done the job. Fatma had expected to feel pleased but found instead that it left her unsettled. It felt as though a threshold had been crossed and although Chetin had assured her again that the mistake would not be traceable her own conscience was giving her trouble.

Melahat chewed on a piece of lokum. 'I hope you know what you're doing, Fatma. Don't forget the saying, "sow the wind and you will reap a hurricane".'

Already feeling uncomfortable, Fatma squirmed at the warning and was relieved when her mother turned her attention back to the television and the woman who was now speaking on the telephone to her feckless husband.

She finished her coffee and went back to the pension where Ahmet was dozing with his head on the bar. She woke him and sent him to catch the leaves that the breeze had dropped into the pool. Derya was sorting the linen in the laundry room and Fatma tried to help but every time she heard a car she rushed out to see if it was stopping.

She rang the office of the bus company and got them to put Mehmet on the line.

'What is it Fatma? What's happened?' Her unexpected call had even upset the usually calm

Mehmet.

'Nothing. I just wondered if there are many people around?'

'Oh. Not yet, my dear. The morning arrivals were all booked into pensions in town. There's another bus arriving in half an hour.'

She rang Hilal and listened to her complain about a rival shop being given space in the new bus station.

'I wonder how big a backhander they gave for that.'

'It's terrible, all this corruption, Hilal. By the way, have you had any enquiries about the pension?'

'Not yet, Fatma Abla.'

'Have you got the board where people can see it?'

'It's on the counter, right by the lighters and chewing gum.'

It was almost three o'clock and she was sitting at one of the tables snapping green beans when she heard a car stop on the lane. She jumped up and rushed round to the front of the pension where a man was getting out of a shiny white rental car. He had steely grey hair that stuck out wildly and his clothes looked as though he might have slept in them.

'Meraba! Ee-goonler!' he greeted Fatma in heavily accented Turkish. 'Oda varmi?'

'Hosh geldiniz! Welcome! Yes – we have room!'

The man nodded to his wife who got out of the car and stood looking up at the pension. Fatma motioned them to follow her and led them upstairs to a room with a view of the valley.

'Chok goozel!' exclaimed the man, while his wife stepped out onto the balcony and gave a nod of approval.

'How many days you stay?'

'Bilmiyorum. I don't know. Three, maybe more.' He explained in a mix of English and broken Turkish that he was looking at ancient sites and wanted to examine the theatre and tombs at Ortakoy. They agreed a price for the room including breakfast and dinner and Fatma called Ahmet to carry their bags up.

She had only just finished writing their details in the register when she heard the unmistakeable sound of the little red car labouring along the road. It pulled up and three large, blonde people sprang from it. They all had long hair and brightly coloured clothes but from the beards Fatma saw that two were male and one female.

'My wife,' Mehmet said and left her to deal with the foreigners. They hauled their large packs from the boot of the car and Fatma filled in their details in the book and showed them to two rooms upstairs.

They returned after a short time and jumped in the pool. The water was cold enough to make them squeal but it did not seem to put them off. The amateur archaeologist and his wife came down having obviously showered and dressed for dinner. He had a beer and she asked if they had gin but settled on a glass of white wine. Fatma and Melek served the guests a dinner of wedding soup, meatballs, cracked wheat pilau and green beans in olive oil. Afterwards they passed round some green almonds for the guests to try. Most took a small bite and made a face but the English man ate a number of the bitter kernels and

Fatma hoped he wouldn't regret it as she knew from experience that too many could play havoc with your insides.

Once the guests had all retired and she had cleared the last plates and glasses Fatma allowed herself to sit for a moment looking up at the pension. Lights were still shining from two of the rooms and she could see one of the Dutch people on the balcony smoking, the red tip of his cigarette glowing in the dark. It felt good to have opened again and have guests in on the first day. It reminded her of what the Kismet represented: the result of her hard work and determination, as well as her family's livelihood and her children's future.

Fatma was not going to let anyone threaten those things without putting up a fight.

*

Harun was frustrated. Osman had just told him that the digger they had been expecting for two days was going to be delayed further.

'I don't understand. Is it because of the distance from town?'

'That's one problem but there's also so much work on at the moment. Building work is banned in town over the summer season so everyone is rushing to get things finished,' Osman explained.

'Should I offer to pay extra?'

'I know Rushtem a little and I don't think that will help.'

'Well, isn't there another company we could use? We need to get the land ready before the bungalows arrive.'

'I know, Harun Abi, but if Rushtem is this busy there's no chance any of the others have a digger to spare – they only have one or two each. I'll give him another call later and see if he's any clearer when one might be free.'

With no work being done in the orchard Harun decided to see how the furniture was progressing. On the lane he passed a man leading a donkey laden with rushes, then a woman holding a basket up to a young man who was balanced in the branches of a tree picking glossy, red cherries. Harun felt his irritation fade. He needed to get used to things taking a little longer round here, he thought. After all, the slow pace of life was one of the things that made the village perfect for the retreat.

Outside the workshop the pile of wood that had been delivered the previous week had got smaller. As he approached the door, though, he heard shouting.

'Donkey-head! How many times have I shown you how to set the machines?' The carpenter had his back to the door and didn't notice Harun enter. He was shouting at a young man with a long face and smooth, sallow skin. The boy looked hopefully at Harun.

'Selam Master Carpenter! Is there a problem?'

Metin spun round. His face was red and his mouth opened and closed a couple of times before any sound came out. 'G-Good morning, Harun Bey. I wasn't expecting you!'

'I thought I'd drop in and see how things were going. I hope it's not a bad time.'

'Of course not, you are always welcome.'

Harun looked around the workshop. There were piles of sawn wood stacked in every free space. 'So how is it going?'

'We've been working hard, as you can see,' said Metin. Then his anger seemed to fizzle out and he looked miserable. 'Unfortunately, it appears that this clumsy oaf has managed to change the settings on the machines.'

'What does that mean?'

'It means that some of the wood has been cut...too short.' The carpenter shook his head at the enormity of the mistake.

'How short? Can you still use it?'

'Perhaps, if we can alter some of the pieces. I am so sorry, Harun Bey.'

'How could something like this happen?'

'I was going to ask the same thing.' The carpenter looked at the boy, who sniffed and looked down at his sawdust-covered trainers. 'I can assure you nothing like it has ever happened before.'

'How much of the wood has been wasted?'

'I'm not sure. I only spotted it now because I thought I would put together some pieces for you to see.'

Harun found the smell of the wood suddenly overpowering and had an urge to leave the workshop. 'Metin Usta, I'm going to Ali Bey's for a coffee. Please check the wood that has been cut and see how much is useable and how much will have to be replaced.'

The carpenter was nodding, his eyes closed, his expression one of sorrow.

'And please don't make any decisions yet with

regard to this young man; we'll discuss the matter when I return.'

Harun left the workshop and trudged along the lane to the coffee house. The old men sitting at their usual table under the plane tree nodded at Harun when he greeted them but he couldn't help wondering what they really thought of him.

Inside, the place was empty apart from Ali who was taking apart the wood-burning stove.

'Good morning, Harun Bey. Time to put this old thing out the back until autumn. Even the evenings are warm enough without it now.'

'So summer's officially here?'

'Well, it's just round the corner anyway.' He pulled apart two lengths of stovepipe and a shower of soot fell onto the newspaper he had spread on the floor. 'It doesn't mean there won't be more rain though. Round here they say May's rains make the grain grow.' He wiped his hands on a rag. 'Sweet coffee?'

'Yes, please.'

It was warm inside and the smell of soot from the stove lingered but Harun did not feel like sitting out where everyone could see him. For the first time since he had arrived there the village felt like a foreign place, somewhere that played by rules he did not understand. Was the digger's arrival delayed by more than just a rush of work? Was the problem at the carpenter's workshop a deliberate act of sabotage? Perhaps even Ali's talk of rain was more than just a warning of bad weather?

Ali set the coffee in front of him and Harun

breathed in the rich, earthy smell and felt comforted. He must not let his imagination run wild. He had always shunned the national tendency – left over, he felt, from the duplicitous world of the Ottomans – to explain everything with a conspiracy theory.

There were bound to be a few hiccups in the building of the retreat and he should not be put off by them. Instead, he decided, he would show the locals what an understanding person he was by staying calm and looking for solutions.

# 12

The opposition group had gathered at the Kismet Pension for the second time. The meeting had not yet started and Demir was telling Atilla about the damage the winter storms had done to the restaurant at the beach, while Nazla complained to Dudu about her youngest daughter's latest misdemeanour. Buket was sitting quietly listening to the older women. Chetin and Kerim were huddled together, looking towards the pool where the amateur archaeologist's wife was lying on a sunbed. Her husband had taken his camera and exercise book as he did every day and gone off to study the ruins.

Fatma clapped her hands. 'Greetings everyone! I have called you here so we can learn what effect our efforts have had so far and try to come up with more ideas. Derya do sit down!' Derya had served everyone coffee and was now fussing round the table offering their visitors water and lemon cologne. She took a chair and sat just behind Nazla.

'Nazla, would you please tell the others what you told me on the phone yesterday?'

Nazla put down her cup and sat up a little

straighter. 'A lot of the wood for the furniture has apparently been ruined. Harun Bey is paying for wood to replace it but it's going to hold things up.'

Chetin smiled but it did not improve his appearance. His thin top lip curled and showed stained teeth. 'Was he angry?'

'He wasn't angry when I saw him. A little quieter than usual maybe.'

'Does he suspect anything?' asked Atilla.

'No.' Nazla shook her head. 'He thinks Metin Usta or his apprentice made a mistake with the measurements.'

Chetin gave a snigger and raised an eyebrow at Kerim. His friend gave him a wink and a thumbs-up. Fatma felt a niggle of guilt. She took a sip of water.

'Atilla Bey, did you manage to delay the digger?'

'I spoke to Rushtem. He has so much business that he's struggling to send a digger out here anyway.'

Nazla nodded. 'I've heard Harun Bey talking to Osman about that too, asking why it's taking so long.'

'But I don't think he'll hold off for much longer. Rushtem has a big job that is finishing this week and then he'll have machines sitting idle—'

'And I did hear Harun Bey tell Osman if it doesn't come soon they should use a different company.'

'That's it then! I'll call Rushtem and tell him the rumours were unfounded and he can send a digger.'

There was a moment's silence.

'There are ways to stop the digger once it's here,' said Kerim.

'What sort of ways?' Demir had pulled his cap down to keep the sun off his face but his eyes still narrowed.

'Things you can do to an engine – putting water in the cylinder, for example...very hard to prove.'

Derya got up and started collecting cups and stacking them on a tray.

'I won't be involved in damaging someone else's property,' said Atilla.

'Nor me,' said Demir.

Fatma put her hands out to calm the atmosphere. 'We're not going to do anything to the digger. Does anyone else have an idea?'

Buket cleared her throat, though her voice was still shaky when she spoke. 'I do.'

Fatma nodded encouragingly. 'Yes?'

'I saw something on the news about a village where archaeologists thought there were some ruins buried under the ground. The people weren't allowed to farm their land until the men finished excavating. If we call somewhere official and suggest there might be treasure in the orchard...'

'Yes!' said Demir, excitedly. 'When the German archaeologists were working on the island, they were so afraid of treasure hunters nobody else was allowed to set foot on it all summer.'

'And this man deals in antiques in Istanbul, doesn't he?' asked Chetin.

'He sells antique silver – I'm not sure that includes ancient relics,' said Nazla.

'Well, he wouldn't do it openly, would he? But it means he has the contacts to get rid of anything he found,' said Fatma. 'That's a very good idea, Buket.'

The young woman sat a little straighter in her chair.

'Who do we need to call?' asked Nazla.

'The Ministry of Antiquities, I suppose,' said Demir. 'Their office is in the museum in town. Who wants to make the call?'

Buket shrank in her seat again.

'Fatma Hanum, I believe you have more experience in dealing with government agencies than the rest of us,' said Atilla.

'Yes, Fatma, you would definitely be the most convincing,' said Nazla.

'I suppose I could do it anonymously. They would still have to investigate.'

The meeting broke up and the others left while Nazla stayed to drink another tea with Fatma. Derya took the cups to the kitchen and said she would start preparing the evening meal.

Fatma watched her go. 'Do you think Derya's acting strangely at the moment?'

'She does seem uncomfortable, as if she doesn't want to be here.'

'That's what I thought.'

'If Hamdi's told her not to get involved perhaps she's hiding it from him,' said Nazla. 'And you know how bad she is at keeping secrets.'

Fatma did. Once, when they were at school, Derya had copied the answers from Fatma in an exam and then felt so bad about it that she had told the teacher and they had both been punished. Which was why Fatma thought it more likely that her friend was not hiding things from her husband but reporting their activities back to him.

*

Melek arrived home from school while the meeting was in progress. She went round to the house and sat under the arbour by the front door where she would not hear them talking. Still, she burned with the shame of it. At dinner she helped her mother serve tomato soup and lamb stew with rice to the guests but she refused to speak to her. She continued to ignore her as they joined the rest of the family to eat.

Her grandmother was particularly cheerful. 'Tonight is Hidirellez,' she announced, pulling the soft centre from a piece of bread and dipping it in her soup. 'Who's making a wish?'

The fifth of May was the night the prophets Hizir and Ilyas walked the earth, bestowing good fortune and making wishes come true. Like many people, Melahat always left her purse out and the kitchen cupboards open to receive the blessings.

'I wish our team could win the league. How do I make that happen, Grandma?' asked Ahmet.

'Write it on a piece of paper and tie it to a tree!'

'Ridiculous!' muttered Fatma.

Melek teased her grandmother. 'What happens if someone else asks for another team to win?'

The old lady slurped the last of her soup and wiped the bowl with another piece of bread. 'You can all laugh but there are plenty of people who would swear their wish came true.' She looked at Fatma. 'I made a wish that you would find a husband and that summer you went to Gülsüm's wedding and met Mehmet.'

'You see, my dear, it was supernatural forces that brought us together!' said Mehmet.

Fatma frowned. 'I don't believe in that nonsense. I have a wish but I intend to make that happen myself.'

Melek dropped her spoon into her bowl. 'Mother, why are you so against Harun Bey? He's a very nice man. And do you really think you and that group of oddballs can stop him?'

'That group includes your Nazla Auntie and Derya Auntie, as well as Atilla Bey, so I would thank you to be less rude about them,' said Fatma. 'Anyway, I wasn't talking about stopping Harun Bey, though that would be nice too. My wish is for the Kismet to have a good summer.'

Melek picked up her spoon but she looked unconvinced and ate the rest of her meal in silence. Afterwards she helped clear the table, then returned to her room. She stared at a page of maths homework but the numbers were jumping around. Inside her a battle was going on between her head, which in this matter agreed with her mother that waiting for wandering prophets to make your wishes come true was absurd, and her romantic sixteen-year-old heart. Eventually her heart won, on the basis that making a wish couldn't do any harm.

She tore a piece of paper from one of her exercise books, wrote her wish in tiny letters, then folded it and tied it with a piece of ribbon. It was dark outside and the chickens clucked warily from their coop. There were no trees in the garden but there was a straggly rose bush in one corner. She reached up and tied her missive to a stem and was drawing her hand back, taking care to avoid the thorns, when she noticed a pale shape fluttering further down the bush. She was not the only one who had made a wish that night.

\*

Harun did not make any wishes but if he had he might have been convinced of the power of the prophets. After all the delays, the digger finally arrived the next morning and worked all day levelling the ground for the chalets. The driver was a young man who was so shy he rarely made eye contact and blushed the colour of a ripe peach when he did, but he was skilled at handling the lumbering machine.

On the second day, he was flattening the ground in the middle of the orchard where the pomegranate trees had stood. Osman and Harun were watching.

'This'll be done in no time,' shouted Osman above the din of the machine. 'What do you want him to do next?'

'We need footings dug for the yoga platform,' Harun yelled back, nodding towards the bottom corner of the field. 'Zuhal wants it down there.'

The digger moved a little further away and the sound level reduced.

'I was thinking about that,' said Osman. 'There used to be a borehole somewhere down there. It hasn't been used for years and it might have silted up but if not, it could be useful one day. Besides which, if we hit the pipe and break it we'll have a flood to deal with.'

Harun tugged at his beard. There were so many decisions to be made, sometimes it was exhausting. 'Perhaps in the other corner then. What about the mulberry tree that's there?'

'We'll have to take that down or there'll be squashed fruit all over the deck!'

'That's a shame. Maybe we can take off the lower branches and fix the roof beneath it so it catches the fruit. I'll call Zuhal and ask her.'

By the time Harun had finished speaking to his wife, the central area had been made ready for the kitchen and dining space. Nazla brought out a tray of tea and the digger driver turned off the engine and jumped down from his eyrie. The big machine ticked quietly as it cooled and gave off a smell of oil and mud.

When they had drunk their tea, Osman and Harun measured the new location of the yoga platform and marked the position of the footings. Then Osman left to take Nazla to visit her mother and the driver climbed back into his machine and flicked the switch, making it roar into life. In his hands the digger performed a delicate dance, dipping and scooping, lifting and spinning to empty the bucketful of soil, before turning back and dropping down for the next one. The movement was mesmerising, and Harun was so transfixed that he didn't notice the arrival of a black car or the emergence of two men from inside it.

Only when the machine stopped spinning and the boy turned off the engine leaving a noisy silence did he turn and see a man in a too-tight shirt and unsuitable shoes picking his way across the field and signalling to them to stop working. Another man, older and dressed more casually, was standing by the gate.

Harun took a few steps to meet the man. 'Good afternoon. Can I help you?'

'Harun Bey? We're from the Department of Antiquities. This village sits on top of the remains of ancient civilisations, which means digging here is strictly controlled. I must insist that all work stops until our experts evaluate the site. If they decide it is of importance, you will have to stop altogether.'

'Sir, this is quite unnecessary! We've been digging for two days and haven't turned up anything more interesting than an old cola bottle and a doorknob. I can spot an antique, you know. I have twenty-five years' experience in the business!'

'Yes, we'd heard that,' said the man sternly.

'My manager will be back soon. He's lived here all his life and will be able to tell you if there's anything here.'

'We'll still have to do our own investigation.'

'Is this usual?'

'It is when we have reason to believe national treasures may be being dug up and sold.'

'What on earth makes you think that?' Harun remembered his resolution to stay calm but it was hard when he was being accused of black-market trading.

The man ignored his question, saying instead: 'Come with me please.' He started to walk towards the gate. Dark patches of sweat had bloomed on the back of his shirt and his neck was pink and shiny above his collar.

At the gate, the second man held out his hand to Harun with a genuine smile. 'Harun Bey. I am Fevzi Shen, Director of the local department of antiquities and curator of the museum. I am sorry for the inconvenience but I'm sure you know we have to investigate any possible breaches of the Antiquities Act.'

'I would be happy to meet you in other circumstances, Fevzi Bey, but this is very inconvenient. I was just asking what exactly made you come here today.'

The curator ran a hand through his thick, grey hair. 'We received a suggestion that you may have uncovered something of interest. I'm quite sure you would not be involved in anything irregular but—'

'We have a duty to follow up any leads,' cut in the civil servant.

The museum director looked at him with distaste. He was obviously a reluctant participant in the operation.

'Fevzi Bey will bring a team to inspect your land. When they have finished, if they are satisfied there's nothing of interest, you will be issued with a permit and allowed to continue. Now please sign these papers.'

Harun signed and the men left. He told the driver to go home and he went and sat on the stump of a pear tree. It felt as if he had woken to find himself acting in a particularly farcical play. He could have laughed with the ridiculousness of it all. But this was no laughing matter.

Dealing in antiquities was taken seriously and punished with long prison sentences. It would also be unwise to try to fight the investigation. Civil servants were one of the scourges of the country, envied for their permanent jobs and good pensions, hated for their pettiness and bullish following of the rules.

He did what he always did when he needed reassurance and rang Zuhal.

'Can you believe it? They suggested I'm black market dealing!'

'That's ludicrous!'

'And the worst thing is they said they'd had a tip off. Perhaps the locals are not as welcoming as I thought. Do you think I should try to find out who it is and confront them?'

'No, my love, I think you need to wait. Remember the saying "Patience is bitter but its fruit is sweet". Would you like me to come down there?'

'I'd love it but there's not much you can do right now. Stay there with Barish for the time being. When the bungalows arrive you'll have plenty to keep you busy.'

## 13

Melek was having trouble concentrating. At school she had been so absorbed trying to picture Barish's face that she had missed the teacher asking her a question until Selma had nudged her. After class the teacher, a concerned lady whose own daughter had not yet reached her teens, asked if anything were the matter and Melek lied and said she was worried about the end-of-term exams.

Now, trying to study for those exams, her mind was still wandering. She decided to go to Selma's. Perhaps it would be easier to stay focused if they studied together.

Outside the front door the ginger cat was lying in a patch of sunshine. He had turned up the previous year and made the garden his home but Melek was the only one he allowed anywhere near him. Seeing her now, he rolled over for her to stroke the soft butter-coloured fur on his belly.

'Tiger, how easy your life is! All you do is eat and sleep.'

The cat twitched his impressive whiskers and gave a faint miaow of protest before sitting up and starting to wash one paw vigorously.

Melek went out of the gate and down the lane. She waved to Nurdan Auntie and to Taxi Mustafa who lived next to the old lady. At the entrance to the orchard a digger was sitting idle on the grass verge, its bucket smeared with mud. She was trying to peer round it to see what changes had been made to the orchard when Harun came through the gate. She felt a stab of fear and was tempted to run away. Then she realised how ridiculous that would be.

'Melek! How nice to see you! Are you walking to the village?'

'I-I'm going to Selma's to study,' she said, her voice thin and shaky. 'We have exams soon.'

'I wish Barish would study for his exams! He never seems to work very hard, though he gets decent enough grades so I suppose I shouldn't complain. Do you mind if I join you? I'm heading for the coffee house.'

Melek gave an awkward nod and started walking.

'How are your plans going, Harun Uncle?'

His smile dropped a little. 'They were going well but we've hit a little obstacle.'

'An obstacle?' Melek had visions of a large rock or a concrete drainage pipe that had stopped the digger.

'I have to wait while the Department of Antiquities checks the site.'

'That's odd. Why are they interested?' Melek had never heard of such a thing happening in the village.

'I suppose they sometimes like to check places like this. There are, after all, people who dig up our nation's treasures and flog them to the highest bidder.'

Melek stifled a groan. There were also people like her mother and her friends who would try anything to stop the retreat going ahead.

'I hear the Kismet Pension is open!' said Harun, running his hand through his hair in a gesture just like Barish.

Melek tried to hide her agitation. 'Yes, we opened last week.'

They passed the mosque and turned right for the village.

'That's great. Have you got many guests?'

'Two or three rooms most nights. Do you know when you'll be opening?'

'We have to be ready by the start of June as I have guests booked in.'

'And when will Zuhal Auntie come down?'

'In a couple of weeks, I hope. Barish will stay with his grandmother until term finishes.'

They were in front of Selma's house and Melek was desperate to get away. 'Say hello to them from me. And I hope you get the permit soon, Harun Uncle.'

'Thank you, Melek. Give my greetings to your family!' Harun replied, though they both knew that where he was going he would see her father before she did.

*

A buzz of voices and wisps of cigarette smoke were spilling from the door of the coffee house. Harun stepped in and looked around self-consciously. He was trying hard not to let the events of the afternoon fuel his paranoia again.

It was busy and Ali was hurrying back to the bar with a tray of empty cups and a cloth over his shoulder. In his usual seat Mehmet was sitting arguing good-naturedly with Galip over a dice that had rolled off the table.

'Please join us, Harun Bey!' said Mehmet in his deep, resonant voice. 'My friend here insists on challenging me at tavla, even though he knows he'll lose, and then he tries employing tricks to win!' He laughed.

Galip shook his head. 'Right now, I'm quite happy for you to win, Mehmet. I have much bigger things to worry about.'

'Good evening to you, gentlemen.' Harun nodded to the two men and sat at their table. 'Perhaps we can share our problems, Galip Bey. You tell me yours and I'll tell you mine!'

'What's happened?' asked Mehmet.

'Oh, it's just that nothing seems to go smoothly. I've had trouble with the furniture, trouble with the digger and now I've been ordered to stop clearing the ground until some archaeologists have checked there's nothing valuable on the site.'

The two men, who had resumed their game, exchanged looks. 'Last winter some blackguards were arrested trying to remove one of the carved faces from the theatre,' said Galip, grimacing as Mehmet wiped a row of his chips from the board.

'Really? That's awful.' Harun was relieved to hear there might be good reason for the investigation. 'I just hope they don't take too long looking as we don't have a lot of time. And what's troubling you, Galip Bey? Anything I can help with?'

'Not unless you know any famous singers.' Galip, who had just lost the game, slammed the wooden board shut and motioned to Ali to bring them more tea. 'Have you heard of the Cherry Festival?'

'Nazla was talking about it with her daughters the other day.'

'It's held every year to sort of celebrate and give thanks for the cherry harvest.'

'Really it's an excuse for a big party,' said Mehmet.

'There are stalls selling things—'

'Cherries?' asked Harun.

'Yes, but also food stalls and some ladies sell things they've made – table cloths, head scarves, that sort of thing. And there's entertainment – local dancers and musicians.'

'It sounds very nice.'

'It is but it's a big thing to organise so we do it jointly with Yeshilkoy, one year they organise everything, the next year we do.'

'And this year is the turn of Ortakoy?'

'Yes, and the festival's due to take place next week'.

'And you haven't found a singer?'

The tea arrived and they waited while Ali collected the old glasses and put down the new.

'We did have one lined up – a very popular young man. Unfortunately, last night he was found in possession of some dubious substances and he is now, shall we say, indisposed. Even if he's released and is able to come, I don't think he'll be seen as a good example for our young people. And Yeshilkoy will love it if we have to admit we don't have anyone.'

'The reputation of the village is at stake!' said Mehmet dramatically, dropping a sugar cube into his glass of tea and stirring vigorously.

'So you need a singer to step in?'

'Yes. Preferably someone who's at least moderately well-known.'

'And who's prepared to come down here to perform in a field,' added Mehmet.

'At very short notice and for a modest fee.' Galip groaned at the hopelessness of the situation. 'Know anyone who fits the bill?'

'Actually,' said Harun and both his companions stopped stirring and looked at him. 'Could you give me a minute?'

Outside it was getting dark and the first stars were shining through the branches of the plane tree. Harun took his phone from his pocket and scrolled through the list of contacts until he found the one he was looking for. The person he called was pleased to hear from him and before he had even finished explaining, had agreed to cancel an existing engagement and perform at the festival.

He ended the call and stood for a moment feeling pleased. He always liked helping people but here he felt he had been given an opportunity to prove himself. If there were any villagers who were suspicious of him, surely they would change their opinions after this?

Back inside he smiled at his friends and drank the

last of his tea, which was cold. 'Galip Bey, this is your lucky day!'

The two men listened as he told them the name of the person he had just hired to sing at the festival, a young lady who had become famous after winning a television talent show.

'And she's agreed to come?'

'Yes.'

'Do you think she'll keep her word?'

'Without question.'

The village headman jumped up and pumped Harun's hand. 'You've saved my skin, Harun Bey.'

'I think that's a little strong but I'm very glad to be of assistance. Life is both easier and more enjoyable when we work together. What do they say? "A single stone doesn't make a wall!"'

They agreed to keep the name of the singer secret and leave Yeshilkoy wondering until just before the festival. Mehmet decided the moment deserved to be toasted with raki and ordered them three doubles. Galip left after one but Mehmet persuaded Harun to join him in several more glasses with the result that by the time they wove their way along the lane he had quite forgotten his own troubles.

\*

Dinner was ready but Melek took her time emerging from her room to serve. When she did, she was quiet and stony-faced. Fatma thought it must be all the studying getting to her. They served the guests – cabbage leaves stuffed with a mix of minced lamb, cracked wheat and pine nuts – then the family sat down to eat.

Fatma nodded to a young couple sitting at one of the tables, their heads together, giggling. 'I'm not happy about those two,' she said.

'I thought you'd be pleased,' said Ahmet, who had checked them in that afternoon while Fatma was in the house. 'They've paid for a week up front.'

'Hmm. I think they might be runaways and I think she's underage.'

'She does look very young,' said Mehmet. 'Did you see her ID?'

'She said she'd lost it,' said Ahmet, dipping bread into the tomato sauce.

'If her family send the jandarma to find her there'll be trouble,' said Melahat.

Fatma did not need her mother to point this out. She had already considered the scandal that would be caused by uniformed men arriving to arrest the young man.

'What's the matter with you, Melek? You're very quiet.'

'Yes, what's wrong, my lamb?' asked Melahat, biting the end off a chilli pepper and chewing it noisily.

Melek fixed her attention on her mother. 'I saw Harun Bey as I was going to Selma's. Do you know work on the retreat has been stopped while the orchard is searched for ancient artefacts?'

'He told me that too when I saw him in the coffee house. I thought it was a bit strange,' said Mehmet.

'Do you?' asked Fatma, keeping her eyes on her food. 'Personally, I think it's quite sensible for them to check things out. They did catch those thieves in the theatre last year.'

'But people are digging here all the time without the museum manager coming out to inspect,' said Melek.

Fatma shrugged. 'Maybe they were suspicious because of Harun Bey's business in Istanbul. Or perhaps he talked to the wrong person.'

'Or perhaps someone else spread a rumour about him.' Melek was still looking at Fatma.

'I'm not the only one who doesn't want this thing to go ahead, Melek.'

'Maybe not but you seem to be leading the opposition!'

Melek got up and started collecting the empty plates. She left them in the kitchen and went off to the house without saying any more. Fatma drank tea and ate a bowl of rice pudding with a generous topping of cinnamon hoping it would make her feel better. It was sweet and comforting but it did not take away the bitter taste of her clash with Melek.

\*

Melek went to the house and sat on the settee that doubled as Ahmet's bed whenever their grandmother was staying. She turned on the television and started watching an American cowboy film in which the main characters were all female. Just when the film was getting exciting, she heard the front door open and her mother came in and sat on the chair. Melek ignored her and Fatma sat quietly watching the action. Melek did not change the language or even add the subtitles even though she knew her mother could understand little of the English dialogue.

Fatma waited until the film ended and the credits were rolling. 'I wish you could see things from my point-of-view, Melek. I had to struggle to build this place – a bit like the ladies in that film who had to work twice as hard to prove themselves. Now Harun Bey comes here and thinks he can do it better.'

Melek shook her head. 'He never said that. He said what he's doing is different.'

'Whatever. I have to protect the Kismet and I thought you'd understand that. After all, it will be yours one day. Yours and Ahmet's.'

'But Mother, I'm not planning to stay in Ortakoy and run the Kismet,' said Melek. 'I want to go to university and get a good job. Maybe go abroad.'

She had planned to talk to her mother calmly at some point about her ambitions but her frustration made it spill out.

Fatma's mouth opened and closed but at first no words came out. Then she said, 'When did you decide this?'

Melek shrugged. 'I've known for a long time.'

'Why did you never say anything before?'

'Because I knew you'd make a fuss.'

'I'm not making a fuss. Am I making a fuss? I just think you might have told us you were planning to abandon us.'

'I'm not abandoning you, I'll still visit. And anyway, I have two years left at high school and if I don't get good grades that year, I might have to wait another year and retake the university exams.'

'And then you'll be off?'

'It's quite usual for girls to go away to university these days, Mother. Selma wants to go too and her parents support her.'

'Selma's parents don't have a business she can step into. When I built the Kismet I was thinking of you and Ahmet. I imagined...' Unusually, her mother seemed to have run out of words.

Melek softened. 'Mother, you should understand what it's like when people expect you to do something you don't want to. You didn't listen to Grandma when she wanted you to stay at home and learn to cook and sew.'

'That was different! I was helping my dear father and I was still here where she could keep an eye on me. You're talking about going away to some big city where all sorts of dreadful things happen.'

'I can take care of myself. You're always saying how sensible I am.'

'I used to think so,' muttered her mother as she stood and left the room, but not before Melek had seen that her eyes were shiny with tears. She felt miserable. She could cope with her mother's anger but seeing her sad was much worse.

# 14

Harun and Osman were watching the men survey the field. They had arrived that morning – three days after the work had been stopped – and were turning over the areas where the digger had exposed the soil. The museum manager showed little interest in the inspection. When they had stopped to drink the tea Nazla had brought out, he had asked Harun about the silver shop and invited him to come and have a special tour of the museum.

By contrast the two young men with him were doing work experience and were keen to show him how thorough they were. So far, they had uncovered three bent teaspoons, a piece of rope and a rake of the sort used to knock olives off the tree.

Harun was resigned to the further delay and currently his attention was focused on another matter. Having arranged a singer for the festival he needed to find somewhere for her to stay. The retreat would have been perfect had it been ready but it would be a while before it was ready to welcome anyone. If she stayed in one of the hotels in town someone would have to drive her back and forth and he would see little of her. The solution, he suddenly realised, was simple: he would ask Fatma to put her up at the Kismet Pension.

He was well-enough acquainted with the young lady in question to know that she sometimes found the glitzy world she now moved in overwhelming and would be quite happy with the simplicity of the little guest house. Her mother and sister, who were coming with her, would also be charmed by the place. In addition, the move might act as an olive branch and convince Fatma of his good intentions. He was so excited with this idea that he left the men sifting through the soil and set off to talk to her straight away.

He walked slowly, enjoying the gentle warmth of the May sun on his face. At the back of the pension he found Ahmet cleaning the pool.

'Kolay gelsin! Let it be easy!' said Harun, the accepted greeting to anyone engaged in hard work. 'Is your mother around?'

'Thank you, Harun Bey! I think she's in the laundry. Mum!' he shouted.

Fatma emerged from one of the doors in the pension with a laundry basket full of sheets and a cross expression.

'What is it? Oh...' She saw Harun and a look of surprise replaced the frown. She handed the basket to Derya. 'H-hello Harun Bey. What brings you here?'

'Fatma Hanum! My apologies for disturbing you – I can see you're busy. I came to ask a favour of you.'

'A favour? From me?' Fatma hesitated. 'Let's sit down. Would you like coffee, or do you prefer tea?'

'Coffee would be lovely, if it's not too much trouble.'

Fatma called to Derya who stopped hanging the laundry and went to make the coffee. She led the way to one of the tables and sat down heavily.

'How is Zuhal Hanum?'

'Well, I think. I speak to her every day and she's looking forward to coming down here again. I bumped into Melek yesterday on her way to study with her friend. What a lovely girl she is!'

'She is but...' Fatma shook her head. 'Well, you know – teenagers.'

Harun nodded in agreement. They made polite conversation for a few minutes more and when they had established that all members of both families were well and that the May weather was perfect Harun put down his cup and took a deep breath.

'As I said, I need to ask a favour of you. You may have heard that the singer who was due to perform at the Cherry Festival had to pull out.' There could not be many people in the country who did not know what had happened to the young man since it had been on every news report and in every paper. 'Since I'm lucky enough to know – he told her the name of the singer he had lined up – I asked her if she would step in and she agreed.'

'Really? She's coming to sing here?'

'Yes. There's just the small problem of where she's going to stay. My place is nowhere near ready so I wondered if you would be good enough to put her up here at the Kismet? She'll need two rooms as she's coming with her mother and her sister. Galip Bey tells me the festival budget includes something for accommodation.'

'You want her to stay at the Kismet? The bigger stars usually prefer to stay in town.'

'Maybe, but I know this young lady and I know she'll be happier at the Kismet than in one of those big, impersonal places. That is, of course, if you have room for her.'

'Oh, I think we have two rooms,' said Fatma.

'Splendid! I'll talk to Galip about the money.'

'That won't be necessary, Harun Bey, I don't want payment. We all have to do our bit for the village.'

\*

Fatma watched Harun leave. She had drunk three cups of coffee that morning but that wasn't what was making her head spin; rather it was the mix of feelings his visit had excited. She looked around for someone to tell.

Ahmet was no good. He would be so excited by the news that this young lady was coming to stay at the Kismet that he would entirely miss the significance of Harun asking her for a favour. Melek was at school and even if she'd been here, their conversation the previous day had put a distance between them. For anything else she would have immediately called Derya but she still wasn't sure where her friend's loyalties lay when it came to the subject of Harun Bey.

In the end she went round to the house and found her mother sucking on dry mulberries and watching one of her beloved soap operas.

'Harun Bey just came round to ask me for a favour.'

'Mmm?' Her mother was immersed in the drama in which the maid had just turned out to be the long-lost sister of the lady of the house.

'I said Harun Bey was here. He wants Alya to stay here when she comes to sing at the cherry festival.'

'Alya? *The* Alya?' There was nobody, young or old, who didn't know that name. 'She's coming to Ortakoy? And staying here?' The old lady pursed her lips and whistled in amazement.

'Yes. Why do you think that is?'

'Because there's nowhere else to stay in the village?'

Fatma gritted her teeth. Sometimes her mother could be exasperating. 'But usually these people stay at one of the hotels in town and don't spend a minute longer than they have to in the village.'

'How is it that she's coming at all? Last I heard, Galip Bey was in a tizz because that young man had been arrested.'

'Apparently Harun Bey knows her – don't ask me how, he doesn't look to me like the sort to hang around with pop stars – and he's sure she will be more comfortable here than in town.'

'Well, that's it then. That's why he's asked you to put her up.'

'You don't think he's trying to get in my good books by sending her here?'

'Honestly, daughter, I don't know when you got so suspicious!'

Fatma snorted at the irony; her mother had once believed that the government was spying on homes through television sets.

'He's a nice man and he's sending you business. Don't complain!'

'I thought you didn't approve of him?'

'He went to visit Nurdan the other day and they talked for two hours about Hasan Abi. He told her his mother was happier with him than she had ever been with his father.'

'So Nurdan Auntie now sees him as family, does she?'

'She just said what a polite and kind man he is. He offered to help with anything she needs – shopping, a lift to town....'

Fatma was disappointed to hear that her mother and her best friend had been won over. It was not as though Nurdan Auntie could have done anything to help and she had known all along that her mother was only coming to the meetings for entertainment. But the stakes in this struggle were high and losing any allies was a blow.

\*

Harun rang the museum every day and was always told the same thing: the team had finished their investigation but had not yet come to a decision. In fact he knew he was going to be given permission to continue because the curator had told him before they left, but these things always took time. He spent the days driving around learning more about the area and putting out word that he was looking for people to help – most importantly a lady, preferably from the village, who could clean and cook.

Finally in the middle of the following week he

was told he could go to the office in town and collect the permit. They had already decided to finish the landscaping without waiting for a digger and Osman found a couple of strong men who spent the next two days digging the remaining footings for the yoga platform and trenches for the cables and pipes.

On Friday evening, Osman went to the airport to collect the singer Alya and her mother and sister. He returned with some unexpected guests. Zuhal had hidden the news that she was finishing classes a week early and coming to stay in Ortakoy. She brought Barish to spend the weekend in the village and enjoy the novelty of the Cherry Festival. Harun was so delighted to see them he felt as giddy as a child before the Sugar Festival.

'I can't believe you didn't tell me you were coming!'

'I wanted to surprise you!'

'Well, it's good to have a pleasant surprise after all the bad ones I've had recently! How is Alya?'

'She's well. Relieved to get out of the city, I think.'

'And what did they think of the Kismet Pension?'

'They looked quite happy. Fatma and her son came rushing out to greet them. I'm sure they will be looked after very well.'

'I'm sure they will. And perhaps they'll put in a good word for me while they're there!'

For the rest of the evening Harun described the ups and downs of the past weeks in more detail than he had been able to on the phone. Nazla hovered around keeping their tea glasses full. She still seemed uncomfortable around him but when he told Zuhal he'd started to think there was a conspiracy against him and she burst into laughter, Nazla joined in.

'I think you've been letting your imagination run away with you, my darling!'

'Yes, Harun Abi, your wife is right,' said Nazla. 'The people of Ortakoy couldn't agree among themselves for long enough to conspire against anyone!'

## 15

The arrival of the celebrated Alya at the Kismet brought the family together. Melek had forgotten that she wasn't speaking to Fatma, Melahat forewent one of her favourite soap operas and Mehmet did not return to the coffee house after dinner. Even Ahmet had changed, becoming suddenly the most solicitous of hosts, concerned about whether the three ladies needed extra pillows or blankets and what they would like to drink.

'I don't think we need anything extra, thank you,' said Alya. 'The rooms are perfect. I would love some tea though and I expect my mother would too!'

Ahmet looked slightly crestfallen. Fatma had seen him studying a book of cocktail recipes earlier and he had obviously been hoping to demonstrate his skill. Fatma, on the other hand, was pleased to discover the young lady was not the diva she had expected.

'Melek my love, go and put on a fresh pot of tea, would you?' She turned to Alya. 'It was good of you to come at such short notice.'

'I didn't have anything important on,' said the girl, who looked not much older than Ahmet. 'And I was happy to be able to help Harun Abi.'

'How do you know Harun Bey?' Unlike the rest of her family, Fatma was not starstruck; she was, however, keen to find out more about her rival and in particular to discover whether there was a hidden motive behind him putting the guests in the Kismet. Was this girl some sort of spy?

'Asya,' she pointed to her sister, 'goes to the same school as Barish. When I enrolled her there some of the parents were a little...unwelcoming.' Fatma saw the girl's mother frown at the memory. 'But Harun Abi and Zuhal Abla were very kind to us.'

Melek brought tea and Alya told them about the family's incredible change in fortunes. They came from a village in the southeast of the country. Her father had been killed in a fight over land, leaving her mother to bring up the two girls alone. She had moved to the nearby town and taken jobs in factories and cleaning, whatever she could find. At the mention of these times her mother pursed her lips and shook her head; Fatma thought she saw tears in the older lady's eyes.

Alya finished middle school and started working with her mother, assuming that would be her life, until a music teacher whose house they cleaned heard her singing and told her she should enter the competition.

'I didn't want her do it,' her mother said. Alya looked at her fondly.

'Mother was worried what would happen to me. Some of the past winners haven't coped so well with the sudden fame.'

'Alya is a good girl but there are always people waiting to take advantage. It's not easy being a mother, is it, Fatma Hanum? You always worry about your children. But sometimes you have to let them take a chance.'

'And then I won and started getting bookings and earning big money. I brought Mother and Asya to Istanbul to live with me and put Asya in a good school so she can go to university and get a proper job. I *did* have to learn not to trust everyone but I've got quite good at looking after myself.'

\*

When Melek heard that Asya was at school with Barish she waited until the others were all engrossed in Alya's story and then asked in what she hoped was an innocent voice, 'What's Barish like? Is he popular at school?'

Asya, a dreamy girl who loved any hint of romance, saw Melek blush and immediately guessed her feelings. 'He's very popular because he's handsome *and* nice, but don't worry – he isn't seeing any of the girls at school. Anyway, you can ask him yourself because he flew down with us!'

Melek couldn't hide her surprise. 'Really? His father said he wouldn't be down until term finished.'

'Harun Uncle didn't know they were coming – Zuhal Auntie wanted to surprise him!'

The following morning Melek had to help with breakfast. Aside from the singer and her chaperones, the guests at the Kismet consisted of four middle-aged English ladies who went out walking every day, a German couple and three young Ukrainians who were studying in Istanbul. The suspected runaways had left the previous morning, thankfully without causing a scandal.

'You know we can't leave all these guests alone in the pension. One of us will have to stay here this evening,' said Fatma.

Melek was about to say that there was no way she was missing the festival, when Ahmet, who had developed a serious crush on Alya, spoke up.

'That's not fair! We've never had a singer as famous as Alya and we all want to hear her. Why don't we ask the guests if they'd like to come? Meli, I'm sure you can persuade them.'

Melek went round the tables and asked the occupants of each if they would be interested in attending a traditional village festival and they all jumped at the chance to experience a bit of local culture. It was arranged that dinner would be served at six o'clock and Mehmet arranged a minibus to transport the guests to and from the event and even Fatma had to agree that there was no need for anyone to stay behind.

After breakfast Ahmet offered to drive the guests down to the beach. Alya and her mother agreed but Asya stayed behind with Melek. The two girls spent the day sitting with their feet in the pool – the water was still too cold to get in – comparing life in the village with life in the city. Asya, who had experienced both, assured Melek that some things were better in the village. She hated the snobbery of the city and the way people judged you on how you looked and who you knew. As Alya's sister she had been welcomed by the cool girls in school but she found them shallow and hypocritical and her best friend was a girl whose father was a taxi driver, who was there on a scholarship.

From time to time, Melek's attention wandered as she remembered she would be seeing Barish that evening. Several times she shivered with excitement at the thought. Asya enjoyed fanning the flames of love and made Melek blush by promising to leave the two alone once they found Barish. Melek knew, however, that with her family and most of the village present it would be a miracle if they found a place to be alone.

Late in the afternoon, Melek took her new friend to her room to help her find something suitable to wear. Melek pulled out most of her clothes and had tried on several outfits before they decided on a pretty white top and her jeans. Alya insisted Melek leave her long hair loose.

Dinner was served, eaten and quickly cleared away and the minibus arrived to take the guests. Galip came to drive Asya and her mother to the festival and Ahmet managed to talk his way into accompanying them. Fatma, Melahat and the two girls squeezed into Mehmet's small car and headed for Yeshilkoy.

As they neared the field where the event was taking place, the narrow road became crowded with people until eventually Mehmet could drive no further and they all got out of the car and joined the throng. Melek and Asya quickly lost Fatma and Mehmet, who had to walk at Melahat's pace. They were swept along towards the bright lights and the sound of music.

On the stage, the first act was already playing. It was a band made up of four local boys who were screeching their way through a popular song, accompanied by the occasional whine from the speakers. Asya made a face and Melek, who knew that one of the boys was the son of Yeshilkoy's headman, laughed. The girls wove their way between the groups of people and just as the boys launched into their second song Melek saw Barish standing alone on the edge of the crowd. He waved and smiled and a flutter of butterflies took off in Melek's stomach.

'Hi, Melek. How are you?' he shouted above the noise.

'Hello.' Melek had spent the day imagining what she would say when they met but now she could think of nothing at all.

He leaned close so she could hear him and Melek could hardly breathe. 'Mum's come down to help Dad. She said I could come too, just for the weekend.'

'Asya told me you were here.'

'I hope you haven't been talking about me?' he asked Asya but he was smiling.

'Only good things – you can ask Melek. I'm going to find Alya.' She gestured towards the stage. 'She gets nervous before a show and Mother and I have to calm her down.'

Melek stared dumbly at her friend's disappearing back.

'Shall we sit down?' Barish pointed at the rows of plastic chairs. Most people were still milling around talking to friends, buying things to eat and drink but Melek knew that when Alya came on there would be a race to sit down. The lights that hung over the field threw a harsh glare and they would be very exposed. She looked around. In the shadows on the edge of the field was a large boulder that would make a good perch. They would be less likely to be spotted there and it had the added advantage of being behind the speaker so they might actually be able to hear each other talk.

'Let's sit there,' she said waving at the rock and Barish nodded and led the way. They sat side-by-side and watched as the band left the stage and were replaced by a group of children folk dancing.

'Are you looking forward to the school holidays?' Barish asked.

'I'm looking forward to the end of the exams but when school finishes, I'll have to spend more time helping in the pension and my mother and I aren't exactly getting on at the moment.'

'Mothers can be a pain sometimes!'

'I don't imagine yours tries to rule *your* life. I told mine that I want to go to university and now she's angry with me!'

'Mum's cool, I guess. The worst thing she does is trying to get me to talk about how I'm feeling.' He made a face and Melek giggled.

'What about you – are you still planning to come here for the holidays?'

'Definitely.' He looked at her pointedly and Melek felt her insides melt. 'The bungalows are coming this week. Dad says the place should be finished in two weeks.'

The next act was a local lady who sang folk ballads. She came on stage wearing a sparkling red dress that clung to her curvy figure and with her bottle-blonde hair heaped on her head. She claimed to be in her forties though she had been performing for almost thirty years, but she was popular and the audience now welcomed her with loud applause and some calls for her most popular numbers.

Barish and Melek took little notice of the lady on stage. Melek told Barish about Ahmet's crush on Alya and he told her about the boy who had been suspended from his school for organising games of poker.

Barish went to buy them a drink and Melek inspected the crowd. She spotted her mother and grandmother sitting in the middle of one of the rows of chairs. They were far enough away and the lights on the stage were sufficiently dazzling that it would be impossible for them to see her but she still shrank a little in her place. Her father was nearer the back with a group of friends from the coffee house and Ahmet was standing right by the stage, waiting for Alya to appear.

The heavy smell of meat roasting on a barbecue wafted from the stalls and smoke drifted up to cling round the lights. Barish returned with two bottles of cola and they sipped their drinks and watched the folk singer perform her final number and leave the stage. Then Alya came on and the crowd went wild. In the dark, Barish felt for Melek's hand. Melek froze.

It was wonderful to see him again after all the

daydreaming she had done, and his hand was warm and assured her she had not been mistaken about his feelings. But it was all so complicated.

Some of the villagers were so old-fashioned they still thought young people should be chaperoned and would be sure to tell her mother if they saw her with a boy. Her mother's feelings about the retreat meant she would see Melek having anything to do with Barish as a betrayal and while Melek might try to reason with her mother she knew that now more than ever she should really be trying to keep the peace. It was fine to make grand statements about forging her own path in life but in reality if she were ever going to get to university she would need her mother's approval, not to mention her money.

Barish sensed her confusion. 'What's up, Melek?'

He looked so concerned that for a moment she thought of trying to explain to him. But she was afraid of spoiling the moment or, worse, scaring him away.

'Nothing,' she said, squeezing his hand. 'I'm just happy.'

And that was true too.

\*

The morning after the Cherry Festival it was quiet at the Kismet Pension. Although no alcohol was served at the event, the English ladies had seemed more than a little merry by the end of the evening and did not make it to breakfast. Melek also failed to appear and Fatma served breakfast to the German couple and the Ukrainians on her own.

Unusually, Ahmet was next to appear. His thick

black hair was damp from the shower and he smelled strongly of aftershave. Asya and her mother appeared just as the other guests were going out for the day and Melek followed soon after them. Alya came out last, dressed in a pretty summer dress and high-heeled sandals, with oversized sunglasses perched on her head.

'Alya Abla, you were wonderful!' gushed Melek. The young woman smiled coyly and looked to the others for confirmation.

'Yes, Abla, you were very good,' said Asya.

'It was the best festival ever!' said Ahmet. 'Everyone said so.'

The visitors did not have to leave until the afternoon and over a leisurely breakfast and a large amount of tea they discussed the night before in detail and when that subject was exhausted, they quizzed Alya for stories of the famous people she had met and the places she had been. Her mother and Melahat meanwhile compared traditions in their respective villages.

Fatma joined in from time to time but mostly she served tea and coffee and watched from a distance. Ahmet was still looking dreamily at Alya and Fatma hoped he wasn't going to do anything to embarrass himself – or her. He liked to act the gigolo but she had never seen any evidence of his success in that field and suspected he was actually quite gauche. She wished he would stop running after unsuitable girls and find himself a sensible, hard-working wife, one who could help in the running of the pension. Unpretentious though she was, Fatma could not imagine Alya cleaning rooms and serving guests.

She was very happy to see Melek smiling again and had resolved to forget their recent disagreement. The truth was that students, even good ones like Melek, rarely got into the university they wanted to and when they did the costs of hostels and books were often prohibitive. There were many things that might force Melek to change her plans and there was no point in them falling out about something that very likely would not happen anyway.

For her part, the visit of the famous star had left Fatma feeling perplexed. She liked the girl, particularly the fact that fame and fortune had not changed her basic values. She was not so keen on the way Alya repeatedly mentioned Harun Bey and how kind he had been to them.

The first time she said it, Fatma thought it was her way of explaining why she'd agreed to come and sing at such an obscure event. When she heard her singing his praises for the third time she began to wonder if the man had wanted her to stay at the Kismet so she could persuade Fatma of his virtues. If so, it was a ridiculous plan.

Unlike her children, Fatma was not an impressionable teenager. She was also not like Alya who, shunned by the other families at the school, had needed someone to stand up for her. Fatma had always managed very well on her own – at least she had until he arrived in the village.

# 16

Harun woke from a deep sleep. It still surprised him every morning to find himself in this place, with the sun blasting through the thin curtain and the bucolic sound of the cockerel crowing, sometimes a donkey or a cow chiming in. This morning his pleasure was even greater when he looked over and saw Zuhal sleeping in her usual tangle of limbs and bedclothes in the room's second small bed.

For a moment he relished the satisfaction engendered by the success of the weekend. Alya had been a huge hit at the Cherry Festival and Galip, delirious with relief that the event had gone so well, had hugged Harun heartily and told him repeatedly that he owed him a favour. Alya and her family had enjoyed the occasion and their stay at the Kismet Pension. He hoped their visit might have gone some way towards softening Fatma's feelings towards him but only time would tell.

Then he remembered the chalets were due to arrive that morning and jumped out of bed. He dressed quickly and was heading out of the door when he saw a bracelet of blue eye beads belonging to one of the girls sitting on the chest-of-drawers. Mindful of the way things had gone up to now, he slipped it into his pocket for luck.

Downstairs the girls were having breakfast. Eda had her nose in a book and the younger two were still half asleep and much quieter than usual. Once they had left for school, Harun and Osman sat down. Harun was too excited to eat much. He was drinking his second glass of tea when the company called to say the lorries were on their way and would be there in approximately three hours.

'I'm going to finish picking the cherries this morning,' said Osman.

'Do you need help?' asked Harun, needing something to occupy himself.

'Not really. Why don't you take Zuhal Hanum to the carpenter's? She's been asking to see the furniture.'

So after breakfast he and Zuhal set off along the lane. Zuhal exclaimed over the bright yellow mimosa pompoms adorning the trees and the splashes of red poppies in the fields. They saw the Imam leaving the mosque and Harun wished him a good day, to which he muttered a reply and hurried off ahead of them. Harun repeated to Zuhal what he had been told about how respected the old Imam had been and how unpopular his over-zealous replacement was.

Entering the workshop, their senses were assaulted first by the sound of a radio playing and a man's voice singing along with more enthusiasm than talent, then by the heavy smell of paint. The carpenter saw them and dropped the paintbrush he was using. Harun was relieved to see that this time he looked happy to see them.

'Harun Bey! Zuhal Hanum! How nice that you came!' He waved at his apprentice who stopped singing and turned down the volume on the radio. 'We have some finished pieces to show you.' He put down the brush and led them to the corner of the workshop. 'It'll all look like that when we've finished,' he said, pointing to a bed, a round table and a couple of chairs that had been stained and varnished and looked perfect for a rustic cottage.

'Those look wonderful!' exclaimed Zuhal. 'Now I know what the furniture looks like I can start on the decor!'

Zuhal started sketching the furniture and making a note of the measurements and Metin's wife brought coffee. Harun talked to the carpenter about the gazebos he wanted for the dining area but he was too excited to sit still and instead drank his coffee pacing between the machines and the furniture, which together took up most of the space in the workshop.

Back at Osman's house, Zuhal sat down immediately to work out how much material she needed for cushions and curtains. Harun went back and forth from the orchard to the house. He was trying to come up with a name for the retreat and every time he came inside he tried out a new one on Zuhal and Nazla.

'The orchard?'

'Not very inspired,' said Zuhal.

'Peace camp?'

'Sounds like a hippy commune.'

'Mountain view?'

'Too common.'

He was about to go in and suggest 'Paradise Lodge' when he heard the rumble of a lorry labouring along the lane. His heart fluttered with a mix of excitement and anxiety and he stuck a hand in his pocket and touched the beads. As he reached the lane the first lorry rounded the bend and he waved to the driver, who pulled over onto the narrow strip of grass in front of the open gate. Osman appeared, his fingers and clothes stained with the juice of the fat, sweet cherries he had been picking, and told the driver of the second lorry to continue along the lane and park in the middle of the village until they had unloaded the first one.

A whole team of men jumped down from the cab and started undoing straps and tarpaulins. Smaller pieces were passed down manually while a winch fixed to the bed of the truck was used to lower the larger crates. It took an hour to unload the first lorry, after which Nazla brought tea and the men took a break. Then the lorries swapped places and they got to work unloading the second one.

Harun was impatient to see a chalet rise up out of the piles of wood, but he knew the men must be hungry so he took them all down to the restaurant on the main road to eat trout with rice and salad. Then the two drivers got back in the trucks and the other men waved them off as they returned to the factory. Finally, they were ready to start.

Harun watched as they joined frames, attached panels and locked steel bolts into place. The first chalet grew on the spot that he and Osman had selected at the top of the field beside a plum tree. Zuhal left her designing and came out and stood with him for a while, talking about going to town and the best place to buy material and bed linen. He pretended to be listening but really he was too nervous to hear her. His idea was materialising in front of his eyes and he was terrified it would not match up to his vision.

But when the first chalet was finished it was even better than he had hoped. The inside was not exactly spacious but certainly adequate and the small porch on the front would comfortably fit a table and chairs. The weatherboard walls and shingled roof blended into the trees so well that from the gate you could hardly see it.

When Nazla and Zuhal brought more tea, he grabbed his wife and planted a loud kiss on her cheek.

'What was that for?'

'Because you believed in me and let me go ahead with my crazy scheme!'

'We still have a long way to go, you know.'

'I know, my love, but it feels as though we've turned a corner. Everyone can now see I'm serious about building this retreat. Nothing can stop it now! And by the way, I've thought of the perfect name.'

He had abandoned 'Paradise Lodge' as a bit pretentious but as he stood on the porch of the first chalet looking out over the orchard another name popped into his head.

His mother's name was Kadriye and Hasan's affectionate nickname for her was Kado.

'Kado's Garden,' he said, saying it out loud for the first time and liking the way it echoed with memories.

'Without Mother and Hasan, we would not have been able to do this and I would have kept plodding on until I either felt better or – more likely – had a meltdown and had to see a shrink.'

Zuhal raised her almost empty tea glass in a toast. 'To Kado's Garden. May it save many more people from meltdowns!'

\*

Fatma had seen the two enormous lorries trundle past the pension and guessed they had brought Harun's bungalows. She felt the bitterness of disappointment: their efforts had not put Harun off. Had he been planning a different business or starting it elsewhere, she might have admired his tenacity. As it was it annoyed her more. Even his sending Alya to stay now seemed duplicitous, like a false gesture of friendship.

She finished serving breakfast and went to the house to call Nazla.

'What's going on there, Nazla?'

'The bungalows have arrived and the men are already putting them together. Do you think we should give in, Fatma?'

'Certainly not. We can't do anything for the moment but that doesn't mean we surrender. Harun will soon find how difficult this business is and if we send a few extra challenges his way…'

'I did have an idea, Fatma.'

'Yes?'

'Harun Bey is looking for a cleaner. He's spoken to a couple of young women but he wants someone from Ortakoy. I could suggest Buket for the job.'

'That's a brilliant idea. She'd be our spy on the inside. Do you think she'd take it?'

'I'm sure she would. She needs the money – there are five of them trying to get by on her father's small pension. And where else would she find a job in the village?'

Fatma felt better after the phone call. Having someone working at the retreat would make it much easier to find little ways to disrupt the business. She would leave it until Harun was ready to open, then call a meeting of the opposition group so they could all come up with things for Buket to do.

She was on her way back to the pension when a car pulled up and a lady got out. She was tall and elegant, dressed in a long, brightly coloured dress and with a scarf tied round her head. She rushed towards Fatma.

'Merhaba! What a lovely place! Do you have a room?'

Fatma was taken aback by the woman's enthusiasm. 'Room, yes, we have room. How many days?'

'I'm not sure. I was just driving along without a plan and I ended up here and I have a good feeling. I like this place!'

She beamed at Fatma, who smiled back even though she had understood little of what the woman said.

'I'll stay a few days – four or five, maybe more. My name is Claudia. Clau-di-a.'

Fatma smiled and nodded, the ends of her head scarf bobbing with the movement. 'Welcome, Mrs

Claudia. I'm Fatma.' She showed the new arrival to one of the upstairs rooms.

'What an amazing view!' The woman leaned on the balcony railing and gazed out over the valley. 'Yes, this is perfect.'

Fatma called Ahmet to carry the new guest's bags up to the room. Hoping to tempt her to stay a few extra days she offered the woman a good rate, including breakfast and dinner. She agreed so fast that Fatma wondered if she should have asked for a little more.

She was curious about the new arrival. She was older than Fatma, perhaps even as old as Melahat, but she dressed in the style of a much younger woman. She seemed to be travelling alone and had ended up in Ortakoy and – perhaps strangest of all – wanted to spend some time here. Fatma hoped Melek would find out more about the lady later. Her own English was adequate for greetings and agreeing prices and Ahmet's went as far as discussing football and trying to fathom the words of American rap music; for anything else they relied on Melek.

\*

Melek was reluctant to do her mother's snooping but she too was curious about the new guest, who had come down to dinner wearing a long orange dress, with her hair piled on her head and some large hoop earrings. She did not have to try hard to get the lady to talk.

After dinner she stopped by her table. 'Would you like something else, Madam?'

'Another glass of wine would be lovely.' The woman beamed at her. 'Are you Fatma's daughter?'

'Yes, I'm Melek. That's my family there,' she pointed to the table, 'and at the bar, he is my brother.' She called to Ahmet to bring another glass of wine.

'Pleased to meet you, Melek! And please call me Claudia.'

'I can't, I mean it's not …polite here, calling an older person with their name.'

'Then what do you call them?'

'Big sister or auntie.'

'Then call me Auntie!'

'Where are you from, Auntie?'

'I'm German but I've travelled all over the world. I used to be an air hostess, you know.'

'Lovely! I want so much to travel.'

'It was fun. It's very good to see the world. But then the airline decided I was too old. I was only fifty-three but they like younger girls. Pretty ones like you.'

Melek blushed.

'So I lost my job and then my husband decided he liked younger women too and he left me. And my children grew up and left home and barely bother to call me.'

'I'm sorry, Auntie.'

Claudia shrugged and gave a very German 'Mehhh. At first I was sad. Then I said, "Screw them!"'

She said it loudly and an English couple who were playing cards at the next table looked round. Melek didn't understand exactly what the German lady had said but she guessed from their surprised expressions that it was rude.

'Now I only have to please myself!' the woman continued. 'I can go where I want, when I want. I booked a holiday to one of those big hotels in the town down there but I didn't like it so I rented a car and started to drive around and see other places. Today I came to your village and I got a good feeling, and I saw the Kismet Pension and I believe in kismet so I thought I must stay here.' She took a sip of the new glass of wine, leaving a smudge of bright pink lipstick on the rim.

Melek smiled. 'We are happy you came! Now please excuse me, Claudia Auntie – I must study for an exam tomorrow.' She stood and would have gone straight to the house but her mother caught her and quizzed her about their newest guest. Melek gave her the edited version of Claudia's story.

# 17

Work in the orchard proceeded rapidly. The men were sleeping on site in one of the chalets so they started early and worked until the light was fading, when Nazla and Zuhal brought out pans of food and a large pot of tea. Harun had his dinner inside but went out to sit with the men and drink tea. Stars twinkled in the wide, purple sky and lights mirrored them in the valley below. The men were all from the city, tough guys who worked hard and earned barely enough to keep their families and they told him how nice it was to have a few days away, even if it was a working holiday.

On the second day five more chalets went up. Galip dropped in to see the progress and Mehmet stopped on his way to the coffee house. He tried to tempt Harun to go with him for a few games of backgammon but he could not be drawn away. On the third morning the men started early and finished the last three chalets before lunch. They spent the afternoon putting in the connections for the pipes and cables and finished late in the afternoon. Harun gave them all generous tips and Osman took them to town to have dinner in a lokanta and catch the night bus home.

When they had left Harun looked about him. On the mountain peak opposite, the last remnant of snow was shining luminously in the mauve dusk and the sky above him was streaked pink and orange where the sun had set. In the fading light, the chalets blended into shadows between the trees. He went to the bungalow in the top corner of the field that would be their home. It had a tiny second bedroom for Barish. The three of them would be living in a space smaller than the living room of their apartment in Istanbul but, as Zuhal had pointed out, they would only really be in the chalet to sleep.

As he stood on the small terrace, Zuhal came to find him.

'Shall we sleep in our new home, darling?' he asked.

'Oh Harun, I know you're excited about the chalets and I don't expect luxury but I don't think I can manage with a blanket on the floor like the men.'

'Ha! You underestimate me!' he said, opening the door wide and ushering her in.

While she had been in town buying material for curtains and cushions he had got Metin to bring round some furniture. Nazla had given him a wool mattress and a quilt and he had bought some candles from the village shop and put them in old jam jars.

'Wow, you made everything ready!'

They spent the first night in their new home, lying together under the quilt because the air was still damp and cool, listening to the night music of the crickets.

Exhausted from all the stress, Harun was asleep in minutes.

*

With the chalets in place, everything else started to take shape. Metin had left his apprentice to finish staining the furniture and was working on site building the gazebos. Electricians and plumbers were connecting cables and pipes and the labourers were back to lay paths and fill in trenches. Harun helped with anything he could. At night his body ached with the unaccustomed activity but he loved the feeling of having built something tangible.

Zuhal was busy at the sewing machine, emerging from time to time with arms full of curtains and cushions to decorate one of the chalets. Her hair was flecked with the raw cotton she was using to stuff the cushions and her habit of sticking the pins she removed into her shirt made her look like a walking pin cushion but she looked happy.

One day Harun came across her hunched over a plank of wood, painting, and she threw herself round to hide her work from him and ordered him to leave. When he returned later from a quick visit to the coffee house, he found her supervising Metin as he hung the piece above the gate. She had made a hand-painted sign decorated with flowers and fruit that said 'Kado's Garden'.

It was a huge relief to Harun when he found someone to do the cleaning and cooking. The young lady in question was called Buket and had been introduced to him by Nazla, who explained that she needed work as she had two young children and no husband. He hadn't asked the details, there were too many sad stories around and he was happy to have found someone for the position. They had also organised for Zuhal's friend Oya to do yoga and he had found a man who could lead the trekking – a qualified guide who had moved out of town for a quieter life and had a smallholding down in the valley.

With just six days left until the first guests were due to arrive he was confident they would be ready. Then he had a call from Istanbul.

Timor, the man who sold silk scarves and delicate Angora shawls in the shop opposite his in the Grand Bazaar, said the silver shop had been closed all day and there had been no sign of Talat. Harun's stomach dropped. He thanked his friend for letting him know and ended the call. Then he tried not to panic while he considered all the possibilities.

Had Talat been taken ill? Perhaps he had been in some awful accident? Maybe one of Talat's family was ill and he had had to take them to hospital and would be back in the shop tomorrow. But why had he not called Harun to tell him? They had spoken a couple of times a week since he had left Istanbul and the young man had always said that everything was going well.

He called Talat but there was no answer. He continued to call every half an hour until the afternoon when it no longer rang and a message said the number was temporarily unavailable. Harun sat miserably on the front porch of their chalet and neither the sight of the last jobs being completed nor Zuhal's efforts to distract him made him feel any better.

*

The new guest at the Kismet pension headed off on foot after breakfast and did not return until mid-afternoon, when she sailed up to the table where Fatma was picking through a bowl of lentils for the evening's soup.

'Fatma, something wonderful has happened!' Claudia had a broad smile on her face and a slightly feverish look in her eyes.

Fatma felt the panic that always hit her when guests tried to have a conversation with her in English. 'Tea?' asked Fatma, 'Coffee? Wine? Eat something?'

'Maybe a cold beer. I want to celebrate! I've come home!'

Fatma jumped up and went to the bar. Ahmet was playing backgammon with a young man who worked in finance in Istanbul and had arrived the night before on an impressive motorbike so Fatma fetched the beer and fussed around pouring it into a glass, hoping the lady would sit by herself to drink it. She was disappointed.

'I went to the theatre today and I climbed to the top and sat down and I had the strangest feeling – like I'd been there before. Then I went round into the field where the tombs are and I understood something. This was my home – here, Ortakoy,' she spread her arms to indicate the place, 'a long, long time ago, when the theatre and the tombs were built. I lived here in another life, do you see?'

Fatma did not see at all. The only words she had understood were today, home and Ortakoy. She could see how excited the woman was and wondered if something had happened that day and she needed to leave the village and return home. Her heart sank and she gave a nod.

The boy playing backgammon with Ahmet had heard what Claudia said. 'She says she lived here in another life,' he translated for Fatma and Ahmet.

'I felt it here,' Claudia continued, clutching one fist to her heart. 'I was a part of this village, I had a family here, I was loved. I knew when I arrived yesterday there was something special. I was called back here.'

The boy gave a quick translation, circling one finger discreetly at the side of his head to suggest the lady might not be in control of her senses.

Fatma now understood what Claudia was saying and was pleased that she was not planning to leave them. It did not, however, make it any easier to find a response.

'Good! Lovely!' she said eventually, feeling it would be rude not to acknowledge such a significant discovery. 'Home!' she said, 'Ortakoy your home!' Then she grabbed her lentils and escaped to the kitchen.

\*

Melek was also treated to the details of Claudia's epiphany.

'Have you ever had this feeling, Melek – like you've been somewhere or done something before, even though you haven't.'

'Yes. The name is…dejavu!'

'Oh, I don't mean those little hiccups of memory. I'm talking about big things, things that make your whole life seem different. Perhaps you are too young, my dear.'

Melek nodded.

'I feel different already, Melek, and I want to find out more about my old life. I'm going to stay here for the summer and see if I remember other things. Maybe I'll write a book about it all. What do you think?'

'I think that's wonderful, Claudia Auntie,' said Melek. She liked the idea of this lady staying.

'In this life, little Melek, you have to follow your dreams! Don't ever let anyone stand in your way!'

Melek thought about what Claudia had said. It was a good philosophy if you were an adult and could please yourself but it was not easy to follow if you were a child and were expected to listen to your elders.

As far as her own dreams were concerned, she had decided not to raise the subject again for a while. She would help out as much as she could in the pension and try hard to keep the peace with her mother. That way she hoped when she needed to start making decisions about university Fatma would find it harder to refuse her.

# 18

The sky over Istanbul was heavy and white and the air was thick with exhaust fumes. There was a line of taxis and a queue of people waiting for them. They all looked harried and miserable.

Harun had hardly slept and had got up at six o'clock and tried calling Talat again. When he got no answer, he booked a ticket on the nine o'clock flight to Istanbul and got Osman to drive him to the airport. Now he took his place at the end of the taxi queue and shuffled along until his turn came. He told the driver the district where Talat lived, hoping when they got there he would remember the way. He had only been to the boy's house once before.

The journey took almost an hour. The traffic never eased in the city and the air resonated with the beeping of horns and the shouts of angry drivers. His own driver muttered curses a couple of times but did not try to engage him in conversation, for which he was grateful.

As they got close, Harun saw a mosque he remembered for its gleaming white dome. He saw the narrow street that was the entrance to the area Talat lived and asked the driver to let him out, knowing it would be easier to find the house on foot. He tried two streets before he found the right one. He remembered it because in the middle, between two apartment buildings, was an old one-storey house in a garden. Talat had told him that developers had offered the old man who lived there a lot of money to sell but he had refused. Now the house had been stripped out and Harun guessed the old man had died and the house was going to be flattened and replaced with another unattractive block.

Talat lived with his mother and sister in the apartment building next door. There was no crowd of people outside, no weeping and wailing, so there had not been a terrible accident or a death in the family. He looked up at the flat which was on the first floor and saw the net curtains move. He thought he saw the shadow of someone passing behind them. He pressed the buzzer a couple of times but there was no response. He heard the sound of traffic out on the main road, a siren somewhere further off, a simit seller boasting of the freshness of his wares, hoping to tempt people out of their houses to buy the crisp, sesame-coated bread rings.

Harun stood back and looked up at the apartment windows again. He took out his phone and pressed redial on Talat's number but got the same message. As he put the phone back in his pocket, he saw the curtain lift and then drop back into place. He tried the buzzer again but still nobody answered. He was about to go and find a cafe to wait when a young woman came out of the building. She smiled at him and held the door open.

'The automatic lock doesn't always work,' she said. 'I'd go up, if I were you!'

'Thank you.'

Harun went up to the first floor. He heard muffled voices inside and pressed the doorbell. The voices went quiet but nobody answered the door. He had almost forgotten about the shop as he tried to imagine what might have happened to this family to make them behave so strangely. Had something frightened them? Were they in some sort of trouble? Hoping to reassure them, he spoke through the door.

'Shaziye Abla, this is Harun, Talat's boss. I'm so sorry to disturb you and I hope there's nothing wrong but the shop has been shut for two days and I really have to find out what's going on.' He thought he heard a sob from inside. 'Is Talat here? Can I speak to him?' It was quiet in the building. He heard water running in the pipes and the cooing of pigeons at the window over the stairs. 'Please Abla, I need to sort this out.' He heard the faintest whispering. 'I won't go until I know what's going on.'

There were soft footsteps and the door was unlocked and opened. Talat's mother stood there looking down at the floor. There were no lights on in the flat and the hall was gloomy but he thought she looked as though she had been crying.

'What is it, Abla?'

She beckoned him to come in and closed the door, then led the way to the small kitchen and pulled out a chair at the table. The air was damp from the teapot that was boiling on the stove. She poured a glass and put it in front of him.

'Are you hungry? Will you eat something?' she asked.

'No thank you. I need to know why Talat has not been to the shop. Is there something wrong? Has he had to go away?'

The woman let out a sob and Talat's sister Serap rushed in and hugged her mother. 'Don't upset yourself again, Mother. You need to stay calm.'

Her mother pulled away and sat at the table as the girl filled two more glasses and joined them.

'Hello, Harun Bey. Hosh geldiniz,' she welcomed him, though her voice was grim.

'Hosh bulduk, I think. But I really have to know what is going on.'

The girl looked at her mother who nodded quickly. 'Talat has made a terrible mistake. He did it for a good reason but that does not make it acceptable.'

Harun felt his stomach clench. He was not sure he wanted to hear what was coming.

The girl told him how a man had come to the shop several times, talking knowledgeably about the antiques and dropping hints about his business and the money he earned. Then one day he asked Talat to lock the door and explained that he ran a counterfeiting business and together they could make a lot of money. Talat would let him take some of the pieces from the shop – nothing too large and conspicuous but good quality valuable things – and he would get them copied and then return them to the shop. He would sell the copy as the original and they would split the money. The sums were large.

Talat, his sister explained, had been trying for two years to save the money to rent an apartment and buy furniture so he could get married but their mother only got a small pension and she herself was a student and it was difficult to put money by.

'He saw a way to make money quickly that wouldn't hurt anyone.'

'It would hurt the people who bought the copies.'

'Yes, you're right of course, Harun Bey. But Talat didn't have to deal with them and anyway, he said, if they had money to splash out on antiques they would not be much affected by it.'

'So because they are rich they deserve to be cheated?'

'No, no!' The girl stared at her tea glass.

Her mother took over. 'Harun Bey, you know my son has always been a good boy. His father died when he was small and he has had to be the man of the house, running errands, helping at home. When he was twelve, he started working in the shop along the street for a couple of hours each evening to earn some money for us. I think now he wanted to do something for himself.'

'What happened with this man?'

'He took some of the pieces but of course he didn't bring them back,' the girl took over again. 'Talat waited a few days. We could see there was something wrong, he looked awful. Two days ago he told us what had happened.'

'And where is he now?'

The girl fiddled with a teaspoon. 'He said he was going to go round antique shops and see if he could spot any of the pieces.'

'He's wasting his time. These people come in from out of town and will have left with the goods. I'm going to the shop now. Please speak to Talat and tell him he must come and see me. We might be able to work this out but not if he won't talk to me.'

He left the apartment feeling punch drunk. The young man he had spent so much time nurturing had let him down. There were a lot of crooks in their business but he had never imagined Talat would fall for their schemes. He had talked of his girlfriend and how they were hoping to get married. If only he had shared his financial struggles, Harun might have been able to help him.

He had walked some way along the dirty street and come to a taxi rank where he asked the driver to take him to the Grand Bazaar. He stared out of the window at the city rushing by. He was hurt by the betrayal but there was more at stake here than broken trust. If he had nobody he could rely on to manage the shop he would have to return to Istanbul and abandon his plans for the retreat. He had come so close but he could not risk everything he had for a dream.

\*

Fatma was sitting at the Kismet watching a couple who had arrived the previous day playing in the pool. The boy was a local not much older than Ahmet but his partner was an English lady at least thirty years his senior. Fatma had heard of such relationships but she found it disturbing to see the two frolic in the water, sit entwined on one sun bed, feed each other the melon she had served up at dinner.

She overheard the young man boasting to Ahmet about the car he drove, the villa he lived in, the trips abroad. Even Fatma could see how appealing these perks must be to someone who was otherwise destined to live his life getting by on a meagre waiter's wage. For once she was thankful that Ahmet set such store by looks.

Melahat was so scandalised by the English woman and her young lover that she had not even come round to the pension for breakfast. Fatma got up and was on her way to the house to check on her mother when she saw Nazla coming along the road. She waited for her friend, who was quite pink in the face and breathing hard.

'Fatma, you'll never guess what's happened!' she called out before she had reached Fatma.

'What is it, Nazla?'

'Harun Bey has disappeared off to Istanbul.'

'Really? Why?'

'There's been some disaster at his shop. The boy who was running it has disappeared.'

'How wonderful!' Fatma exclaimed, then looked round guiltily to make sure nobody had heard her. 'Let's go inside and have coffee and you can tell me everything.'

In the house Fatma bustled about making a sugary coffee which she took into the living room for her mother and then two medium-sweet coffees for her and Nazla. They settled themselves at the kitchen table.

'So, tell me all about Harun Bey.'

'I don't really know much more, Fatma. Apparently, something's happened to the boy and the shop was closed all yesterday. Harun Bey's gone up there to try to sort it out.'

'Will he be back soon?'

'I'm not sure but I heard Zuhal tell him that if he couldn't find someone reliable to run the shop he should stay there.'

'And what will happen to this place?' Fatma waved a hand dismissively to signify the retreat.

'I've no idea. Zuhal has gone off for a walk with her sketch pad. Osman is in the orchard carrying on as though nothing has happened but he's in a foul mood.'

'Perhaps our efforts were not in vain!'

Fatma ate one of the flour cookies Derya had baked the day before. It was sweet and powdery. The thought of the retreat being abandoned before it had even opened made her giddy with relief. It would be another folly, another great monument to bad judgement, like the grand hotel sitting half-built on the edge of town after it was found that a third of it was located on government land, or the restaurant up the mountain that had never been finished because the forestry commission stopped the owner using their roads to get to it. In the case of the retreat, Harun might be able to sell the bungalows. If not, they would slowly rot and melt back into the orchard.

# 19

There were more people in the main avenue of the covered market than lived in the whole of Ortakoy. Feeling a sense of panic at the crowds washing towards him Harun looked up at the beautiful, tiled ceiling and almost bumped into a Chinese tourist who was studying his mobile phone. The two danced around each other and Harun hurried on to reach the shop as quickly as possible. Even though he knew what he would find, he still experienced the heavy drop of disappointment when he saw the shutters pulled firmly down on the front of the shop.

As he was undoing the padlock Timor called across to him. 'Harun! Welcome back!'

'Thank you, Timor, but I can't say it's nice to be back. How do you put up with this?' He waved at the crowds.

'They're the reason we're here. "The busier the better", you used to say.'

'I did, didn't I? I must have been crazy!'

He rolled up the metal front and unlocked the door to the shop. Inside, everything seemed to be in order. He went round behind the counter and started looking through the sales book.

Talat had carefully logged all the sales he had made and the money taken, as well as the money he had paid out for some new items. Harun looked round the shop and noticed that a particularly fine silver coffee set was missing. He checked the book again and could not see it listed. It must have been one of the pieces Talat had let the man take.

He had been in the shop for ten minutes when the first customer came in. After that, there was a steady stream of them. He sold several of the replicas to tourists and a man came in to examine a particularly fine Ottoman oil lamp and left saying he would be back to buy it. Spending a few hours in the cramped shop trying to secure sales and haggling over prices made him more depressed. By late afternoon he was desperate to get some fresh air and call Zuhal.

'Talat's been had by a conman,' he explained when he had shut the shop and was sitting at a café in front of the Ahi Chelebi Mosque drinking tea. He liked this spot and the mosque, which was dedicated to a fifteenth century Ottoman physician, but he was also sitting at the table to escape the press of people heading for the waterfront and the ferry terminal.

Zuhal's voice was comforting. 'I'm so sorry, my love. What did they take?'

'I'm not exactly sure yet. I haven't seen Talat. The worst thing is that he handed things over knowingly.'

He explained to Zuhal what Talat's mother and sister had told him. 'I asked them to make it clear to him that he needs to come and see me but he didn't come today. I'll stay here and open the shop tomorrow and hope he comes then.'

'Go to my mother's. She'll be happy to see you and you can see Barish.'

'I don't think I'd be much company. I think I'll just get a fish sandwich from the boat here and go back to the apartment.'

'Alright. But don't drink too much whisky!'

In the apartment in Tophane, he ate part of the sandwich but he did not have much appetite. He poured himself a few fingers of scotch and sat by the window, looking down onto the street. He had got so used to the huge sky and open spaces of Ortakoy that the city felt suffocating. He wondered where he could possibly find someone he could trust to take care of the shop.

After a few sips of the warming drink he had an idea. There was an old man, the person who had taught him the antiques business, who had been complaining of boredom the last time Harun saw him. He would jump at the chance to get involved in things again. But an arthritic knee had forced him to sell his own shop the previous year. Would he be capable of running another one?

Harun poured himself another glass. He thought of Talat and the responsibilities and duties he had been trying to fulfil. He was not a bad person really, just one who had made a bad choice. By the time he went to bed, Harun thought he had come up with a solution. He just needed Talat to put aside his shame and come and see him.

\*

The next morning Harun was in the shop early. It did not open until half past ten but he liked to get there before the streets were busy. He went through the inventory book and identified which pieces were missing and their value. He ordered a coffee from the kahvehane and was rearranging some of the tourist pieces when he heard someone come into the shop.

'Put it on the counter, thank you,' he said, thinking it was the waiter from the café.

'Harun Bey?'

He turned to see Talat standing looking miserable. He had never been a violent man but his hands itched to grab his protegee by the shoulders and give him a good shake. Instead, he fired a question at him.

'Why did you do it, Talat?'

Talat hung his head. 'I thought I wasn't hurting anyone. It was wrong, I know that now and I'm so ashamed. You trusted me and I let you down, Harun Abi.'

'If you needed money, you could have asked me.'

The boy said nothing but took some keys out of his pocket and put them on the counter.

'What are you doing?' asked Harun.

'I'll start paying you back the money when I find another job.'

'Why, is this one not good enough for you anymore?'

'You said…I thought…you don't want me to carry on working here, do you?'

'I certainly do. How else am I going to make sure you don't do anything stupid again?'

The young man looked at him in amazement.

'I've spoken with Zeki Bey who is bored of retirement and is happy to come in for a few hours each day to keep an eye on the place – and on you. I will lend you a sum of money so that you can go ahead with renting a house and marrying that girl of yours. You will pay me back that and the money for the pieces that have gone missing, a little each month.'

'Abi, you are a very good man! I don't deserve this.'

'Everyone deserves a second chance but if you mess up again, I'll not only fire you, I'll go to the police too.'

'I promise I will never do anything like this again.'

'Now go home and tell your mother and sister so they can stop worrying. I'll look after the shop today but tomorrow morning you need to be in early to do a stock take. Zeki will be here about eleven o'clock.'

At the end of the day Harun closed the shop, said goodbye to Timor and escaped the confines of the bazaar. He hadn't eaten all day and he was ravenous. He stopped at one of the cafes on the Galata Bridge and ate İskender kebab and drank a beer. He took his time as his flight was not until eleven at night. By the time he had finished his meal the sun had dipped below the horizon and the city twinkled with a million lights, reflected back in the water of the Golden Horn. It looked lovely but it did not tempt him to stay.

## 20

The first guests were due at Kado's Garden the following day. Metin was putting a last coat of varnish on the yoga deck and the electrician was running cables to lights in the trees. Zuhal was organising the laundry and kitchen with the help of Buket. The young woman was nervous and jumpy and Harun was a little worried he had made a mistake in hiring her but Zuhal thought they should just give her time.

The last traces of snow had vanished from the tops of the mountain and the first crop of grain was already turning golden in the fields down in the valley. After his trip to the city Harun appreciated the scenery and the clean air even more than before. In the afternoon as everyone raced to finish their work a white cloud appeared behind the far peaks, building rapidly into a billowing tower which then spread out and blocked the sun.

'There's a big storm coming,' said Osman. 'Better make sure all the doors and windows are shut,' and he went round the chalets checking.

The cloud turned silvery then, as the light faded,

dark charcoal grey. After dinner, Harun sat on the tiny terrace of their cabin enjoying a glass of raki. A breeze was stirring the leaves of the trees and lightning was dancing over the mountains. He heard a distant rumble of thunder.

He went into the cabin where Zuhal was reading and got into bed. The thunder was moving nearer and the wind was whistling between the chalets. Harun thought he would not sleep but exhaustion took over and he managed a couple of hours. He woke just as the storm broke.

The wind had died down and the first drops of rain tapped lightly on the shingled roof. Soon the tapping turned into drumming and water poured off the overhang onto the terrace. Then it sounded as though a dam had been opened and water was pouring from the sky.

He got up and opened the door. All he could see outside was a watery blackness and the noise was so loud that Zuhal stirred in her sleep. He shut the door quickly and spent half an hour huddled under the covers hoping that the rain would stop before the guests arrived.

Then, as quickly as it had started, the torrent died away. Harun pulled on a jacket and went to sit on the terrace. A gold halo was sitting on the mountain opposite and the valley was emerging from the darkness shrouded in mist. The trees, the grass, the chalets all looked washed clean. The halo grew until a ray of white light reached over the mountain and the sun appeared, watery and pale at first but quickly gaining strength and heat.

Zuhal came out wrapped in a blanket, her hair tangled round her face.

'How long have you been out here?'

'An hour or so. Since the storm finished.'

'How beautiful it all looks!'

The sun was catching at the raindrops in the trees making them sparkle.

'It *is* beautiful. I hope our guests think the same!' said Harun.

'I'm sure they will. And you know what they say: rain brings blessings!'

They dressed and went to the kitchen where Zuhal made tea. Osman wished them good morning as he hurried down to the truck and set off for the bus station in town to meet the guests who were arriving on the overnight bus from Istanbul.

Zuhal finished her tea and went to check the cabins. Harun dried the tables and put cushions out in the gazebos. When the truck pulled into the field, five young people tumbled out of it. A taxi pulled up behind it and another four emerged from that. Harun had spoken to the girl who had booked their stay and knew they were students celebrating the end of term.

'Hey – look at that!' said one of the boys, waving at the view.

'Sweet – these cabins are so sweet!' said a girl with a gold hoop in her eyebrow and a diamond stud just above her mouth.

'Melisa – look at the mountains!'

'Ozan – are you going to leave your guitar in the taxi?'

The group stumbled around, bleary-eyed after

the long journey and dazed by their surroundings. Harun introduced himself and Zuhal and showed them to their chalets while Buket put out a breakfast of cheese, eggs fried in olive oil, tomatoes, cucumber, honey and flat bread, along with the last of the season's cherries. They devoured the food, then fell asleep stretched out on the cushions.

Harun found his eyes growing heavy too. The rush to finish work on the retreat, the anxious trip to Istanbul and the lack of sleep combined to make him bone-weary. But he also felt a blissful sense of accomplishment. Kado's Garden was finished and ready for guests; surely the rest of it would be easy?

\*

At the Kismet, the storm had brought a new crop of frogs to the pool. It was a curious phenomenon that each time it rained they abandoned the bubbling stream that ran down the slope behind the pension in favour of a tank of chlorinated water. Fatma had dragged Ahmet out of bed to catch them before the guests came out for breakfast. He was dancing around the pool scooping at them with the net but they were lightning fast as they dodged it. Fatma snapped at him to stop messing around and get a move on.

She was feeling irritable. She knew from Nazla that Harun had returned from Istanbul and that the first guests were arriving at the retreat. If only that infuriating man had listened to her advice and gone back to Istanbul!

Still, the fact that the retreat was opening did not mean they had to give up. A few extra problems, a few disappointed guests on top of the usual dramas of running such a place and she was sure Harun would abandon his dream and go back to his easy life in the city. After breakfast she went to the house to call her allies.

Demir apologised but said that as the yachting season was starting, he and Dudu were moving down to the beach and would be too busy to help. Atilla said that discouraging someone was different from actually damaging their business and that he was not prepared to get involved with the latter. Chetin said he couldn't see much point in continuing as this man obviously had more money than sense. Fatma knew the real reason he had lost interest was that the chance to ruin his brother's business had passed. She didn't even bother to ask about Crazy Kerim.

With each desertion she felt worse. Finally she called Nazla.

'You're not deserting, are you?' she asked miserably.

'No, I'm not. Osman's already acting differently, putting on a posh voice, driving round in that flashy truck.'

'Then start thinking of things we can do. Have they got any classes set up?'

'Well obviously Zuhal is going to do painting classes and her friend's coming to do yoga. I think Harun Bey has found a man to lead the trekking. Can you believe that he's looking for someone to demonstrate kilim weaving?'

Fatma grimaced. 'Yes, I can.' She remembered the awkward tea party when her mother had suggested the craft – her mother who knew almost all the women who might help Harun Bey by demonstrating it. 'I think he might find that harder than he imagines.'

When she had ended the call, Fatma went to find her mother.

'Do you remember suggesting carpet weaving to Harun Bey?'

Melahat chuckled at the memory. 'Our mothers used to weave all our rugs. They taught us to do it and my fingers bled from the rough wool and I was always getting them pinched in the frame. And these people are going to pay to try it?' She shook her head as she slurped her tea.

'Actually, they're not going to get the chance because you're going to stop it.'

'Me? How am I going to do that?'

'You know all the ladies round here who could take kilim weaving classes. You're going to have a word with them and tell them not to work for Harun Bey. Tell them he's a rascal or tell them about Nurdan's curse – I'm sure you can find something!'

'Fatma dear girl, give up this fight. The man has opened his business. It might last, it might not but you're only hurting yourself by waging this war. There are whispers in the village about you consorting with Chetin.'

'Yes, well that association is over – thankfully. But I'm not going to give up just because everyone else has. And as you're the one who came up with the ridiculous idea of kilims, you can be the one to put a stop to it!'

Her mother grumbled about her aching legs

and the heat and said she thought she might go back to Hilal's where there was air conditioning but eventually she went to the phone in the hall and started calling her friends. She warned them against working for Harun and asked them to pass on the word. Then she spent the whole day in the house saying she felt ill.

At dinnertime she still would not go round to the pension and Fatma put some food on a tray and gave it to Melek to take to her. Strangely, the mystery illness did not stop her eating a large helping of chicken and rice and a slice of semolina cake.

*

Melek had spent the day studying. Her head felt heavy and her body stiff. Even with the window open the small room was hot and stuffy. A fly had been ricocheting off the furniture in ever decreasing circles and she realised she had been staring at the same page for ten minutes, daydreaming of Barish. She thought a walk might help clear her head and decided to visit Selma.

Outside, the sun was high and bright and the sky was achingly blue. A warm breeze carried the smell of wild thyme from the slopes above the road. Looking up, Melek saw two brown ears and a curious face appear over a rocky knoll.

'Leyla?' she called.

'Hello, Melek Abla.' The girl appeared and patted the young goat.

'How are the babies doing?'

'Oh they're big now. They go quite a way from

their mother sometimes but they always come running back when something scares them.'

'Don't forget you're going to come to the pension when school's finished so I can teach you to swim.' This agreement had been made at the Children's Day party when Melek had caught the young girl gazing longingly at the pool.

'I won't forget, Melek Abla!'

Melek walked on. As she got near the retreat she heard music and singing. Her heart started beating faster. She drew level with the gate and saw a crowd of young people sitting around on cushions. One boy was strumming a guitar and the others were singing. Melek held her breath and scanned the group for Barish's face but she could not see him. She relaxed a little.

'Melek! How lovely to see you!'

Melek spun round and saw Zuhal coming from the other corner of the field. She had a large shirt on over her clothes and the shirt and her hair were flecked with paint. 'Do come and have a drink with me!'

'I-I don't want to disturb you.'

'You won't be disturbing me – we're just having a break from our lesson. I'm afraid Barish won't be here until next week.' She gave a mischievous grin and greeted Melek with a kiss on each cheek.

'Then I'd love to,' said Melek quickly.

The older woman pulled off the shirt. 'Phew! It's hot with that on but if I don't wear it my clothes get covered in paint!'

The guitar player finished one tune and started

another and his friends joined in noisily. Zuhal went into the kitchen and reappeared with two glasses of lemonade. She kicked off her sandals and climbed onto one of the koshk, lying back on the cushions and stretching her legs in front of her. Melek slipped off her flip flops and sat on the cushion opposite.

'How are your exams going?'

'I've done half of them but we still have physics and chemistry to go and they're my worst subjects!'

'Barish loves sciences and hates Turkish!'

'How many guests do you have in, Zuhal Auntie?'

'There's this lot,' she gestured to the singers, 'and two more couples came yesterday – those are the ladies taking the painting class. They own a small café where I often have lunch.' She told Melek about the café and how the owners had some of her pictures on the walls. 'How are things at the Kismet?'

'Getting busier now.'

'If you have time, you're always welcome to come here and join in our groups, you know. I'm doing the painting, of course, and we're doing trekking. My friend Oya is arriving today to take yoga classes and Harun is trying to find a lady to teach weaving. I think we have your grandmother to thank for that idea!'

'I'm sure Grandmother didn't suggest it seriously.'

'No, I suppose it must seem strange that people now want to do it for entertainment. Times change!'

'Not in Ortakoy, they don't. At least, not very fast!' said Melek with feeling.

Zuhal picked up the paint-splattered shirt and felt with her feet for her sandals. 'Excuse me, Melek,

I'd better get back to work or we won't finish our pictures before dinner. Do come again – you're always welcome!'

Melek got up to go. As she did she saw Buket walking across the field carrying an armful of sheets. She froze. Had Buket seen her? Would she tell her mother she'd been at the retreat? But it appeared that Buket was working there, in which case she must have changed sides, accepted the retreat and left her mother's ridiculous group.

Still, Melek hurried out of the field with her head down. It was hard to know who you could trust with so much intrigue going on.

# 21

The students had left Kado's Garden. They seemed to have enjoyed their holiday and Harun thought they had been the perfect first guests as they had not been at all bothered by teething problems such as a hot tap that had been connected to the cold water supply, a bathroom door that wouldn't shut and Buket forgetting to knock before entering one of the chalets and finding one of the boys fresh from the shower and completely naked. In fact, Buket had been much more upset about this last event than the boy.

Zuhal's friends from Istanbul had spent only four days at the retreat but they had promised to promote it amongst the customers at the café and to return as soon as they had another chance. This week's guests were a group of women, one of whom lived downstairs from their apartment in Tophane, a British couple who ran a textile business and had been visiting their suppliers and two families who wanted their young children to get close to nature.

The trekking was popular and Harun was pleased with the guide he had found for it. The man not only knew all the tracks and paths around but could also point out wild flowers, identify bird calls and entertain people with the history of the area. Oya was giving yoga classes twice a day and Zuhal was kept busy – it seemed everyone considered themselves a budding artist.

There were two things currently concerning Harun. The first was Buket. The young woman was still too nervous to look him in the eye and if he came across her suddenly in the kitchen or going between chalets, she startled so badly she often let out a shriek. Her hands shook so much that she often spilled drinks and she had already dropped a few pieces of crockery. One time, after letting several tea glasses slide off a tray, she had stared down at the broken glass and burst into tears.

Zuhal had told him to give the young woman time but Buket did not seem to be improving.

'I overheard the Istanbul ladies talking about her this morning,' said Harun to his wife when she had finished her painting class. 'They think she's rude and don't understand why we hired her.'

'I don't think she means to be rude, she's just always in a hurry to get away from people.'

'And she never smiles,' said Harun.

'According to Nazla, her husband treated her very badly. I suppose it's made her wary of people.'

'What's she like with you?'

'She's timid but she does talk to me and she works hard. Let me have another word with her.'

Harun sighed. He did not want to fire the young woman or to have to look for someone else to do her job. 'Alright. But please make it clear, my love, that if things don't improve we'll have to let her go. I can't have her upsetting the guests.'

The following afternoon they were sitting together in one of the arbours. Buket brought out tea and the glasses rattled on their small saucers but she managed to get them to the table without accident. Harun thanked her and she gave a quick smile and scuttled back to the kitchen.

'Have you had a word?' he asked Zuhal, tilting his head in Buket's direction.

'Yes. I explained she comes across as surly and she promised to try to smile more. Have you found anyone for the weaving classes?'

'No and I've tried all the ladies Osman recommended now.'

This was Harun's other problem. Kilim weaving was listed as one of the things offered at the retreat and a few people had already enquired about it but despite his efforts he had not managed to find anyone willing to come and teach the class. 'Some of them hardly let me explain why I'm calling before turning me down. It's almost as though someone has put them off.'

'Now, sweetheart, don't start with those crazy conspiracy theories again! You heard Melahat Hanum say her fingers are too stiff to weave now. Most of these ladies are probably the same, or perhaps they just don't want to go out in the heat of summer.'

Buket had come out of the kitchen and was hovering near them.

'Well, I think we'll have to drop it from the list of activities.'

'Then we'll find something else we can offer,' said Zuhal.

Buket took their empty glasses and returned with them full. She put them on the table but this time she did not hurry off.

'H-Harun Bey.'

'Yes, Buket.' He thought the young woman was probably going to beg him not to fire her.

Instead, she said, 'I-I-I hope you won't be angry but I heard you talking with Zuhal Hanum about weaving.'

'I'm not angry, Buket. I would welcome any help. I've been trying to find a lady to demonstrate kilim weaving but I've had no luck. Do you know anyone?'

She was standing very straight with her fists clenched. 'N-not who makes kilims but one of the villages in the valley is known for making dastar – traditional cotton cloth.'

'That sounds interesting. Tell me more!'

'It's woven from pure cotton and it's mostly uncoloured but they weave patterns into it.' The young woman put a hand up and patted her head. 'They use it for scarves and tablecloths.'

'Do you know someone who makes this dastar?'

Buket nodded. 'My aunt lives in that village and she's one of the best dastar weavers.'

'Do you think she'd come here and demonstrate her craft – for a fee, of course?'

'I-I think so. I can ask her if you like.'

'That would be wonderful! You would be saving the day, Buket.'

The young woman gave a shy smile but there

seemed to be a different swing to her walk as she left.

The next day she came to find Harun with an older woman dressed in the village women's usual attire of baggy trousers and long-sleeved top.

'Harun Bey, this is my Nermin Auntie, Auntie this is Harun Bey.' Buket pointed to the scarf draped over the woman's head, which was loosely woven from cream thread and had zig-zag lines through it. 'And this is dastar.'

Harun invited the woman to sit down. He asked her about her craft and showed her where he imagined the lessons might take place. He was pleased to find that unlike her niece she was a relaxed, happy woman who readily agreed to everything he suggested. As the Istanbul ladies were keen to try a local craft, they decided that Osman would drive Nermin home to collect her spare loom and she would give the first class that afternoon.

Later he watched her skilfully guiding the shuttle back and forth and drawing the lines tight on the frame. It was amazing how she took a mass of loose threads and turned them into cloth. When it was time for the guests to have a go, Nermin was patient and encouraging and proved herself a natural teacher. Buket came over to have a look and when he caught her eye and smiled she actually nodded and smiled back.

Zuhal had turned out to be right again, thought Harun: Buket had just needed time to settle in.

*

At the Kismet Pension Claudia was proving a

colourful addition to the place, taking it upon herself to welcome any new arrivals and tell them of her own personal epiphany. The other guests currently consisted of two couples from Georgia, two Turkish families each with a small child and three boys from Sweden with their Turkish friend and guide. These last were noisy but they were good customers as they liked to drink beer every afternoon and until well into the night.

It was early afternoon and Fatma had left Ahmet in charge and escaped to the house. It was not much cooler inside but at least it was shady and quiet, apart from the noise of the television. When she went to look, she saw that her mother had nodded off and she turned the sound down on the game show she had been watching – a particularly ridiculous one in which a mother picked a bride for her son from a group of hopefuls.

She went back to the kitchen and had just poured boiling water onto the tea leaves and turned down the heat to let the pot simmer when Ahmet came running in.

'Mum, you have to come. There are some men here to see you!'

'What sort of men?'

'I don't know – something about the pool.'

Fatma heaved herself up, stuck her feet back in her plastic sandals and followed him round to the pension. They passed a white car with the black number plate of an official vehicle but even without it she would have known the two men peering into the swimming pool were government workers.

She took a deep breath, forced her mouth into a smile and marched towards them. 'Good afternoon, gentlemen. Can I help you?'

'Are you the owner of this establishment?' asked one of the men. He was squat with a square face and reminded Fatma of the toads she sometimes saw by the stream. She introduced herself and the man said he and his colleague were from the Health Department.

'We're here to check your pool. There are regulations about pools used by the public.'

'The pool is new,' said Fatma. 'My son here is the one who looks after it. He's been doing everything properly.'

She felt confident as she said this. Ahmet had been taking care of the pool with a commitment that had surprised her.

'We'll know that when we've tested the water,' said the other man, whose shirt was missing a button and gaping open to show his vest underneath. Neither man, thought Fatma, looked like a keen swimmer.

The man with the vest opened a case and both men took out small vials which they filled from the pool. They each added something from a dropper bottle, closed the top and shook them. Then they held the test tubes up and examined the results. Ahmet brought over two glasses of soda water and the men sat at one of the tables.

'The level of chlorine is just within the limit,' said the toad. 'But the pH level is too high.' He held up one of the tubes in which the water had turned pink. 'It should be six or seven but it's more like nine. Do you have a testing kit?'

'Oh yes!' said Fatma and sent Ahmet to fetch it.

He gave it to the man with the vest, who opened the box and emptied the contents onto the table. 'This hasn't been used! You should be testing the water every day otherwise how do you know how much of anything to add?'

Fatma looked at Ahmet. He shrugged. 'The water looked alright.'

'Just because you can't see something doesn't mean it isn't there and some of the things that live in pools can make people very ill,' said the man, looking at the pool with distaste.

'Of course,' said Fatma, glaring at Ahmet. 'We're still learning all this but I'll make sure Ahmet tests it every day from now on.'

'Do you have a logbook?' asked the man.

'Logbook?'

'When you test the water, you should write the results in a logbook.'

'Is there a trained lifeguard here?' asked the toad, looking pointedly at Fatma.

'Er, no. Do we need one?' she asked.

'If there isn't, you should have a sign telling people.' He put another tick on his form. 'You also don't appear to have a lifebuoy.' He shook his head. 'We could fine you for these omissions.'

'Please don't do that,' said Fatma, her chest tightening at the thought of a fine. 'We'll get them all sorted this week.'

The man finished filling in his form and handed her a copy before saying, 'We'll let you off with a warning this time but we'll be back soon to check.'

The men finished their sodas and put everything back in the case.

'Next time,' said the man with the vest, 'we won't be so lenient.'

When they had gone, Ahmet disappeared behind the bar and sat on his stool disconsolately. Fatma actually felt sorry for him. Who could have known one small pool would require so much attention?

\*

Melek got off the minibus and waved to Selma as it carried on along the lane towards the village. Instead of going round to the house to change she went straight to the pension. School was almost finished for the summer and they were no longer required to wear uniform. In three days they would collect their reports, lower the flag and sing the national anthem for the last time for three months.

In the bar Ahmet was sitting on a stool watching a video of Alya on his phone.

'Where's Mum?'

'In the house. Some men came to check the pool.' He poured a glass of cherry juice and put it in front of Melek.

Melek sat on one of the bar stools. 'Was there a problem?'

Ahmet shrugged. 'We have to put some signs up and I'm supposed to test the water every day.'

Melek was just taking a sip of her drink when she saw him look up and smile.

'Hey bro, what's the news?'

Melek turned to find Barish standing just behind

her. Her heart leapt into her throat and she choked on the juice. She put the glass down and turned away, trying desperately to swallow and not spray cherry juice everywhere. How had he come before term had ended? How was it possible that he was even more handsome in real life than in her imagination?

'Hi! How's it going?' he said. 'Are you alright, Melek?'

Melek grabbed a tissue to wipe her lips and nodded, though her eyes were watering with the effort of not coughing.

'When did you get here?' said Ahmet.

'Last night. Exams finished so I got permission to leave early. What about you, Melek, are you still going to school?'

'Yes,' she squeezed out, 'until Friday.'

'How's it going at your dad's place?' asked Ahmet.

'He said it was a bit of a panic to get everything finished for the first guests but they seem sorted now. Everyone looks happy, anyway.'

Melek, desperate to say something interesting, looked around and saw Claudia sitting on her balcony. 'We have a German lady staying who thinks she lived in the village 2,000 years ago!' she blurted out. Ahmet looked at her strangely.

'Really? That's wild.' Barish gave his dazzling smile and she was speechless again.

The Swedish boys and their Turkish friend came back from a trip to the beach and jumped in the pool. They called out to Ahmet for beers and he took them over and stayed to chat with them.

Barish turned back to Melek. 'When can I see you?'

'I-I don't know. When school finishes, I have to help here.'

'What, all the time?' Barish moved a little closer.

'Not all the time.'

'So we can hang out sometimes?'

'Yes, but not here!' Melek was caught between wanting Barish to stay and wanting him to leave before her mother came back and saw him.

'Then come to the retreat!'

Melek reluctantly moved away and Barish followed. At the front of the pension she said, 'I'll come on Saturday afternoon.'

Barish caught her hand and gave it a quick squeeze. 'See you on Saturday!' He set off along the lane and Melek walked back round to the pension. She could still feel the warmth of his fingers wrapped round hers.

# 22

Fatma had not slept well. The bedroom was hot and a mosquito had taken advantage of the hole in the screen that she had been asking Mehmet to fix for a month and spent the night whining around her head. Twice she got up, turned on the light and, armed with an old farming magazine she kept for this purpose tried to find it, but the creature obviously sensed danger and kept quiet until the minute she put out the light and got back into bed, when it started up its serenade again.

Now her eyelids were heavy and her head felt fuzzy. With Melek's help she served breakfast to the guests, then poured tea and went to sit with her mother. Melahat was enjoying her breakfast, wrapping pieces of hard-boiled egg and cheese into bits of flat bread and pushing them into her mouth. She chewed the latest morsel, then took a sip of tea and smacked her lips.

'I spoke to Latife yesterday,' she said, looking at Fatma pointedly. Latife was Buket's mother and another old friend of Melahat's. 'Did you know Buket is working for Harun Bey?'

'Nazla did mention it,' said Fatma. 'Some people are so fickle.'

'That girl isn't in a position to turn down work. Anyway, Latife thinks they're nice people.'

'Hmm.' Fatma took a sip of tea and burnt her tongue.

'They invited her to go in with Buket and have a look round the place. She says the chalets are lovely.'

'And Latife would know, being such an expert on design!' said Fatma thickly, because her tongue was throbbing.

Melahat ignored her. 'And they're giving classes in dastar weaving.'

'Dastar?'

'Yes. Apparently Latife's sister is taking the classes.'

It was not hard for Fatma to guess who had suggested dastar weaving to Harun. It seemed that Buket had forgotten the reason she was at the retreat and was going out of her way to be helpful.

The afternoon was quiet. Selma had come to visit Melek and the two girls were splashing about in the pool laughing. Fatma was just considering going over to the house to try to get an hour's sleep when Claudia returned almost as animated as before. She perched on a sunbed and proceeded to regale Melek and Selma with the news of her latest adventure. Fatma looked on, curious. Perhaps, she thought, Claudia had remembered more details of her previous life. Then she heard the names Harun and Zuhal mangled by Claudia's accent and her heart dropped.

Claudia asked Ahmet for a beer and continued

expounding animatedly to Melek and Selma. The girls, trapped in the pool, stood listening and sometimes nodding in agreement. Fatma heard the word 'yoga' and was sure. Her best customer was going to leave the pension and move to the retreat!

She sat miserably, shelling some fresh kidney beans and thinking how much easier things had been before Harun came to the village. Finally Claudia went off to her room with a cheery wave at Fatma as she passed and the girls climbed out of the pool and grabbed their towels.

'What did she say?' Fatma demanded, making Melek frown and Selma look alarmed. 'I mean what was she so excited about?'

'Claudia Auntie? She saw people doing yoga at the retreat and she does a lot of yoga in Germany so she went in to ask if she can join their classes.'

'And what did they say?'

'Zuhal Auntie showed her round and said she was welcome to join in any of their classes.'

'Of course she did. And once Claudia Hanum starts visiting there for classes they will persuade her to stay there too!' Fatma should have felt relieved that Claudia was not moving but she was sure it was only a matter of time.

'Mother, calm down! Harun Bey would never steal a guest from you.'

'How do you know that, Melek? You hardly know the man.'

'Anyway, he doesn't need to; he has plenty of his own.'

'And how do you know *that*?'

Melek lifted a hand to her mouth and coughed.

'Claudia Auntie said it looked quite busy when she was there,' said Selma with a nod.

'Talk to her, Melek. Ask her to pay for her room for the next month. If she's already paid, she's less likely to move elsewhere.'

Fatma took the beans into the kitchen and put them to boil. She cut onion and garlic, then carrot and potato and cooked them in olive oil and tomato paste to make the pilaki for the beans. She had just turned it off when Derya's husband Hamdi arrived with a delivery of vegetables.

Fatma had always liked Hamdi and admired him for inventing a business that didn't exist until he started it. The farm he and his two brothers inherited from their father could not support three families and Hamdi hated working in the fields anyway. The only thing he looked forward to was the weekly visit to the market. He was a good-looking man who dressed with a certain panache and had a way with people. In charge of the stall he was in his element and the customers – many of them women of a certain age – queued up to buy from him and once there usually ended up buying more than they had meant to.

It was these ladies bemoaning the fact that the market only happened once a week that gave him the idea for his new business: he became a mobile greengrocer, driving round the better streets in town taking fresh produce to his customer's doors. He was never too busy to listen to their woes and if one of them asked him to pick up some anchovies from the fishmonger or some tablets from the pharmacy he always obliged. The ladies called him 'Farmer Hamdi', which was ironic since he had never been called that when he had actually been a farmer.

Fatma called him with an order every two or three days and he delivered it on his way home.

'Hello, Fatma Hanum. Where do you want this?'

Fatma pointed to the side. 'Put it over there, Hamdi. How's business?'

'Business is good. I have more houses than ever on my round and of course there's this new place in the village.'

Fatma stopped chopping parsley for the pilaki. 'You're delivering to Harun Bey?'

'Every day,' said Hamdi, innocently. 'They seem to be very busy.'

When Hamdi had gone, Fatma went round to the house to call Nazla.

'I'm tired of hearing about Harun Bey and his retreat. It seems to be all anyone's talking about!' she wailed.

'Me too! Osman talks about him all the time,' her friend sympathised. 'He's there from early morning, running about as soon as one of those fancy ladies needs anything. I can't even get him to fix the bathroom door. Dila got stuck in there for half an hour the other day.'

'Come round tomorrow,' said Fatma. 'It's time we came up with our next move.'

*

Melek spent the last three days of school daydreaming about visiting Barish. Her feelings veered between excitement and nerves.

'What will I say to him?' she asked Selma on the bus back to the village on the last day.

'I don't know. What did you talk about at the Cherry Festival?'

'Not much. We were listening to Alya most of the time.'

'You'll be fine when you're with him, Meli,' her friend assured her.

She was still nervous as she walked along the lane. She looked both ways to make sure nobody could see her before turning in under the sign that read 'Kado's Garden'. Barish was sitting in one of the gazebos watching his father and another man playing backgammon. When he saw her, he jumped up.

'Melek! It's nice to see you!'

'Hello. I said I'd come on Saturday.'

'I know. I was just worried you wouldn't be able to get away.'

'I told my mother I was going to Selma's,' she said.

'Ahh.'

Melek looked around nervously and Barish seemed to notice. 'Come on, let's go somewhere quieter.'

Melek hesitated; she had never been alone with a boy before, apart from Ahmet.

'I promise I'll behave,' he whispered and led the way through the orchard to a chalet that was bigger than the others.

'Welcome to our house!' he said, with a flourish. On the terrace the table was laid with a plate of biscuits and a bottle of cola in a bucket of ice. Melek felt a fuzzy warmth when she realised he had prepared for her visit.

He pulled out a chair and she sat down. The veranda smelt of wood stain and the sharp scent of pine from the forest behind.

'How was your report?' Barish asked.

'OK. Physics and chemistry were my worst marks but everything else was good. What about you?'

'Same. I mean OK. I like sciences and maths. Turkish is my worst subject.' He opened the bottle and filled two glasses with cola. 'I want to be an engineer so it isn't so important. All those different sorts of endings – who cares?'

Melek giggled. 'I don't really like the grammar but I like literature.'

'Do you know what you want to do – for a job, I mean?'

'History maybe, or archaeology.'

'I went to look at the amphitheatre and the tombs yesterday. Dad says they're two thousand years old.'

Melek found herself telling him about the Lycians who had lived in the area and left traces of their lives at so many ancient sites.

'What did they use the theatre for?'

'Plays, gladiator fights. I go and sit there sometimes and try to imagine it!'

'Perhaps you lived here in another life too?' said Barish.

Melek blushed.

'I'm joking! I like that you know so much about it.' Barish leaned closer and she felt his breath on her cheek. 'I really like you, Melek.'

Melek felt as though her heart might explode. Her hand trembled as she picked up her glass and took a drink.

'Is something the matter?' Barish asked, looking concerned.

'No! It's just...'

'I know your mum doesn't like Dad much.'

'It's not so much that she doesn't like him.' Why was it, Melek wondered, that she was exasperated at her mother most of the time but now felt the need to defend her? 'It's more that she's afraid of losing business to the retreat. She worked hard to get the pension going.'

'Dad would never take business from her.'

'I know that. But my mother is...well, she can be stubborn.'

'Does it mean we can't see each other?'

'No! But we'll have to keep it a secret. For now, at least.'

'OK.'

'And we'll have to be careful because there are people everywhere who'll tell Mum if they see us together. Top of the list is Nazla Auntie.'

'Then we'll have to make sure she doesn't see.' He leant towards Melek again and this time she didn't back away.

\*

Harun and Zuhal had just watched Nermin give another weaving class and were drinking salty ayran, said to be good for cooling the body in extreme heat. They saw Melek scurry out of the gate and soon after

Barish came to join them.

'How was your date?' asked Zuhal.

Barish shrugged nonchalantly but his smile gave him away.

'Has Fatma stopped seeing me as the enemy?' asked Harun, hopefully.

Barish raised his eyebrows. 'No. Melek didn't tell her she was coming here.'

'Oh. Never mind, it's quite romantic. You'll be like Romeo and Juliet!'

Zuhal frowned at him. 'Have you forgotten what happened to them?'

'Well of course I don't mean the ending. Anyway, it won't be for long. I have another plan to win over Fatma Hanum and this time she won't be able to resist!'

\*

While Melek was at the retreat, Nazla was with Fatma. They made tea and took a glass in to Melahat, who was watching a dating programme for the elderly. Then they took theirs out to the arbour that leaned against the front of the house. The bench was warm beneath their legs and the sun winked through the ancient grape vine but it was quiet and away from prying eyes.

'Is it me or does the weather get hotter every year?' said Fatma, mopping her brow with the corner of her head scarf.

'It is hot for early July,' said Nazla. 'I bet your pool's popular!'

Fatma nodded. 'I'm almost tempted to get in it

myself!' The two women laughed at the thought. When they were young, they had sometimes gone to the beach but they only ever waded up to their knees in the water and neither had learned to swim.

'How is Harun Bey coping with the heat?'

'It doesn't seem to bother him. He says it's worse in the city surrounded by all the buildings.'

'No more problems with his business there?'

'There don't seem to be. I heard he's got someone more experienced keeping an eye on the shop.'

'Wouldn't it be better for everyone if he just went back and took care of it himself?' said Fatma bitterly. She took a sip of tea. Even on the hottest day chai was still a comfort. 'Have you come up with any ideas?'

'I wondered if we could put something in the food.'

'Do you mean poison?'

'No! Maybe laxatives? It would be easy enough for Buket to add them to something like tash kebab or turlu and I don't think anyone would taste them.'

'How would we know how much to use? Too little might have no effect and too much might make people seriously ill – or worse!'

'God save us! You're right, Fatma; these things look easy when they do them on the television, but in real life....'

Fatma poured more tea and they both stirred in sugar. For a moment the only sound was the tinkling of the spoons on the glass.

'I was thinking of the things we often have to deal with,' said Fatma. 'Blocked drains, power cuts, that sort of thing. Could we make one of those happen?'

'I don't think we should mess with electricity – that could be dangerous,' said Nazla, 'but perhaps we could block the pipes.'

'If they have a bad experience the guests might write about it on...wherever it is that people write these things—'

'And a blocked drain can be a really bad experience! So how do we go about it?'

'I don't know,' said Fatma, 'I've only ever done the unblocking. But we've found everything down there from whole toilet rolls to socks and underpants, even a toothbrush!'

'A toothbrush? Why would anyone put that down the toilet?'

'I imagine with most of them it isn't intentional – something falls in and they don't want to put their hand in to pull it out.'

'Do they think it will flush away?'

'I don't think they care. They just hope they'll be well away before it causes a problem.'

'I have to tell you, Fatma, Buket isn't happy about doing this.'

'I thought she was on our side?'

'She says she's changed her mind about Harun Bey. And she doesn't want to lose her job.'

'Well remind her that she wouldn't have the job if it hadn't been for us – well, for you.'

'I did and she said she'd do one more thing. But after that she doesn't want to be involved.'

# 23

When Harun had first put his idea for the retreat to Zuhal, one of her questions had been how he planned to find guests. He had assured her that with all his contacts it would not be hard. He had had some simple leaflets printed which he got Talat to put out in the silver shop and to take round to other shops in the market. He had a few friends who worked in large offices and one who lectured at the university and he had asked them to post information about the retreat on the notice boards in their workplaces. This week there were two couples at Kado's Garden who had seen just such a notice in the office of the textile company where they worked. Harun had also paid to have a website set up, though he was dismayed at the number of sites that showed up in a search for guest houses or even retreats.

So far, word-of-mouth had been the most effective marketing tool for them and they currently had a family with teenage children and two young Englishmen who worked at the Embassy, all of whom had come as the result of recommendations. Harun was getting enquiries every day and though the place was not yet full, he had bookings through to September. And he still had his trump card to play.

Birol Bey had come into the silver shop the previous year and asked questions about some of the pieces they had in at the time. He was, it turned out, not a potential customer but a journalist who was writing an article on the markets of Istanbul. Though the man was a local, Harun offered to give him the insider's tour of the Grand Bazaar and they had spent a pleasant morning wandering the vaulted lanes and poking around in some of the oldest shops, followed by lunch in his favourite restaurant.

Birol Bey had sent him a copy of the article when it was printed. There was a photograph that showed the front of the shop and Harun was referred to as the owner and an expert on antique silver. In the months that followed, a number of customers had said they had first read of the shop in the article. Harun had kept in touch with Birol and they had met several times for a drink. He had called to tell him about his new venture and Birol had wished him luck and promised to write about the place when it was finished.

Now the initial glitches had been ironed out and they had all got into the swing of things Harun felt confident enough to invite the journalist down. An article in the national press would be great publicity for Kado's Garden and should also raise their profile on the internet. And Harun had an additional reason for inviting Birol Bey to Ortakoy, one that involved reaching people much closer to home.

*

Fatma put the aubergine to roast in the oven, then chopped the onions which made her eyes water and her nose run. She fried them with pepper and garlic, then added minced lamb. When it was done, she piled it into the aubergine and put the tray back in the oven.

Outside she looked around. Ahmet was sitting at the bar talking to his friend Huso. Melek was in the pool giving Leyla a swimming lesson. She had found a swimming costume left behind by one of the guests for the little girl to wear and was showing her how to hold the side of the pool and kick. Leyla was an enthusiastic pupil and was making quite a splash with her skinny legs. It was nice, Fatma thought, to see the little girl behaving like a child.

Claudia and a young German couple who were staying had spent the day at the beach. She had asked Mehmet to collect them at six and he had set off before Fatma had gone into the kitchen. When she came out, she was surprised to see that he still was not back.

'Ahmet, what time did your father leave?'

He shrugged. 'I don't know. Why?'

'Don't you think he's been a long time?'

'He's probably stopped to chat with Demir Abi.'

Fatma had to agree that that was a possibility. Her husband was never one to pass up the chance for a chat, though she hoped he wasn't keeping the guests waiting.

Melek got out of the pool and took Leyla to the laundry room to change back into her clothes. Two English ladies who had arrived the previous day and spent the afternoon bobbing around in the pool in large inflatable rings gathered their things and went off to their room. Fatma went to check on the stuffed aubergine, which were nearly ready. Mehmet still had not returned.

The beach road was steep with many twists and turns, some of which bordered precipitous drops. In addition, it was in such a sorry state that in places huge potholes or large rocks meant vehicles had to drive close to the edge. Fatma tried to banish a vision of the little red car plummeting down the mountain with Mehmet and the three Germans inside.

'Do you think something's happened?' she asked Ahmet.

'Like what?' He continued watching a video on Huso's phone.

'I don't know. Perhaps he's had a flat tyre.'

'I could go with Huso on his motorbike to see!' he said more enthusiastically.

'Let's wait a little longer,' said Fatma, though she could feel her chest tightening with worry.

She took the dinner out of the oven, fetched her mother from the house and settled her at the table with a glass of cherry compote. Mehmet still had not returned. She could not leave it any longer.

'Go and see what's happened, will you? And if he's chatting with Demir tell him to get back here straight away!' she shouted after the two boys who had already slid off their stools and were heading for the road. Fatma heard the motorbike start up and pull away.

She poured herself a glass of compote and sat down with her mother but after listening to Melahat tell the story of a man whose car had plunged off a road in town taking him – and the woman who was in the car with him who was not his wife – to a watery grave, she went to the kitchen to finish getting the evening meal ready.

Fatma was cutting up a watermelon when she heard the sound of a motorbike pulling up. She and dropped the knife and ran – or hurried as fast as she could – round to the front of the pension. But the motorbike that pulled up in a slew of small stones and a puff of diesel fumes was not Huso's sleek new machine but a heavy old Java, and the passenger who climbed awkwardly off was not Ahmet but Claudia. The driver was Demir and Dudu's good-for-nothing son, Murat. Fatma was confused.

'Hello, Fatma! Oh! That was so exciting,' said Claudia, giggling like a teenager and smoothing down her skirt. 'Thank you for the ride, Murat!'

Murat did not even glance at Fatma. 'Is my pleasure,' he said, with a suggestive wink. 'I am here tomorrow at eleven o'clock. See you then!'

Claudia waved one red-nailed hand at him as he turned the bike round and roared off back towards the village. Then she turned to Fatma.

'Mehmet has car problems. It is…kaput! Murat offered to bring me back.' She swung her beach bag onto her shoulder. 'Ciao!' she said and disappeared into the pension.

Fatma's relief at the news that her husband had not met a dreadful end was quickly replaced by dismay at the fact that Claudia had met Murat and was seeing him again the following day.

Murat was a constant source of disappointment and shame to his parents. The only thing he had ever showed any interest in was chasing after women – mostly older, foreign ones. For a while he had lived with an English lady who had given him the money to set up a small water sports business at the beach. When that lady's family eventually persuaded her to give up her Shirley Valentine dreams and return home, Murat quickly sold the boat and spent the money.

Fatma was still standing by the road considering the situation when Huso and Ahmet drove up.

'Don't panic, Mum, they're all OK. The car broke down. Huso collected the mechanic from Yeshilkoy and he's fixing it now.'

But Fatma had already moved on to worrying about other things. She went to find Melek.

'Claudia has just had a lift back from the beach with Murat *and* he's coming to pick her up tomorrow.'

'What for?'

'I don't know. I imagine he's hoping to charm her into giving him money like he did with the last one. You have to tell her not to go.'

'Mother, Claudia Auntie is older than you. I can't tell her what to do or who to see.'

'No, but you can warn her what he's like and if she's got any sense she'll stay away from him.'

'I wouldn't bet on it,' muttered Melek.

It was another half an hour before Mehmet arrived back with the German couple. Fatma and Melek served the aubergine, which was a little dried out but still tasty.

All the worry had left Fatma famished and she was enjoying her own dinner when Mehmet said, 'That car has done good service but I think the time has come to change it.'

Fatma stopped, a forkful of aubergine and lamb poised in the air. She was amazed; Mehmet had always loved the little red car. 'Really? What did you have in mind?'

'I don't know but collecting guests, carrying supplies, tackling the beach road, these are jobs for a sturdier vehicle. Maybe something like Harun Bey's pick-up truck. I was talking to Osman the other day and he was saying how economical it is to run.'

Fatma felt a vein throbbing in her temple. 'And did he say how much it cost to buy?'

'A truck like that wouldn't be cheap but it would keep going forever. It would be a good advertisement too – we could have Kismet Pension written on the side...'

He went on extolling the virtues of Harun's truck but Fatma had stopped listening to him. She was watching Melek talking to Claudia. Melek looked serious and the German lady seemed to listen for a minute. Then she threw back her head and laughed. Melek came back to clear the plates and shrugged.

'I told you she wouldn't listen.'

'What did she say?'

'She said we don't need to worry about her, she's just having some fun.'

Fatma felt the throbbing spread across her temple. Claudia's words had done nothing to reassure her.

*

The next day Melek visited Barish. As before, she looked around carefully before entering the retreat and they retired to the small veranda of the chalet, which was conveniently placed so that it was easy to see anyone approaching, unless of course, they were coming through the forest at the side and even Melek thought that was unlikely.

They talked about families. Barish told her about his grandmother and Hasan Dede and in particular, how enthusiastically he had stepped into the role of step-grandfather.

'You would have loved him – he was really into history.'

Melek had heard people talking about Hasan Chelik all her life but she was too young to remember him from his stay in the village.

'He liked dragging me round museums but then he'd make up for it by taking me to a match. He even played video games with me!'

'My grandfather was lovely too. He taught me the names of all the flowers and birds we saw. When Mum left school, she started helping him on the farm and in the end, she was running it alone.'

'Really? So she's always been different!'

'She has.' Melek could still feel proud of her mother, even though she infuriated her. 'I just wish she'd let me do my thing too.'

Selma had been right: she and Barish never had any trouble finding things to talk about. And the more they talked the more Melek liked him.

Back at the pension she tried to behave normally but it was difficult. She was so worried about letting her secret slip that she said as little as possible and she spent a lot of time daydreaming. Even the usually unobservant Ahmet noticed a change in her.

'What's up, Meli? You haven't said anything all day.'

'Nothing! I think I might have stayed in the pool too long with Selma and got a bit of a chill. I'll be fine,' she lied. It was not that she thought Ahmet would disapprove of her relationship with Barish – he'd probably actually be quite impressed – but he was terrible at keeping secrets.

She knew her mother had also noticed a change in her because she had overheard her talking to Derya. Derya had assured her that it was a phase all teenage girls went through and reminded her how her own daughter had been sullen and unhelpful for at least three years.

One person did discover their secret. Claudia called her over the evening of her visit to the retreat and gave her a knowing wink. 'So, little Melek, you are in love!'

Melek was horrified. She sat in the seat opposite and leaned over the table. 'Who told you, Claudia Auntie?'

'Nobody told me. I was at Kado's Garden for yoga and I saw you with Zuhal's son. I could see from your faces,' Claudia said in a whisper that was still louder than Melek was comfortable with. 'Young love is a wonderful thing!'

'Please, Claudia Auntie, don't say anything to my family.'

'Pshht,' Claudia waved a hand dismissively, 'I

won't say anything. But why is it such a secret?'

'Things are difficult in the village – people are very old-fashioned, you know. Also Mum's decided Harun Uncle is the enemy...'

'Would you like me to speak to her?' asked Claudia.

'No! No, Claudia Auntie. She'd go crazy!'

'You like him, though, no?'

'I really like him!' Melek blushed. She did not wholly trust Claudia not to let something slip but it was also nice to have someone other than Selma to share her excitement with. Her friend was pleased for her but Melek did not want to bore her by going on about Barish too much.

'Well, then you'll have to keep meeting in secret. Maybe I can help you – carry messages between you or cover for you when you are together. I'm a great supporter of love,' she said with a wink.

# 24

Birol Bey arrived on the early morning flight and Osman collected him from the airport. As the truck pulled up at the gate it was barely nine o'clock and the sun was bright but not yet vicious, the sky was brilliant blue and the orchard was so vibrant and green that it looked freshly painted.

'What a fantastic spot!' said Birol Bey, shaking Harun's hand vigorously.

Harun showed the VIP guest to his room. Zuhal had made sure everything was perfect and even added a small vase of wild flowers and a basket of peaches and apricots. When Birol Bey returned he had changed out of his city clothes into khaki shorts and a white shirt.

'So how did you discover this gem of a place, Harun?' he asked.

'You could say it found me.'

Harun told him about his mother's death and inheriting the land. 'Once I came here I fell in love with it. There are ruins, you know, a theatre and tombs and a beautiful beach in a sheltered bay. And because it isn't well-known it hasn't been spoiled.

You can still see traditional village life.'

'It sounds idyllic. But you haven't told me where the idea to set up a retreat came from?'

'A magazine article, actually!' Harun told him how fed up he had been feeling when he read about the health benefits of retreats. 'That same day I learned about the orchard here and…well, you could say it was fate!'

'Can I put that in the article?'

'Of course!'

'What else do you want me to write about?'

'I thought perhaps you'd like to spend the morning in Kado's Garden. Have a look around, join in if you want to, take some pictures. Then this afternoon I'll take you on a local tour and you can see for yourself what an amazing place it is.'

Birol Bey did as Harun suggested and spent the morning wandering round the orchard, taking photographs and talking to the guests. He watched Zuhal's painting class and Nermin's weaving class, though he declined both offers to have a go. At lunchtime he joined Harun and they ate courgette fritters and a cracked wheat salad dressed with pomegranate molasses.

'What do you think?' Harun asked.

'I think you've made a perfect escape.'

'Do you think your readers will want to come and stay?'

'They'd be crazy not to! It's hot here, but at least the air is clean and you get that bit of breeze from the mountains. In Istanbul I swear you can see the stink of exhaust fumes and rubbish hanging over the buildings!'

When they had finished eating and savoured a cup of thick, smooth coffee, Harun took his visitor on a tour. He showed him the theatre and the tombs. They walked around the centre of the village and stuck their heads in at the village shop and the coffee house, where Harun introduced Birol to Mehmet. They took the roller coaster ride down to the beach and Demir ferried them across to the island where they scrambled up the loose path to the ruins of the monastery and looked out at the view of the sea – the same one the monks must have enjoyed hundreds of years before.

Harun knew the journalist was excited about writing the article but he had one more request and he waited until dinner to put that to him.

'So you agree, my friend, that Ortakoy is the perfect place to get away from it all?'

'Certainly! I wish I could stay a week!'

'You are welcome to visit any time you can get away but Kado's Garden is not actually the first place welcoming people to the village. There's a place that's been here for a while, a family-run pension that sometimes struggles to find guests. I think we should put them in the article too.'

*

Fatma was waving off the German couple when she saw Murat sauntering out of the pension having obviously spent the night there. He even had the nerve to nod at her.

'Morning.'

'Hello, Murat. Can I have a word?'

'What about, Fatma Abla?' He smelled of sweat and of Claudia's perfume.

'I want to know why you're pestering Claudia Hanum.'

'Pestering? Is that what she called it?' He leered.

'That's what I'm calling it. I know exactly what you're doing, trying to get money out of her.'

'I haven't asked Claudia for a single kurush.'

'Yet.'

'Did she ask you to speak to me?'

'No but she is a nice lady and I don't want you taking advantage of her.'

'I think you'll find she's quite happy with our arrangement.' He smirked again. 'If there's nothing else?'

Fatma lost her temper. 'There is, actually. I can't stop you seeing Claudia Hanum, but I can stop you staying here. It's illegal anyway: all our guests have to be registered on our system.'

'Then you'd better register me as a guest,' said Murat. He was no longer smiling and his grey eyes were hard and calculating. 'Because if you won't let me stay here, I'll get Claudia to move to that new place – what do they call it, Kado's Garden? I'm sure *they* don't meddle in their guest's private business.'

He got on the motorbike, kicked the starter and revved the engine, producing clouds of grey smoke.

'Good day, Fatma Abla. I'll see you again soon, I'm sure.' He swung the bike round in a wide arc and headed back towards the village.

Fatma was shocked. She had not expected him to

listen readily but she had not expected him to be so unpleasant. And threatening to move Claudia to the retreat – did he know this was exactly the thing she was most afraid of?

The previous evening Mehmet had told them about the man Harun had introduced him to.

'He's a journalist and he writes articles for all sorts of newspapers and magazines. He's going to write one about the retreat.'

It was so unfair! She had been trying to get people to visit Ortakoy for years and now Harun turned up and after five minutes he had people ready to write about him and his dratted retreat. Fatma's breakfast was sitting heavy in her stomach. She went round to sit in the shade of the bar and took a soda water to try to ease the indigestion.

She was still there when a man in blue shorts and a pale blue Lacoste t-shirt appeared. Assuming he was looking for a room, she jumped up, wiped her face with a corner of her headscarf and tried to look business-like.

'Can I help you?'

'I'm looking for Fatma Hanum.'

'That's me. Do you want a room?'

'Not this time,' said the man, holding out his hand. 'I'm Birol. I'm a journalist and I'm here doing research for an article.'

Fatma shook his hand. She was confused.

'Harun Bey called me as we've known each other for some time, but he's keen for me to write about your place as well as his. The Kismet Pension, isn't it? I love the name!'

Fatma was still lost for words.

'So Fatma Hanum, tell me a little bit about the Kismet – how you came to build it, what you offer here, what sort of guests you cater for. Then perhaps I can see a room.'

Fatma sat down and called for Melek to make coffee. Birol asked for his sweet and she chose to have hers sweet too, feeling a need for the extra sugar. She found herself telling Birol about working with her father on the farm and how she had sold some of their land to build the pension after he had died. She told him it was their ninth season.

'And as for guests – well you can see some of them here.' She waved a hand.

Claudia was lying by the pool in a swimming costume and large straw hat, reading a magazine. Three Chinese tourists that Mehmet's taxi-driver friend had brought the day before were taking selfies with the backdrop of the valley and the mountains. A Turkish family with two children and the grandmother in tow had left the children to play in the pool while they collected their things to go to the beach.

'We have some other guests who have gone out for the day,' said Fatma.

'So, I would say you attract quite a variety of people!' said Birol.

'Yes,' Fatma agreed. 'We have all sorts.'

She took him to look at one of the upstairs rooms and he took pictures of the inside and of the view from the balcony. As they went out of the room, they met Claudia going into hers.

'Welcome to the Kismet Pension!' she said. 'You

will love it here!'

Birol, who spoke passable English, explained that he was not staying at the pension but writing about it and it was another fifteen minutes before she finished telling him about how she had found the place by chance – kismet, they both agreed – and how she had instantly felt at home there. She even told him of her conviction that she had lived in Ortakoy in another life.

Downstairs, Birol thanked Fatma for her time.

'I love honest, unfussy pensions like the Kismet. I hope my article will get the word out and you'll be full for the rest of the season!'

\*

Drainage systems are unpredictable. Sometimes relatively large objects slip through easily and other times something small catches on a ridge or a bend in the pipe and stops everything that follows from getting through. The wad of paper towel and handful of ear buds that Buket had unwillingly put down the toilet in one of the chalets appeared to have passed through without incident but in fact they had united in the waste pipe between the chalets to form a barrier that had been partially blocking the pipe. Now, several days later and shortly before Birol Bey was due to leave for the airport, something caught in the remaining gap and the pipe was blocked completely. The nearest chalet to where the blockage occurred was the one where he was staying.

Birol and Harun had enjoyed another relaxed lunch together, talking about other activities that people might enjoy in the area – cycling, sailing, horse-riding, scuba diving – before Birol went back to the chalet to collect his bag. Harun was about to check his laptop for messages and emails when Birol called out to him. He had opened the door of the chalet but was standing outside. The note of urgency in his voice worried Harun.

'Quick, come here. The bathroom's flooded!'

Harun stepped through the door, took one look at the bathroom floor and stepped out again. The smell carried even outside.

'Ay! Birol Bey, I am so sorry.' He closed the door. 'Osman!'

Osman was cutting back the brambles at the side of the yoga platform that seemed to grow a metre a week. He put down the scythe and trotted over but after looking inside the cabin and seeing the mess he shrugged.

'These things happen, especially with a new system.'

'You stay and sort this out,' said Harun. 'I'll drive Birol Bey to the airport.'

On the way they talked about the Kismet and Fatma. Harun asked what Birol had made of her.

'She's an interesting lady. Is she a widow?'

'Oh no! You met her husband Mehmet at the coffee house, but she's the one who runs the business.'

'She must have been quick to tread on his foot!' said Birol. At a wedding, after the vows had been said, bride and groom raced to step on the other's foot as it was said that whoever got there first would rule the home.

Harun laughed. 'I don't know about that but she's definitely a strong lady.'

'And do I get the impression she has not welcomed you to the village?'

'You're right there, though I'm hoping that your article will show that I really have no bad intentions.'

At the airport Harun apologized again for the blocked drain.

'Don't worry about it. Osman's right – there are often problems with new places. I'm certainly not going to mention it to anyone.'

When Harun got back, Osman was still trying to unblock the pipe. He had tried pushing a length of wire and an old piece of hose down the toilet in the chalet but these attempts had both been unsuccessful. Now he had dug up the pipe outside and was pushing the length of wire into the bubbling mess inside. The stench in the hot air almost took Harun's breath away. Osman hardly seemed to notice it. He pushed the wire in a bit further.

'The problem is on this section.' He wiggled the wire and suddenly a surge of filth poured along the pipe, with clumps of paper and a flotilla of small plastic sticks. Harun was fascinated and disgusted in equal measure. Thankfully, most of the guests had gone to the beach for the day and those that were around appeared to be having a siesta.

'What are all those?' he asked Osman.

Osman poked around with the wire. 'They look like those things people use to clean their ears with.'

'Who could have put those down the toilet?' He looked at the nearby chalets. One had been occupied until the previous day by a family with teenagers. 'I bet it was those kids!' The siblings – a girl of about sixteen who was never apart from her phone and a sulky boy a couple of years younger – had made it clear that the retreat was not their idea of a holiday. 'I ought to message their parents and tell them what they did.'

Privately though he knew he wouldn't. He was just relieved that nobody had woken to find their chalet flooded with something unthinkable and that Birol Bey had been so understanding.

*

In the Kismet, Melek confronted her mother.

'Now do you see that Harun Uncle isn't trying to steal your business? He actually sent that journalist to cover the pension as well as the retreat.'

Fatma had spent most of the afternoon trying to work out why Harun had done it and got nothing for her efforts except a headache. Now she thought about it again.

'I do think it's a bit strange. And that man said he likes "honest, unfussy" pensions. What does he mean by that?'

'I suppose he means places like this that are simple and comfortable,' said Mehmet. 'In town it's all mini-bars and Jacuzzis.'

'Well, I hope he's not going to make the Kismet sound like some cheap hostel,' said Fatma grumpily.

'Why do you always think the worst?' asked Melek.

'I prefer to think of it as being realistic,' said Fatma.

'It does seem good of Harun to get the Kismet in the paper,' said Mehmet, looking hopefully at Fatma.

'And in my experience when people do a good deed they usually want something in return.'

'What could Harun Uncle possibly want from you?' said Melek, angrily.

'I don't know...perhaps he's going to ask for commission. At the very least I'm sure he'll tell everyone what he's done so they all know how marvellous he is. You all seem convinced already,' she said crossly, though Melek had already left the table with a huff of disbelief.

## 25

Melek was laying the tables for breakfast when Claudia got back from an early-morning yoga class.

She looked around theatrically before whispering, 'He says you are to meet him at two in the theatre. Wear your walking shoes.'

It had been Melek's idea for them to go for a walk together to get away from the village and all the prying eyes. Now she spent the whole morning trying to hide her excitement. She told her mother she was going on a picnic with Selma and after lunch slipped over to the house and called her friend to warn her of the subterfuge.

She changed into her favourite shorts and a clean t-shirt and brushed her hair before tying it up. It was a muggy day and she put two bottles of water and some apples in a rucksack. In the garden the ginger cat was lying in the shade of the grape vine. His vivid, orange coat was covered with dust.

'Tiger, look at the state of you! Cats are supposed to be clean animals.'

He opened one green eye and twisted onto his

back to expose the soft, butter-coloured fur of his belly. Melek bent to stroke him before hurrying off along the lane. The air hung heavily over the valley and the mountains opposite had almost disappeared in a haze of dust and humidity.

Shortly after the turning for the village, Melek veered off the road and pushed her way under the branches of a fig tree and into the lower area of the theatre. Barish was sitting on one of the elaborately carved stone seats that had obviously once been reserved for the local dignitaries.

'Hi Melek!' He jumped up and picked up his own backpack. 'How hot is it in here?' It was true, the pale stones soaked up the sun's heat and reflected it back with blinding force. 'Mum's made us a picnic.' He held up his backpack. 'She wanted to put in a melon but I said it was too heavy!'

Melek led the way out of the other side of the ancient theatre, round the back of Selma's house and up onto a little ridge above the village. Clustered by the track were several sarcophagi, mostly broken open by earthquakes or grave robbers. Sitting in the shade of one they saw Leyla. The mother goat was cropping noisily at the dry grass, the kids had skittered off at the approach of strangers and were looking at them warily with their alien eyes.

'Hi Leyla!'

'Hello, Melek Abla.' The little girl had jumped up at their approach and looked shyly at Barish.

'This is my friend, Barish.'

'Hello, Leyla!'

Leyla gave a wave of greeting.

'Leyla's learning to swim,' Melek told Barish.

'That's great!' he said, encouragingly.

'Melek Abla let go of me and I didn't sink,' said the little girl proudly.

'You're a natural! Come for another lesson soon. And Leyla, please don't tell anyone you saw us – you know how people gossip!'

'Don't worry, Melek Abla. My mother says I'm good with secrets.' She lifted her chin and looked proud, though Melek thought it was sad that a child so young should have learned to keep secrets.

They carried on along the track which turned uphill and disappeared into the forest. The air was still warm and heavy with the scent of pine but at least it was shaded. A thick carpet of needles made the path springy. Melek was in front, trying to find a pace that was lively enough but did not make her puff unattractively, and wondering what her rear view looked like. She was so absorbed by these thoughts that she was surprised to suddenly emerge from the forest.

They were on a wide, flat strip between two mountain peaks. Ahead and below was the sea, a patchwork of light and dark blue stretching away to the hazy horizon where it merged into the sky. A faint breeze tickled their damp skin and the bright sun made them squint.

'Wow!' said Barish, taking in the view in front, then looking back at the faint smudge of white walls and red rooves that was Ortakoy.

They chose a spot in the shade of an acacia tree and flopped down. Melek took a long drink of water.

Barish opened his rucksack and took out filled meatballs, dolma and some peaches.

'I picked those from a tree in the orchard,' he said proudly. 'I know it probably doesn't seem odd to you but it's new for me to be able to collect my own food!'

'One of the better things about living in the village,' said Melek.

Barish ate hungrily. Melek was too excited to eat much and was also afraid of dropping pieces down her or getting pieces of parsley stuck between her teeth. She nibbled a couple of dolma and then took a peach. It was warm and so ripe that the juice ran down her chin. When they had finished eating they lay on their backs and watched the sun glinting through the gently wafting branches of the acacia.

'So what did your mum think of Birol Bey?'

'She was impressed.'

'Is she pleased the Kismet is going to be in the paper?'

'Mmm.'

'That doesn't sound very enthusiastic.'

'Oh Barish, I'm sorry. She should be grateful to your father and I said that to her but she's still... wary.'

'She doesn't suspect anything about us, does she?'

'No. She's more worried about Claudia Auntie and Murat.'

'Your Claudia Auntie has been doing some painting with Mum. She's quite a character. I imagine she can look after herself.'

'That's what I said but these foreign ladies do sometimes seem to lose their minds when they come here!'

'It's love,' said Barish dramatically. 'It sends people crazy!' Then he turned towards her and planted his warm lips on hers.

Melek tensed. The tingling in her lips seemed to reach her whole body. Being with Barish, she realised, made her tense not just because she was worried about them being seen but also because he made her feel things she had never felt before. She pulled away.

'Come on! We still have a way to go to get back.'

They packed up the remains of the picnic and took a path that led along the slope. Barish stopped to examine a tortoise that was crossing the track and it hissed crossly at him and marched off faster. They stopped and removed their shoes and socks to dip their hot feet in the water of a small pool formed where a stream had hollowed out a large flat rock. A trick of light made the water appear green but its coldness was no trick. Melek explained about the caves and ravines in the mountains where ice survived right through the summer.

The sun started its downward arc and the light got softer.

'Not far now,' said Melek. The path was narrow and steep and she was stepping carefully between boulders when her foot got caught. She let out a shout as momentum propelled her forward and she sprawled sideways on the scrub beside the track. Prickles embedded themselves in the soft flesh of her palms but it was the pain in her ankle that caused tears to spill from her eyes.

'Melek! Are you alright?'

Melek grimaced. She felt clumsy and foolish.

'Sorry – of course you're not.' He bent and examined her ankle. It was already swollen and there was a purple stain beneath the skin. 'Uff – that looks awful.'

Melek managed a weak smile.

'Do you think you can walk on it?'

She took a deep breath. 'Wait a moment until the pain goes away a bit. Then I'll see.' She inspected her hand. Barish took hold of it and pulled out the thorns. Then he folded his own hand over it and squeezed gently. They sat like that for a while, with just the thrum of the crickets for company.

Barish looked at her ankle again. It was now twice its normal size. 'I can try to carry you,' he said.

'You can't carry me all the way down. Help me up and I'll see if I can walk on it.'

Barish took her gently by both forearms and pulled her upright. Melek put the bad foot gingerly on the ground but she winced and hopped back onto her good foot. She tried again but it was too painful. She hopped for a short way, leaning on Barish.

'You can't hop all the way!' he said.

Melek knew he was right; they were still at least three kilometres from the village. But it could not be far to the forestry road and a car could get up there.

'No, but I think I can make it to the track. Then you'll have to leave me and go for help. I'm sure you'll find my father in the coffee house and he can come up in the car and get me.'

She hopped on. It was painful, the jarring movement causing stabbing pains in her ankle but she bit her lip and tried not to cry out too often. After ten minutes, with several rests on the way, they reached the track. Melek sank gratefully onto a mossy tussock.

'Are you sure you're alright with me leaving you here?'

'I'll be fine!' she said with more conviction than she felt. The light was already fading and the trees cast strange shadows about. The thrumming of the cicadas started to irritate her but when they all fell silent for a moment, she found herself holding her breath in fear and waiting for them to start up again.

She tried to calm herself by singing. She had sung most of five songs and still he was not back. The pain in her ankle was starting to make her feel sick. She stopped singing and started trying to name the 81 provinces in numerical order. She had got to 33 when she heard an engine in the distance.

'Thirty-three Mersin…thirty-four Istanbul…'

But the vehicle that was approaching was too large, its headlights too bright to be the little red car.

'Thirty-five Izmir…thirty-six Kars…'

She stayed very still, holding her breath as it pulled up on the track in front of her.

'Melek, my love, what happened?' Her father jumped out of the truck and ran over.

Melek let out her breath and burst into tears of relief.

'Hello, Melek, I hear you've hurt yourself,' said Harun, who had got out of the driver's door. Barish got out of the back.

Her father looked at her ankle. 'Ouch, that looks

nasty. We'll get you back to the pension and then decide if you need to go to hospital.'

He took hold of her on one side and Harun took hold of the other and they lifted her up easily and put her gently on the back seat of the truck, sitting sideways with her leg stretched in front of her. Barish sat by the door and as she took up most of the seat it felt quite natural for her to lean back against him. The truck pitched about on the rough track, making her ankle hurt. Still, thought Melek, the journey was more comfortable than it would have been in the little red car.

At the pension her father went in and found her mother and by the time they came back Harun and Barish had lifted Melek out of the truck.

'Melek. What happened?'

'I'm OK, Mum, I just fell.'

She looked from Harun to Barish. 'This young man found her and came to call me,' said Mehmet. 'But Harun Bey kindly offered to drive as his truck is better suited to off-roading.'

'I'm happy to drive down to town too if you think Melek should see a doctor,' Harun said.

Fatma looked uncertain. 'I...you...Melek?'

'I'll put some ice on it for now and see how it is in the morning.'

When they had gone and Mehmet had settled Melek in a chair with her leg up and a bag of ice on her ankle, Fatma hovered beside her.

'Where were you when you fell?'

'Coming down from the ridge.'

'And where was Selma?'

'With me, of course,' said Melek, crossing her fingers.

'What a good job that young man was passing. I would never have thought of him as someone who enjoyed walking.'

'Oo,' said Melek, wincing with only slightly exaggerated pain.

'I'll get you a pain killer,' said Fatma and hurried off.

Melek made a mental note to call her friend as soon as she could to let her know what had happened on their picnic.

# 26

~~

Harun was watching Zuhal who was sitting on the yoga deck sketching Oya. In a few fluid strokes his wife had caught the outline of her friend's body which was curved back into a circular pose she said was called King Pigeon. He had taken a few classes with Oya but he was quite sure that no amount of practice would enable him to twist his body into the shape she had currently assumed.

He looked up and saw Buket approaching. She looked nervous and he hoped she was not going to start behaving oddly again.

'Harun Bey, I-I'm sorry.'

'What is it Buket?'

'I have to go. I've changed all the beds and done most of the washing. There's one load that's still in the machine that will need hanging up.' The young woman was fighting back tears.

'We can hang that. Is there anything I can help with?'

The kindness seemed, as it so often does, to tip the young woman over the edge and she let out a sob and covered her face with her hands. Zuhal put down her sketchbook and looked round. When she saw Buket crying she jumped up and took her hand.

'What is it, dear?'

'It's my father,' wailed Buket.

Harun and Zuhal left Oya in her pigeon pose and led Buket to one of the arbours. Harun fetched tea, leaving Zuhal to fuss over the younger woman.

When Buket had started working at the retreat he had invited her to bring her family along for a visit. Her sons were lively boys of six and eight who played a game of chase between the chalets and had noisy pretend gunfights with bits of wood. Her mother Latife was a quiet, gentle woman with sad eyes who had thanked Harun and Zuhal over and over for giving their daughter a job. Her father Mumtaz had stayed strangely silent.

When they had gone Buket had explained that he seemed to be suffering from some form of dementia. He had not been officially diagnosed because that would involve a trip to the doctor which he would not agree to but she and her mother thought his condition might be the result of years of breathing toxic fumes in his job as a tinsmith.

'He used to go round the villages and the ladies would bring out their pans for him to recoat. He knew all their names and their husbands' and children's. Now half the time he can't even remember his own!' she had said bitterly.

As Harun returned with the tea, she said, 'My father has decided he's dying.'

'Is he ill?' asked Zuhal.

'Not that we know of. He just keeps saying he

hasn't got long to go.'

'Older people often talk about death,' said Zuhal. 'My grandmother used to say she was looking forward to having a bit of a rest!'

'Father has dug his own grave and keeps going to the cemetery and sitting in it!' said Buket and let out another sob.

'Oh!'

'He's cross with us.'

'Why is he cross?' asked Harun.

'Because he wants the boys to have their sunnet – their circumcision.'

'Well that's not hard to arrange,' he said.

Buket fiddled with the tassles on the edge of the tablecloth. 'But he wants a big celebration and we can't afford it.' She shook her head and took a sip of tea. 'There's a rich man in town who's going to organise a big sunnet party for lots of local village boys.'

'That sounds like a good solution.'

'But it's not until winter and Father says he won't last that long.'

'I'm so sorry, Buket. It's such a cruel illness,' said Zuhal, shaking her head.

Harun remembered his own sunnet and how pleased he had been with the hoard of gold sovereigns he had been given. He remembered, too, Barish dressed in the finery of a prince, sitting on a throne in his friend's swanky restaurant by the Bosphorus. As a family they had been blessed and blessings should be shared. 'He who eats his bread alone will carry his burden alone,' the saying said.'Buket, I think I might be able to help with your problem.'

She looked at him hopefully.

'I can't make your father better but I can make his wish come true. I will pay for the boys' circumcisions and we can have the celebration here.'

'Really? You'd do that for us?' Buket wiped her eyes and blew her nose.

'I'd be delighted to. Now go and help your mother take him home. And tell him he'll get his wish soon.'

\*

Fatma was in a dilemma. She could hardly complain that Harun had rescued Melek but somehow it seemed too convenient that his son had been the one to raise the alarm and he had happened to be with Mehmet and offered to go.

Fortunately the swelling on Melek's ankle had started to go down by the following morning and Melek assured them that a trip to the hospital was unnecessary. The foot was still a nasty purple colour and walking on it was obviously painful. Still, she hobbled round to the pension and sat at a table polishing cutlery and rolling pastries.

Fatma watched her daughter for signs of guilt but it was hard to tell when she had been behaving out-of-character for some time. Derya had said it was a phase all teenage girls went through but Fatma had her own theory. Melek had changed since Harun had arrived in the village and she thought the proximity of these city people with their fancy clothes and pretentious ideas had turned her head.

Nazla had called to tell her their first attempt at drain blocking had finally brought results. 'It took a few days but it made quite a mess in the end. Of course it was Osman who had to sort it out. I made him wash in the garden afterwards and I threw away all the clothes he was wearing.'

'And what did the guests have to say about it?' asked Fatma.

'I...I'm not sure they knew much about it. It was that journalist's chalet that got most of it.'

'Really?' Fatma felt a rush of hope. 'Do you think he might mention the plumbing problems in the paper?'

'I don't think so. Apparently he was very understanding.'

'Then it wasn't much of a success, was it?' Fatma had said gloomily.

Now she was speaking to Nazla again. 'We need to do something else.'

'Must we?' Nazla sounded unsure.

'You're not giving up as well, are you?'

'No, but if things start happening too frequently won't it look suspicious?'

'Pff – things happen frequently anyway in this business. The other day one of our guests got very upset because they saw a cockroach in the room. She came running down to ask me if there was another room they could move to – as if the creature hadn't already disappeared down the same hole it had come out of.'

'Do you want me to put a cockroach in a room?' asked Nazla.

'Don't be silly, I should think there are plenty of bugs running round in those chalets already. No, I was thinking of something a little bigger and furrier.'

'A mouse?'

'Exactly.'

Living in the village they were used to finding mice and even rats. These creatures made nests in the outhouses and ate the chicken feed that was stored there. The ginger cat kept them away from the house, the only thing he was good for in Fatma's opinion, but one had got into the washing machine at the pension the previous winter and eaten through all the rubber hoses.

'I imagine the sort of ladies you have staying there will have a fit if they see a mouse!' said Fatma, enjoying imagining one of the guests running screaming out of her rustic chalet.

'How will I get it in though?' asked Nazla.

'You have a box trap, don't you? Catch one in the wood shed and let it out in one of the rooms.'

Fatma finished the call and was returning to the pension when she heard the sound of an old motorbike coming along the lane. Murat had been picking up Claudia almost every day and often staying over. Fatma looked round crossly and was surprised to see not Murat but his father pull over and turn off the bike's noisy engine. Despite the heat, his flat cap was still pulled down firmly on his head. The cigarette clamped in his mouth had burned down to a stub.

'Good day, Demir, are you well?'

Demir spat out the end of his cigarette and clicked his tongue to say 'no'. 'The jandarma have been down to the beach and closed the restaurant. They say my licence has been cancelled.'

'That's awful!' There had been problems with the restaurant's licence before but the authorities had never shut it down during the season. 'Come in and tell us what happened.'

Mehmet had finished breakfast and was reading the newspaper until such time as it was acceptable to go to the coffee house. When he saw Fatma coming over with Demir he folded the paper and stood up to welcome the visitor.

Demir flopped in a chair and scratched his head under his cap. He told them how a jandarma sergeant and two young recruits had come from town in a boat and made him pack up the tables and chairs before fixing a tape and seal across the kitchen door.

'Why have they come in the middle of summer?' he asked miserably.

'It's a political thing,' said Mehmet. 'The Government and the municipality are arguing over who should get rent from the beaches.'

'Well, I wish they'd argue in the winter when I'm not trying to make a living.'

Ahmet brought tea and Demir added five lumps of sugar and stirred for some time. 'What am I going to do now? The flotilla group are due to come tonight for a barbecue. We do it every week. If they have to go elsewhere, they might not come back to the beach.'

'We'll have to go to town to sort out the licence,' said Mehmet. 'But these things take time. I doubt they'll let you open today.'

'Still, we might be able to help,' said Fatma. She understood how frustrated Demir felt, seeing his business threatened through no fault of his own. 'We could have the barbecue here tonight. Leave it to me – I'll organise everything!'

When they had finished their tea, the three of them got into the red car and Mehmet drove them down to town where he and Demir visited the local government offices. They succeeded in getting a new licence issued, though as Mehmet had suspected Demir would not be allowed to reopen until the following day when the jandarma would come out again; breaking the seal himself was, the clerk informed him with a severe look, illegal and carried a large penalty. While they were dealing with the tedious red tape, Fatma was shopping for the barbecue.

At the Kismet everyone was roped in to help with the preparations. By six o'clock the meat was marinating, the mezes and salads were ready and the rice was washed and waiting to be cooked. The fridge in the bar was full of beer and there were a couple of extra bottles of raki and one of whisky on the shelves, because Demir said the sailors liked a drink.

At seven o'clock Mehmet and Demir went down to meet the flotilla and explain the change of plan. They returned with the first group and their leader, a young Australian who did not seem at all bothered by the change of venue. A minibus arrived shortly after with the others. They were of varying ages, mostly couples though there was one man who had his teenage son with him. Fatma supposed that the day's sailing must require focus and gravity because they all seemed to be making up for it now by talking and laughing loudly.

The pension guests came out and sat down, quiet by comparison. They had been told of the special night being organised, all except Claudia who had left after breakfast and not yet returned.

Fatma laid the meze out on a table – roasted aubergine in garlic yogurt, red cabbage fried in olive oil, spicy tomato and pepper salsa, fried pastries with feta and herbs – for the guests to help themselves. Mehmet was already at the barbecue fanning the coals to get them to the perfect temperature. Ahmet was rushing between the tables with a notepad and a tray of drinks trying to keep up with the orders.

For a while the noise died down as the guests addressed themselves to the food. Eventually plates were pushed away, legs stretched out and the hum of chatter resumed. Some of the sailors lit cigars.

The belly dancer arrived with an older woman who was her mother and her manager. Mother and daughter both ordered a whisky. The girl told Fatma she was happy not to have to go to the beach restaurant where her heels sank into the sand and creepy-crawlies dropped out of the thatched roof onto her head. When she had finished her drink she took off her coat to reveal an outfit comprising scraps of red chiffon and gold coins that jangled as she moved.

As Ahmet dimmed the lights and put on her soundtrack, she moved into the middle of the floor and started her shimmying, twirling dance. Every man in the place was mesmerised. Fatma watched the girl's mother and wondered how she could stand to see her daughter being ogled that way.

After dancing alone for a while, the girl called

up the men who almost fell over each other in their eagerness to join her. They watched and tried to copy her moves but most had not the slightest sense of rhythm or flexibility. The women performed slightly better but were still stiff and awkward compared to the dancer. She did a tour of the tables, inviting the guests to tuck tips into her barely-there outfit and left the floor to much cheering and whistling. Ahmet put on some lively pop music to which some of the guests started jigging around.

Relieved that the evening had gone well and was almost over, the tiredness caught up with Fatma and she sat down on one of the bar stools. She did not see Claudia arrive, take in the party atmosphere and throw herself enthusiastically onto the dance floor. Nor did she see Murat follow her, put his hands on her hips and start dancing suggestively close. Fatma only noticed they were there when she heard the cheers from the other dancers, who had formed a circle around them and were encouraging the racy display. Unfortunately, the noise also attracted the attention of Demir who had finished most of a bottle of raki with Mehmet.

Murat's father stood up and darted across the floor remarkably fast for someone who had drunk so much. Even in the dim light Fatma could see his expression was one of rage. Murat, pressed against Claudia, did not see his approach. Claudia saw someone rushing towards them and stepped away leaving Murat gyrating alone.

'Ayyyiiiippp!' roared Demir. 'Disssgracefulll! You bring shame on your family!'

In his anger, Demir seemed to grow to twice his usual size. He pushed the surprised Murat in the middle of his chest and the younger man staggered backwards. Before he could regain his balance, Demir threw a punch and his son took another step back, except his foot found only air and then water. He fell backwards into the pool and Demir, carried forward by the force of his punch, followed him. They thrashed around for a moment before finding their feet and standing up facing each other. Demir's cap floated in the water between them.

Fatma sat frozen in horror. She watched as Mehmet helped Demir out of the pool and Murat hauled himself out and disappeared, dripping, round the side of the pension. She hardly dared look at the guests. When she did she had another surprise. The shouts of laughter and mock punches they were throwing told her that they had found the incident highly entertaining. The only one who looked upset about it was Claudia.

Once the sailing enthusiasts had been loaded onto the minibus and returned to their vessels and the Kismet's guests had staggered off back to their rooms, Fatma watched Ahmet collect the last glasses and count the money.

He whistled in amazement and shook the small metal box they kept the cash in. 'We took almost a thousand,' he said. 'Demir Abi was right when he said those guys like a drink.'

Fatma suppressed a snort as she remembered Mehmet retrieving Demir's cap from the pool, wringing it out and placing it on his head. She was sorry for his humiliation but she was also secretly pleased with the turn of events. The loss of face would, she hoped, be enough to deter Murat from visiting the Kismet for some time.

# 27

The heat lay over the village like a dense, prickly blanket. The breeze no longer blew down from the mountain and instead the Meltem wind brought hot air from inland. The fields down in the valley were a patchwork of yellow, brown and ochre.

At Kado's Garden yoga sessions took place at seven in the morning, painting and weaving late in the afternoon and trekking had stopped all together. Most days the guests wanted to go down to the beach. Sometimes they stayed down there and ate at Demir's restaurant, returning to the village after dark when the heat had softened a little. Harun had taken to getting up early to enjoy the cool and quiet of the dawn.

This morning he had made a pot of tea and was sitting in one of the gazebos. The jasmine that wound round it was filling the air with its delicate fragrance. He was thinking of Fatma. The way Mehmet had described Melek's accident and rescue to her had made it clear that her opinion of him had not improved. He still hoped that when Birol Bey's article came out in that weekend's paper it might finally do the trick.

He remembered something Mehmet had said to him not long after he arrived in the village. They had been sitting outside the coffee house drinking tea and Mehmet had been telling Harun about the trouble with the pool workers.

'Some people think Fatma should know her place as a woman, they feel threatened by her, I suppose. But her spirit was the thing that first attracted me to her. She can be bossy sometimes and she doesn't like to admit she's wrong but she always sees reason in the end.'

Harun hoped this was true.

He poured himself another glass of tea. The outline of the chalets and trees could now be seen in the half-light. Someone was walking along one of the paths and he called out thinking it was one of the guests up early.

'There's tea ready if you'd like a glass!'

The figure gasped in shock and froze. 'Good morning, Harun Bey.'

'Oh Nazla, hello! I thought you were one of the guests. You're out early.'

'I-I-I...' The light grew and Harun saw Nazla was holding something. 'I was just taking this little fellow down to let him go in the lane.' She lifted the object, which Harun saw was a small cage with a mouse trapped inside.

'Where did you find him?'

'He keeps coming into the shed and eating the apples that are stored there. I catch him and put him outside and he comes straight back in.' She was shifting from one foot to the other.

'I suppose there are a lot of them around.'

'Yes. They're everywhere!' Nazla agreed. 'Enjoy your tea!'

She hurried on through the orchard and out of the gate and a few minutes later Harun saw her go back up towards the house. Only after she had gone did it occur to him that when he had first seen her she had not been heading in the direction of the lane at all.

\*

Fatma had been right about Murat. Being scolded and pushed into the pool by his father in front of so many people was too humiliating and nobody had seen him since the barbecue. Claudia spent a couple of days by the pool getting over being abandoned. Melek, whose ankle was still weak, kept her company. When Fatma asked her whether Claudia was upset about Murat's disappearance she shrugged.

'She says it was just a bit of fun and she knew it wouldn't last.'

While Claudia licked her emotional wounds, another guest was suffering from a more physical – and much more evident – infliction. A young English girl had arrived at the pension accompanied by her Turkish boyfriend. He worked at a restaurant in the town and said he had brought her to stay in the village so she did not disturb him at work but Ahmet had cynically suggested that in fact he had another girl on the go and was making sure the two did not meet. Whichever was the case, he showed up late at night and left in the middle of the morning, leaving the girl on her own for most of the time.

When she arrived, Fatma had noticed her milky skin; the locals cruelly referred to foreigners as pale as this as 'white cheese'. On her first day at the Kismet, the girl had spent several hours by the pool, talking to Claudia and Melek, jumping in the water frequently to cool down and slathering on sun cream at regular intervals. On the second day, she seemed a little less assiduous with the cream. On the third day she fell asleep in the sun for two hours.

She did not appear for dinner that night. When her boyfriend arrived sometime after midnight, he found her sweating and shivering and as there was nobody around at the pension ran over to knock on the door of the house. Fatma took one look at the girl and went to call Mehmet to drive them to town.

A few hours at the hospital on a drip had sorted out the sunstroke. The burns were not so quick to heal. The backs of her legs were raw and had to be anointed regularly with a thick lotion. Walking was agony as it stretched the damaged skin but every day before he went to work the boyfriend helped her hobble down to lie on her front on a sunbed in the shade. She spent the day eating, drinking and reading magazines left by previous guests.

For the first two days, she cried out frequently in pain and Claudia and Melek felt sorry for her and did their best to make her comfortable. When the wounds started to itch, the girl got irritable and they did their best to entertain her. Once the burns were better, she was bored and started moaning about the heat, the primitiveness of the village and the perfidy of men; the boyfriend who had initially been so attentive had stopped visiting.

Claudia suddenly felt much brighter and started going to yoga and Melek found her foot really did not hurt so much to walk on. By the time the girl was due to leave even Fatma was relieved. As Mehmet piled her bags into the little red car, she hugged them all and promised she would return. Fatma hoped she would not. She was hoping that Birol Bey's article would bring such an influx of monied guests that they would not have to deal with problems like this girl.

The article was coming out in the Saturday paper. Fatma had asked Atilla to order five extra copies of the newspaper for her. That morning, as soon as Ahmet finished cleaning the pool, she sent him to the village to collect them. With the excuse that it was too hot to walk, he took his father's car.

Fatma served breakfast with a lot less care that morning. She was excited and nervous in equal measure and as time went on she got impatient. Ahmet had been gone a long time. He was a terrible driver and she began to wonder if he had had an accident, though really between the pension and the village shop there were no steep drops, no sharp bends and it would be hard even to find a tree you could crash into.

The guests had all finished eating and Fatma had sat down with her own breakfast when Ahmet finally returned. He was carrying the stack of newspapers and wearing the smug expression he used when he had some news to impart.

'Guess what they're putting up in the village?'

'Guess what who's putting up?' asked Fatma, who did not like riddles. She reached for the top newspaper and started rifling through.

'The road people.'

'Not traffic lights, I hope. There are so many sets of traffic lights in town now —' Fatma was still searching for the article. She hoped she had not bought five newspapers for nothing.

'Signs for the ruins!'

Fatma stopped scanning the paper and looked at Ahmet in surprise. Most of the historical sites around were marked with brown signs, some had booklets written about them and the larger ones had ticket offices and a man collecting entrance fees. Ortakoy's ruins, on the other hand, had never even been marked on the map. Fatma, who had grown up playing amongst them, had always assumed they were too badly destroyed to be of interest.

'Atilla said there's one down on the main road, another at the junction and one just in front of the theatre,' said Ahmet.

'What's made them put them up now?'

Ahmet shrugged. 'I don't know.'

Fatma pushed her plate aside, spread the paper on the table and started going through it from the back. After a few pages she came to the article, which was titled 'Ortakoy – a village where the past meets the present'. There were a few photographs – a view of the bay and the island, one taken from the road looking down into the valley and a picture of the entrance to Kado's Garden. She could see nothing about the Kismet. Had it all been a trick?

Then she looked further down the page. There was a picture taken along the road showing the front of the pension, the sign and Fatma standing in front of it. She was not used to having her photograph taken and had not thought to change from her usual working outfit of baggy trousers and an outsized t-shirt but the picture was black and white and her clothes were thankfully not very clear. What was clear was that she was not smiling; in fact it looked as though she was glaring at the camera.

Ahmet came to look over her shoulder. 'Oha Mum! You'll scare people away with a face like that!'

She turned a very similar expression on him. Then she went back to the article, skimming through the bits about the village and the retreat to get to the part about the Kismet. Birol Bey had written that it was a 'delightful pension with clean, comfortable rooms and a swimming pool, whose owners, Fatma and her family, welcome the guests personally and provide breakfast and evening meals for a very reasonable price. The Kismet', it continued, 'is perfect for families and anyone who wants to avoid the more crowded and commercial resorts and enjoy the charms of a traditional village'.

Fatma read it again. It seemed a fair description.

'Are you happy with what it says?' asked Ahmet.

'It's alright,' said Fatma. 'Now, let's get on with some work.'

She spent the morning helping Derya clear the dishes and wash up, then change the bedding in two rooms and hang out the washing. In the afternoon she went over to the house for a break from the vicious heat and sat watching a ridiculous game show with her mother, all the time listening out for the phone to start ringing. By the late afternoon there had not been any calls and Fatma had to hide her disappointment.

She was serving dessert – pistachio kadayif that Derya had made – when the phone in the bar rang and Ahmet answered it. He called her over.

The woman on the telephone had a high-pitched, grating voice. She said she had seen the article, then proceeded to ask how large the rooms were, whether the beds were single or double, if they all had their own balconies, whether the balconies had good views. Fatma had never answered so many questions. She started off trying to give as much information as possible, then changed to answering the woman's questions briefly and finally cut to one-word answers.

'When are you thinking of coming?' she asked when she could manage to get a word in.

'Oh I'm not sure yet if my husband can get any holiday this summer but if he does we will be sure to consider your pension as an option,' said the woman and finished the call.

Fatma went to sit down and eat some kadayif, which was one of her favourite desserts. The phone rang after five minutes and Ahmet, who was eating himself, shrugged to show he had no intention of jumping up to answer it. Fatma got up and went to answer the call. This caller wanted to know how far the village was from town, how far it was to the beach, whether there was a market in the village, how often the linen was changed on the beds and the size of the pool. She then asked the price and when Fatma told her, she asked whether there was a discount for a week or ten-day stay and whether they could pay with a credit card.

'No discounts in peak season,' said Fatma.

'Then you are more expensive than the place we usually stay,' said the woman rudely.

Fatma stopped herself from suggesting that in that case the woman should continue to stay there. Instead she said politely, 'Thank you for your call. Do call if you decide to book with us,' and put the phone down.

It rang almost straight away with another caller who asked the price for August and for September, for one room and for two rooms, whether they could put three people in one room and whether there was a charge for collection from the bus station. The calls continued all evening. After the fifth one, Fatma begged Melek to answer and when she got fed up Mehmet took a couple of calls. By eleven o'clock they had one possible booking for the following week and had spoken at length to twelve callers.

'What is wrong with these people? You would think they were buying the place, the number of questions they ask!'

When the phone started trilling again, Fatma pulled the cable out of the wall. 'We will be available again in the morning and I hope that we get more bookings from the people who ring tomorrow.'

# 28

Leyla arrived for a swimming lesson. She was getting braver all the time, both in and out of the water. Instead of waiting quietly until someone spotted her, she now walked round the side of the pension and straight up to Melek, who was talking on the telephone with another potential guest who had seen the article in the paper.

'There's a general store and a kahvehane in the village but there isn't a café, so to speak. There is internet connection but it's a bit temperamental.'

She smiled and nodded to Leyla who hopped from foot to foot and grinned as she waited for the call to finish. Melek thought the little girl was excited about swimming but as she hung up the phone Leyla handed her a folded piece of paper.

'What's this, Leyla?'

The girl shook her head and drew her lips in to show that she wasn't going to say anything. Melek read the note. It was from Barish, inviting her to go to the beach with him the following day.

'See, Melek Abla,' said Leyla proudly, 'I told you I'm good at keeping secrets.'

Melek folded the paper and slipped it into the pocket of her shorts. 'You are, Leyla. Now let's see how good you are at swimming!'

The lesson took most of the morning. When Leyla was dressed and sitting at the bar drinking a glass of cola and watching a video of cats on Ahmet's phone, Melek found a piece of paper and wrote a reply to Barish. As she slipped it into the little girl's hand she thought how ironic it was that her mother, who hated soap operas, was making their lives resemble one.

*

The phone continued to ring frequently and although a lot of the callers asked a string of questions and then said they would think about it or they had to talk to their husband or wife, they had received a number of bookings as a result of the article. Fatma had also raised the prices, as befitted an establishment featured in the national press.

She was in the kitchen chopping garlic and mint to stir into yogurt for a refreshing hydari when she heard a car pull up. By the time she had washed her hands and got round to the front of the pension a woman had climbed down from a very large, black jeep.

'Oh, the heat! Is it always this unbearable?' she demanded of Fatma.

She was in her thirties, dressed in casual clothes that even Fatma could see were expensive and with several heavy gold bangles on her wrist.

'In August yes,' said Fatma. 'We have a pool though.'

A man got out of the driver's side and looked up at the front of the pension.

'Is this the same place? It doesn't look how it did in the pictures!'

The woman looked too. 'The Kismet Pension, yes this is it.' She turned to Fatma. 'We reserved a room with a view and asked for an extra bed.' She opened the back door of the jeep and a teenage girl looked up crossly from her phone, then returned to tapping the buttons rapidly with fingers tipped with long, multi-coloured nails.

'We've arrived, Ela Nur!' said her mother. 'Put your phone away for a minute and let's look at the room.'

'But Achelya and Mert have had an argument and she needs me,' said the girl, still tapping.

'Now!' said her mother in a voice that made Fatma jump. The girl slid down from the back seat with the phone still gripped in her hand.

Fatma led the way into the pension. There was only one room free, the room recently vacated by the sunburnt English girl. Fatma went upstairs and unlocked the door of the room, which was on the back of the pension and looked to the slope above the road.

The woman walked through the room and onto the balcony. 'The article said the view was stunning,' she said.

'It is on the other side,' said Fatma.

'But I especially asked for a room with a view,' said the woman.

Her husband was looking in the bathroom.

'Unfortunately those rooms are all full. You're

here for a week so it might be possible to move you if one becomes free.'

The girl poked at the folding bed that Fatma had got Ahmet to carry up there. 'I'm not sleeping on that!' she said and leaning against the wall started tapping rapidly into her phone again.

Her mother sniffed. 'Are you sure you don't have another room? This one smells like a hospital.'

There was, thought Fatma, a medicinal smell. It must have been from the cream the girl had used on her burns. 'It's the disinfectant we use to clean the rooms with,' she said quickly.

'No air conditioning!' said the man.

'No television!' said the girl.

Fatma, who had had enough, said 'Most of our guests are European. They don't watch television on holiday.'

'That's funny,' said the woman frowning, 'because when we visit Europe all the hotel rooms have televisions.'

'And air conditioning,' said the man.

'We are a simple pension,' said Fatma, fixing her mouth into something like a smile. 'If you are looking for these things perhaps you should try one of the large hotels in town.'

'I think we will,' said the woman, sweeping out of the room, followed by her husband. The girl flicked the mattress on the folding bed and left.

Fatma waited in the room until her anger subsided enough for her heart to stop galloping. She heard the jeep drive away. Then she went down and hung the room key on its hook, crossed out the booking in the register and fiddled for a minute with the brochures on the table. Still prickling with indignation, she went to the kitchen to make herself a restorative coffee.

She sipped the strong, comforting drink and thought about the rude family. It was all about expectations. The foreign guests who visited the Kismet Pension were all delighted when they saw the rooms. Birol Bey's article had been quite accurate in its depiction but if it was going to attract more guests like the ones who had just left she wished she had never agreed for the pension to be mentioned.

Over the afternoon her anger festered and she had to bite her tongue when faced with another barrage of questions on the telephone. Melek was refusing to answer it anymore and Mehmet had spent the whole afternoon at the coffee house, returning just as she served dinner to the guests. By the time the family sat down to dinner she had decided that action was necessary.

'Some of these people who saw the pension in the paper are more trouble than they are worth,' she said.

'Really, my dear?' asked Mehmet. 'I thought you would be pleased with all the callers.'

'That's the trouble – most of them are just that. They call and want to know all about the place, one of them asked me if the furniture was wooden and whether the water was heated with solar energy or electricity. As though you need a hot shower in this weather!' She wiped her brow pointedly with a paper napkin. 'Anyway, I think we should try to get more foreign guests.'

'How are we going to do that?' asked Ahmet.

'I can call Ilker,' volunteered Mehmet. 'Perhaps he can ask the other taxi drivers to bring us guests. Maybe if we offered a little more commission...'

'That won't be necessary because from now on *you* are going to go to the bus station every day.'

'Me? Every day?'

'Do you have some other pressing business?' Fatma asked looking menacing, daring him to answer.

'No, but Fatma...the car...the petrol...' said Mehmet, then gave up.

'I'm sure they can manage without you at the coffee house for a few weeks,' she said drily and the subject was closed.

\*

In her room Melek put on her old swimming costume. It was a bit tight on top and a bit saggy across her stomach where the elastic had lost its stretch. She wished it had occurred to her to go to town and buy a new one but it was too late now. She put a t-shirt and shorts on over the offending item, grabbed a towel and left the house. She looked for the ginger cat in the garden but he had slunk off to some dark corner to avoid the heat.

Barish was waiting for her at Kado's Garden. He was wearing swimming shorts and a t-shirt. His hair was a little longer and streaked from the sun. The sight of him made her forget the guilt she felt for lying to her mother.

'Hello.' He took her hand and gave it a squeeze. There was a gaggle of guests, waiting by the truck.

'Hello, Melek. It's nice to see you!' Harun strode across from the kitchen to the truck. 'Jump in everyone and hold on tight!'

Some of the guests rushed to get inside the vehicle. The others got in the back and Melek and Barish climbed in after them. There were large foam mats on the floor and Melek sat down and hugged her knees. She took out her towel and draped it over her head.

'The sun's very strong at this time,' she said to Barish, though in fact the cover was more to stop anyone in the village spotting her.

The truck pulled out of the retreat, took the right turn by the mosque and went through the centre of the village. The guests were in high spirits, enjoying the bumpy ride and the rush of air on warm skin. Melek saw Atilla outside the shop straightening postcards in a rack and Selma's sister Idil washing the balcony of her home upstairs. Once they had passed the last house, the road faded to a dirt track and they entered the forest. Melek took off the towel and gripped the sides of the truck as they started to be pitched around. Then the road itself fell away and they careered down towards the beach. A couple of the guests squealed with excitement or possibly fear. Barish put a hand over Melek's.

After some minutes of twisting back and forth and plunging down, the track levelled out and they came to a stop beneath a carob tree. The beach was never busy. Locals rarely ventured down there, especially in mid-summer when the sand was too hot to walk on without shoes, and visitors who did attempt the journey often gave up when the road got bad. Still

Melek looked around before getting down from the truck.

There were two boats moored at one side of the bay and a family sitting close to the water's edge who she guessed from their bright blond hair were Swedish or Dutch. The retreat guests jumped down from the truck and headed straight for the sea. Melek led Barish through the trees to a spot further from the restaurant and Demir and Dudu.

She took off her sandals and walked in the shallows where the water rolled lazily back and forth in ripples too small and weak to be called waves. It was tepid but still refreshing. Near the rickety jetty Barish dropped his towel on the stones.

'Come on – I'll race you in!'

He pulled off his t-shirt, hopped on one leg and then the other to remove his socks and trainers and ran towards the sea. Melek peeled off her t-shirt and shorts and raced after him. He dived into the clear water just ahead of her and surfaced further out in an explosion of spray.

'The water's so clear!' he said. 'There's a shoal of calamari just over there – did you see them?'

Melek plunged in and swam under water. She could see a group of the filmy creatures darting along in formation ahead of her. When she surfaced Barish was floating on his back, his head tipped back and face turned to the sun. She lay back and squinted up so that the sun broke into kaleidoscope patterns of light. She could hear the swishing and tinkling of the shingle swirling back and forth on the sea bed.

Water splashed on her face and she jumped and

righted herself. Barish reached out, his hands glowing white in the clear water, and took hold of her round the waist. It felt wonderful and terrifying at the same time.

'Nobody can see!' he said.

Melek stayed there in his embrace treading water. Then she could bear it no longer and pulled away. Her heart was thumping so hard she thought it would make ripples in the water. She scanned the beach to see if anyone was watching. The customers from the retreat had spread out. Some were swimming or snorkelling among the rocks; others were lying on the beach, mostly further back where a stand of pine trees provided some shade.

Barish doubled over and swam down into the clear depths. She could see his shape, shady and distorted beneath her. When he came up he presented her with a long, white shell, its outside rough and dimpled, its inside pearly with the faintest tinge of pink.

They swam ashore, spread out their towels and flopped down on the warm sand. Barish said how nice it would be to sail along the coast, stopping in secluded bays. Melek told him about the flotillas and the barbecue they had put on at the pension with its unexpected drama.

'Was your Mum upset about it?'

'Mum? No, she was pleased. Murat was so embarrassed he's been keeping away. I don't think Claudia Auntie's seen him at all.'

'Ah!' said Barish. 'Perhaps that's why she has been at the retreat so much for the last few days.'

He walked up to the restaurant and bought ice-cold bottles of cola. Melek held hers to her hot cheek before drinking it and savouring the sharp bubbles that tickled her throat.

A family arrived at the beach, two small children straining to get out of their mother's grip and race down to the water and a father laden down with bags, mats and an umbrella. They made a little camp not far from Melek and Barish, then stripped down to their bathing costumes and took the excited children into the sea. The father swam out a little way with the elder child, a boy who could swim with armbands. The mother sat in the shallows with her small daughter balanced on her lap picking shells from the seabed and making shapes in the wet sand. Melek thought how easy things were when you were small. Her own mother had never ventured into the water but they had spent all their time together and Melek had tried to copy everything her mother did. Even the most mundane things – shelling peas or hanging out the washing – had become a game when they did it together.

'I've never seen a beach as quiet as this,' said Barish. 'The ones in Istanbul are packed if it's a nice day and the places we usually go on holiday are full of idiots showing off on their jet skis and motor boats.'

They were lying side-by-side. It was familiar and cosy. Feeling daring, Melek hooked a foot over Barish's ankle. He took hold of one of her damp curls and pushed it behind her ear. Melek closed her eyes and listened to the jurr-jurr drone of the cicadas.

Presently she heard the gentle hum of a small outboard motor and assumed it was sailors from one of the yachts. She heard the thump as someone jumped onto the dock. Barish leant over her and kissed her cheek. She opened her eyes and smiled, then saw a figure standing close by. With a sick lurch she realised it was Murat.

Melek rolled away and stood up, brushing the sand off her in an attempt to hide her confusion. Her heart, already aflutter from Barish's kiss, now thumped with fear. She saw Murat curl his lip in a sneer and walk off up the beach.

'What is it, Melek? What's the matter?' Barish looked worried. He touched her arm and she flinched.

'I feel a bit sick. Maybe I drank the cola too fast. Do you think we'll be going soon?'

'Dad'll take you back now, if you want.' The disappointment in his voice made Melek feel more miserable.

The beauty of the day, the closeness she had felt to Barish had all just disappeared. She had always suspected they would be caught out in the end and a part of her had even hoped that someone like Nazla or Derya would be the one to tell her mother and urge her to be reasonable and understanding.

But Murat was the sort of person who enjoyed other people's misfortune and would do his best to fan the flames of her mother's anger. Plus at the moment he had a score to settle and she had just given him the perfect opportunity to do it.

# 29

The August heat tested the patience of even the calmest of souls. The sun bore down from early morning until it sank dramatically behind the mountain in an explosion of orange. The evening air was warm and throbbed with the sound of cicadas. At the Kismet the pool was, as Fatma had hoped, a big attraction.

The guests spent the day in it or lolling around beside it and the sale of cold drinks and snacks had consequently increased. Ahmet took every opportunity to dive into the water, especially if there were any girls around. Melek and Leyla continued the swimming lessons and Melek had proved herself to be a patient teacher. When Selma came to visit, the two girls chased each other round in the water, practised somersaults and handstands and laughed a lot. At other times Melek was increasingly sullen and irritable. The cooking and laundry were made more onerous by the heat and Melahat grumbled all the time about it.

Mehmet was going to the bus station every day, leaving first thing in the morning. Some days he found guests off one of the early morning buses and after dropping them at the pension escaped further duties to spend the afternoon in the coffee house; on other days he had to wait until later before he managed to snag some customers. His best find had been two Dutch families who squashed into the little car and a taxi and were still at the pension, occupying three rooms, a week later. Their presence and the continuing approval of Claudia had helped Fatma get over the upset of the guests in the large jeep who had declined to stay.

One night Fatma had a disturbing dream. In it, she was careering downhill on a bicycle and could not find the brakes. She woke sweating and anxious, with both legs scrabbling madly for the ground. Given all that was happening in her life it was not surprising that she should feel out of control; what was strange was how vividly she had imagined the experience when she had never ridden a bicycle in her life.

It was not yet six o'clock and she heard the call to prayer echoing faintly in the still air. Knowing there was no chance of sleeping more, she got up and made tea. In the garden she opened the door of the chicken coop and the cockerel rushed out and crowed joyfully at the start of another day. Fatma thought of the day ahead of her.

At this point in the summer the routine always started to get monotonous – preparing breakfast, changing sheets and hanging out washing, making dinner. There was no escaping these tasks, just as there was no escaping the heat, but Derya and Melek could manage without her for a couple of hours. It would make a pleasant change to get away from the pension for an hour or two. She thought she might take a stroll into the village and see the newly erected signs. She might even call in on Galip or Atilla for a chat.

She waited until after breakfast. When her mother heard where she was going she decided to accompany her part of the way and visit Nurdan. While Melahat collected her handbag and her shawl – you never could be too careful, she said – Fatma took off her muslin headscarf, ran it under the tap and replaced it on her head. The damp cloth provided protection for a short time from the blazing sun.

They left the little house and walked slowly along the lane. A ringdove sitting on a telegraph pole peered down at them and cooed lazily. In the valley the cotton harvest was nearly ready, fields of bushes dotted with fluffy, white balls.

Nurdan was sitting on the chair on her front step waiting. The two friends disappeared into the house to drink tea and gossip and Fatma carried on alone. Her headscarf was drying fast and she could feel the heat beating down on the top of her head.

She had planned to pass the orchard without looking and was scurrying past with her head turned firmly the other way when she heard a voice call out, 'Ela Nur, will you leave the phone and come and join the class? Everyone is waiting for you!'

Before she could stop herself Fatma turned to see and what she saw made her stop dead. Parked just inside the gate was a familiar large, black jeep. The girl Ela Nur appeared from amongst the trees and slouched across toward the deck where her mother was waiting. Fatma remembered the girl's refusal to sleep in the folding bed, the family's general disdain for the room. Now she realised they had rejected the Kismet Pension in favour of a wooden bungalow. Her anger surfaced again, mixed with the bitter-sweet understanding that she had been right about Harun and his retreat: it was taking customers from her.

She turned and hurried on, choking with the unfairness of it all. On the lane just before the village she saw the brown sign that pointed to the theatre. It should have brought hope that the village was beginning to be recognised, even vindication for her efforts, but she was too tormented to feel it.

She puffed her way up the slope into the theatre and sat on one of the first row of stones. Fatma remembered playing games of hide-and-seek there as a child with Nazla and Derya. Now she thought of the people who had come here for some entertainment and to escape the worries of daily life. Had any of them felt their position threatened by a new arrival in the village? Had they worried about a daughter who seemed to be growing away from them?

The sweat was beading on her forehead and the glare from the white stones was giving her a headache. She went back through the arch and stopped in front of another sign. This one had a crude map showing the layout of the theatre, the tombs and the barely visible bath house. It seemed to give the ruins a significance, a legitimacy. Perhaps they would attract the interest of some professor who would come with a group of students and spend the summer picking laboriously through the site looking for treasure. What did it matter, Fatma thought bitterly, since he would probably choose to stay at Harun's place and hold court until late sitting on cushions in one of those gazebos, regaling everyone with stories of his findings.

'Hello, Fatma Auntie! What are you doing here?'

Fatma was woken from her non-too-pleasant daydream by Selma, who had just come out of her gate and was looking at her in surprise.

'Hello, Selma. Is your father in?'

'He's in his office.'

The village headman had enclosed the terrace on the side of their house and made it into his office. His wife and daughters teased him that he went in there to escape the family – mainly the twins. Fatma opened the door and went in. The room, being mainly glass, was like a hothouse and a fan purring in the corner just shifted the hot air around and ruffled the stacks of papers on Galip's desk.

'Hello, Fatma. How are you?'

'I'm fine, thank you, Galip. How are you? How is Idil settling into married life?'

'She's very happy. She's actually inside having tea with her mother now. They see each other nearly every day but they still seem to find plenty to talk about!'

'How nice!' Fatma fanned her face with a leaflet taken from the table. 'I've just come from the theatre. Do you know I don't think I'd been in for twenty years? It's great that you got those signs put up.'

'Oh that wasn't me!' said Galip, smiling.

'It wasn't?'

'No. I tried several years ago but they kept putting me off. I'm afraid I sort of gave up.'

'So who…?'

'We have Harun Bey to thank for that. Apparently he got to know the museum manager and they managed it together.'

'H-Harun? The museum manager?' Fatma felt quite faint. She dropped the leaflet back onto the table.

'Are you alright, Fatma?'

She pressed a hand to her temple and took a breath. 'I'm fine, thank you, Galip. It's just so hot. I think I'll go over and get a bottle of cold water from Atilla…'

'Are you sure you're alright? I can get you some water. It is rather hot in here…'

Fatma waved him away and left the small office. She crossed the road to the shop and found Atilla outside putting postcards on a stand. She took a bottle of water from the fridge, drank half of it, then poured the rest into her hand and patted it onto her forehead and her throat.

'Are you alright, Fatma?'

'Oh you know, Atilla, this heat seems to get worse every year. You're selling postcards now?'

'Yes.'

Atilla proudly held out a stack of cards. The picture was taken from the top of the theatre, looking down over the stone tiers to the valley below. He pulled out a card from another pack and Fatma saw a picture of the bay and the island taken from the beach road.

'Where did you get these?'

'A photographer came and took them and I had them made into cards. I've got some with pictures of the town too. I think we'll be getting more visitors now we have the signs...'

'Do you think they're going to make that much difference?'

'I'm sure of it. I've had mugs made too, and fridge magnets. They're coming next week.'

Fatma stared miserably at the stand of cards.

'By the way the article in the paper was good. We all have a lot to thank Harun Bey for.' He shook his head. 'And to think you didn't want him here at first.' He leant close and said in a whisper, 'I'm a bit embarrassed when I remember my own part, actually.'

Fatma pulled a coin from her pocket and put it on the table beside the postcards. 'Thank you, Atilla. I hope you sell a lot of cards!'

She headed back to the Kismet as fast as the heat and her state would allow. It had been a mistake to come into the village. Now she just wanted to be as far from it all as possible.

She went into the little house and sat in the kitchen. From the small front room came the sound of the television and her mother shouting directions to the participants in a game show.

'Not that box – open the other one! Don't bid any more, you silly girl!'

Fatma had not cried since she had lost her dear Baba but right then tears were stinging her eyes. The villagers talked about Harun Bey as if he were some kind of saviour and nothing she did to persuade them otherwise was effective. Her attempts to get him to leave the village had been just as unsuccessful.

The phone rang and she went into the hall to answer it.

'Fatma? You don't sound very cheerful.'

'Oh Nazla, I'm tired of all this. This man is unstoppable!'

'I'm so glad you're ready to give up too!'

'Give up? Who said anything about giving up?'

'I thought…when you said you were tired of it… Harun caught me with the mouse this morning. I had to make up something about letting it go down on the lane but I'm not sure if he believed me. Nothing we've done has worked, has it?'

'But Nazla I've told you – we just need to keep at it. Drop by drop a lake is formed!'

'You really want to carry on? Because honestly, Fatma, I'm not sure I even want Harun Bey to go anymore.'

Fatma sagged onto the chair in the dark hall. 'So you're happy for Osman to hang around these ladies?'

'The thing is,' said Nazla with an embarrassed giggle, 'It turns out he isn't interested in them at all. I got so cross the other day I accused him of flirting with them and he said they drive him crazy with all their ridiculous requests. "More money than sense", that's what he thinks of them.'

'So you're abandoning me?'

'I'm not abandoning you, Fatma, but I don't want to be part of your campaign anymore. I think you should give up too. The retreat hasn't affected the

Kismet, has it? And Harun got you into that article – that must have been good for business.'

'Actually you're wrong. There is a family who were supposed to stay at the Kismet but are now staying at the retreat!'

'I'm sorry, Fatma, but I've made up my mind. I'll come and see you soon but I have to go and make the girls some lunch now.'

Fatma put the phone down. She felt quite alone. Nobody understood her because nobody was in her position. She went back to the kitchen and sat at the table. She thought back to the dinner when Hilal had come and told her that there was going to be another guest house in the village. She had tried to dismiss the suggestion as gossip or at best a half-hearted plan that would never become a reality; how wrong she had been!

'Fatma, I'm croaking with thirst. Are you making tea or not?' her mother's voice called from the other room.

Fatma stood and filled the teapot. She remembered a long time before when she had been upset by her mother taking Hilal's side over her own and her father had explained it to her.

'Your sister is not as capable as you, dear daughter. Your mother knows Hilal needs support, just as she knows that you are quite able of taking care of yourself.'

Fatma had not been convinced at the time and she still was not sure that this justified her mother's favouritism but she did know that she could look after herself. She had done it for most of her life and she would continue to do it now. She did not need anyone else to fight her battles. She would fight on alone.

*

After a restorative four glasses of tea and a piece of baklava that Mehmet had brought back from town, Fatma felt ready to continue with her day. There were guests who would be expecting dinner in a few hours and she had not even decided what she was going to serve. She was on her way round to the pension when she heard the throaty roar of an old motorbike. She was surprised and a little disconcerted to see Murat.

'Hello, Fatma Abla, I'm pleased I caught you!'

He pulled up next to her and turned off the engine but stayed sitting on the machine. His mouth twisted into a crooked smile that made Fatma uneasy.

'Me? I-I...' Fatma stood looking at him, her mouth opening and closing.

'I hope there's no bad feeling between us. I listened to your request and broke things off with Mrs Claudia. She was quite upset.' He leant back on the motorcycle in a pose worthy of James Dean.

Fatma remembered him floundering in the pool and had to stifle a snort of laughter. 'Well, she's quite recovered now and I need to get on—'

'One minute, Fatma Abla. I have something important to tell you.' He sat on the bike looking at her with an expression of satisfaction. 'It's about your daughter.'

Fatma's heart started racing. She had left Melek in the pension when she went to the village and had not seen her since her return. Had something happened? Had she gone out and had an accident?

'What is it? What's happened?' Fatma's mouth was dry and her voice sounded strange.

'I feel it's my duty to warn you. She's a nice girl, I wouldn't want anything bad to happen to her.'

Murat was talking in riddles but at least it seemed nothing had happened yet. Fatma took a deep breath and tried to calm the pounding in her chest. Murat was in no hurry. He took a packet of cigarettes from his pocket, tapped it on the handlebar of the bike to shake one out and lit it.

Fatma could not stand it any more. 'What is it you want to tell me, Murat?'

'Just that I saw your daughter at the beach with a boy.'

Fatma was thrown. 'With a boy? But Melek went to the beach with Selma.'

'Selma wasn't around when I saw her. Actually I think you know the boy. He's the one whose father built the bungalows. And they looked very friendly, cuddled up together on a blanket!' He took a drag on the cigarette, tipped his head back and blew a stream of smoke up into the air. 'He's from Istanbul so he's bound to be a lot more experienced than the kids round here. It would be awful if your Melek got led astray.'

Fatma felt thought her knees were going to give out on her. She needed to think through what Murat was saying but first she needed to get away from him.

'I can assure you that won't happen. Thank you for letting me know,' she said stiffly and turned to walk back to the house.

'Good day, Fatma Abla,' called Murat and she could hear the triumph in his voice. She wondered for a minute if he might have made the whole thing up but there were easier ways of getting back at her that did not involve Melek. She heard the bike heading off along the lane as she entered the house. In the kitchen she collapsed once more onto a chair.

So this was why Melek had become so distant: she had been trying to hide a secret. Derya had told her it was a phase all girls went through but she should have known better. How long had it been going on? Who else knew?

Fatma's mind seethed as she went about the familiar and comforting task of making tea – filling the bottom half of the pot with water, spooning tea into the top half and rinsing it, pouring boiling water from the bottom into the top. When it had brewed for the necessary fifteen minutes she poured herself a glass but found she could not drink it. The lump in her throat had moved to her chest and she could not swallow. She remembered Hilal saying she felt as if something was squeezing her heart and for the first time Fatma thought she knew how her sister felt.

# 30

Melek was helping Derya with the laundry. After her trip to the beach she had been terrified Murat would tell her mother he had seen her, but three days had passed and she had begun to nurture the hope that he might keep her secret. Perhaps, she thought, he was too embarrassed to come to the Kismet after his recent humiliation.

Then Ahmet appeared in the door of the laundry looking grim.

'Mum wants to see you, right now! She looks pretty mad.'

Melek guessed the worst had happened. The washing machine shuddered to a stop and she started to empty the sheets and towels into a plastic laundry basket.

'I'll go when I've hung these up.'

She carried the washing out to the line and started pegging the sheets and towels in a neat row. She concentrated on the task at hand but still her stomach was doing somersaults. When the basket was empty she had no more excuse and she walked slowly round to the house. On the garden path the ginger cat was hunkered down watching a line of ants. She stroked him and felt his body ripple under her touch.

'You understand, don't you, Tiger? You don't listen to anyone.'

The cat gave the tiniest miaow in answer and went back to watching the ants.

Inside, the house was gloomy after the bright sun. Her mother was slumped at the kitchen table with her eyes closed. Forgetting their differences she dropped to her knees beside her.

'Mother, are you ill?'

Her mother opened her eyes and looked at Melek. 'I'm not ill, my daughter, but I'm hurt. Is it true what I've heard? Have you been seeing Harun's son behind my back?'

Melek felt her face flush. There was no point in denying it when her body was giving her away. Part of her was even relieved that the hiding was over.

'Ayyy!' exclaimed her mother, clutching her chest.

Melek stood up. It made her feel braver. 'He's a polite boy from a good family and if you hadn't taken against his father so unfairly I wouldn't have had to hide it from you.'

'Do you think I would approve of you seeing any boy? You're too young.'

'I'm fifteen and things aren't the same as they were in your time.'

'So these days it's alright for young girls to lie to their mothers and to carry on with boys in full view of everyone?'

'We weren't doing anything wrong! Did Murat tell you?'

'Yes. He saw you together at the beach. Who else has seen you and knows what's going on? Am I the last one to find out?'

'No! Only Harun Uncle and Zuhal Auntie know. And Claudia and Selma.'

'And now Murat knows he'll be telling half the village.'

'I don't care. I'm tired of sneaking around and you always say to take no notice of village gossip.'

'Do you plan to carry on seeing this boy?' her mother challenged her.

Melek's throat was tight, her heart pounding but she stood up straight and said, 'Yes, I'm going to keep on seeing him until he goes back to Istanbul. I really like him.'

'And if I forbid you from seeing him?'

'You'll have to lock me in my room.'

Melek turned and walked out of the house and into the lane. This time she really did go to see Selma and when her friend opened the door she burst into tears and poured her heart out to her.

\*

Fatma poured herself another glass of tea. The weight on her chest had lifted enough for her to drink but she felt an ache in the pit of her stomach. Unlike Ahmet, Melek had never disappointed her before. She had been an easy baby and a happy child who was keen to please and always did what was asked of her. She could hardly believe that the same girl had now betrayed her in this way.

When she could leave it no longer she went

to the pension and made a simple dinner of lentil soup, chicken sautéed with peppers and garlic and chips. Derya stayed behind to help serve as Melek had not returned. Fatma noticed Ahmet looking at her furtively. Even Melahat when she came over for dinner was quiet. After the others had eaten and Fatma had managed a few spoons of soup and a couple of pieces of chicken, she confronted Mehmet.

'Do you know what your daughter has been doing?'

Mehmet looked as though he was thinking hard. 'Yes-no-I don't think so. What has she been doing?'

'Going around with a boy. And not just any old boy – Harun's son.' She looked at him for reaction.

Mehmet looked suitably surprised. 'Really? Well I never!'

'Is that all you have to say, Mehmet? Aren't you concerned about your daughter's reputation?'

Mehmet smiled weakly. 'I'm sure she hasn't done anything awful, Fatma.' He took a sip of the raki Ahmet had brought him.

'So you're alright with her cuddling up to this boy on the beach where everyone can see them, are you? And what about all the lies she's been telling? She was sneaking off to meet him when she told me she was seeing Selma. Even when she sprained her ankle she must have been with him all along. What did he say when he came into the coffee house?'

'I-I don't know.' Mehmet added another ice cube to his glass. 'When I heard Melek was hurt I didn't listen to anything else. Do you want me to talk to her?'

'It's a bit late for that!' Fatma threw up her hands

in frustration. Then she softened. 'We both should have talked to her before and tried to find out what was troubling her.'

A thought crossed her mind. If she had not been so preoccupied with her struggle against Harun she would have paid more attention to her daughter. Had her campaign driven her daughter away? She slumped in her chair, guilt adding to her misery.

'And she says she's going to keep on seeing him.'

'Maybe,' Mehmet shook his glass and watched as the ice melted leaving white strands in the milky liquid, 'Maybe we should let her have a bit of freedom—'

'What, and have creeps like Murat going round talking about her?' Fatma shivered as she recalled his smug expression as he had told her.

Fatma did not ask for her mother's opinion but she got it anyway.

'I don't know why you expect her to listen to you when you never listened to me!'

'I never lied to you though, Mother.'

'No, you just ignored me and went ahead with whatever you wanted to do.'

'You mean helping Baba on the farm?'

'I mean refusing to respect your mother.'

Fatma thought back to that time. Her mother had nagged her at every opportunity. She told her she would never find a man who would marry her, never have a family; she threatened and cajoled and sometimes refused to talk to her. It had affected their relationship for a long time; perhaps it still did. She would not let that happen to her and Melek.

But Melek obviously thought she was in love and was unlikely to listen to anything she said. In which case there was only one thing for Fatma to do: she would ask Harun to talk to his son. She had not managed to persuade him to give up on the retreat but surely he would understand the concern of a mother for her daughter? The time had come for confrontation.

*

The next day she did the breakfast service alone. Selma had called late the night before to say Melek was staying with her and she still had not returned in the morning. Hoping to catch Harun and his wife before they were busy, Fatma left Derya clearing the dishes and headed for the retreat. As she walked, she practised what she would say. She waved to Nurdan Auntie who was sitting in her usual place on her front step, but she did not stop to chat.

It was only just turned ten o'clock but the sun was molten and the tarmac of the lane was shiny and soft. By the time she reached the retreat Fatma's forehead and the back of her neck were prickly with sweat. She took a deep breath, swiped a sleeve across her damp brow and walked in before she could change her mind.

Inside the place looked different to how she had imagined it. The remaining trees had recovered from their late pruning and threw shade over much of the orchard. The wooden chalets peeped out attractively from between them. In the centre, the gazebos with their drapes of jasmine were inviting and several people were already lounging on the brightly-coloured cushions inside. One of them was Zuhal. She was sitting alone seemingly lost in thought.

Fatma marched towards her. Zuhal sensed someone approaching and looked round.

'Fatma Abla, how nice to see you! Do come and have a drink. I can't cope with anything but cold drinks in this heat but would you like a coffee?'

'No thank you, Zuhal Hanum, I just came to talk. Actually I was hoping to see both of you. Is Harun Bey here?'

'I'm afraid not. He's gone to town with Osman. Will I do?' She pulled a playful face but Fatma was not in the mood for jokes.

'I suppose you'll have to.'

'Would you like a tea or some water?' Zuhal started to get up.

'No, thank you.'

'At least sit down.' Zuhal herself sat back and drew her legs under her.

Fatma reluctantly kicked off her plastic sandals and plonked her backside on the cushion opposite her. She would have preferred a more formal setting to say what she had come to say.

Zuhal took a sip of her juice. 'What did you want to talk about, Fatma Abla?'

Fatma did not answer. She was watching the a group of ladies standing round a loom on which a local woman was demonstrating weaving cloth. Among them were a scowling Ela Nur, her phone still gripped in one hand, and her mother.

'Those were my guests,' Fatma said to Zuhal. 'I

distinctly remember Harun Bey saying this place wouldn't take business from the Kismet.'

'I'm so sorry, Fatma. I'm sure Harun had no idea. They turned up a couple of days ago without a booking…'

'That's because they had booked to stay at the Kismet.'

Both women were watching the group where Ela Nur was now tapping a message into her phone and her mother was hissing at her angrily.

'Actually you're welcome to them,' said Fatma. 'But the point is this place *is* affecting my business. I came to talk about a more important subject though.'

Zuhal twisted one of her curls around her finger.

'I've just found out my daughter has been spending time with your son. I suppose you knew that?'

Zuhal broke into a smile. 'They are a very sweet couple.'

Fatma winced. 'I don't think it's sweet of Melek to have been sneaking around and lying to me.'

'She's hated having to do that,' said Zuhal passionately. 'She's such a lovely girl!'

'Yes, well she *was* a lovely girl but at the moment she's quite changed. She has no experience with boys, you know.'

'Oh I can assure you Barish is a gentleman. I made sure he respects girls.'

'Maybe so, but what counts as respect in the city is different to here. In the village young people can't just carry on the way those two have apparently been doing.'

'Do you mean young people are not allowed to

see each other?'

Fatma was flustered. It was very warm and she wished she'd asked for a glass of cold water. 'Not at their age. And after the way Melek has behaved I shan't be letting her out of my sight.'

'Perhaps they could meet with one of us around?' said Zuhal hopefully.

'No. Please speak to your son and tell him not to contact Melek or try to see her.'

'Oh Fatma Abla, they'll be so upset!' Zuhal looked distraught. Then her anguish turned to puzzlement and she sniffed the air before turning back to Fatma. 'Fatma Abla, I know you're upset that we came here and set up Kado's Garden but can't we find a way to be friends?' Zuhal put one hand on the table, palm side up, in a gesture of conciliation.

Fatma was disconcerted by the directness of the question. She wondered if Harun and Zuhal knew about her efforts to scupper their plans. Had someone told them? They had never confronted her about it but perhaps they had guessed. Her head spun and her throat was scratchy with the heat.

'Could I have a glass of water, Zuhal Hanum?' she asked.

\*

Leyla was sitting in the shade of a fig tree. She had eaten three of the fat fruit that dangled from its branches, peeling back thick skin to reveal the gooey, pink insides. Now she was feeling slightly sick. She stretched out and rested her head on a tussock of grass.

With her eyes closed, sounds became more intense. She could hear the noise of the goats tearing up the grass and the gentle jangle of their bells when they moved. There were more distant sounds too: a tractor droning, a dog barking, music playing on a radio. Then she heard another sound, a crackling, hissing sound, that she couldn't identify.

She got up and looked around. It was coming from the forest further along the slope. She took hold of the rope and pulled the mother goat off the grassy verge and along the lane. The kids skittered behind them. As she walked along the lane the sound got louder and a spicy smell tickled the inside of her nose. The goats were reluctant to go on. She had to drag the mother. Just before the field where the Istanbul man had built bungalows she looked in amongst the trees and saw orange flames.

Despite her young age, Leyla was not one to panic. She knew the goats would make their own way home and she tied the rope onto the halter and released the mother who turned and set off at a trot towards the village with her two half-grown kids gambling beside her. Leyla ran as fast as she could along the lane and into the retreat.

\*

Fatma recognised the smell of burning. For a moment she wondered if someone was burning stubble down in the valley – it was banned these days but that did not stop some of the older farmers – but the smell was not dry and earthy and it was not drifting up from below; it was sharp and heady and seemed to be coming from the top corner of the field. With a sick feeling she remembered when she had smelled it before. She had been a young girl the last time there had been a forest fire in Ortakoy but the same smell had hung over the village for weeks afterwards.

Before she had time to say anything Leyla came racing into the field shouting 'Fire! Forest fire! In the trees up there,' and pointing towards the forest beyond the top corner of the orchard.

Fatma leapt up, jammed her feet into her plastic sandals and hurried towards Leyla.

'Have you seen it?'

'Yes, Fatma Auntie.'

'Is it big?'

'Not so big yet.'

'Has anyone else seen it?'

'I don't think so, Fatma Auntie. There's no one there.'

'Leyla, run to the pension, quick! Tell Melek what's happening and stay there with her.'

The girl was already heading towards the broken gate.

Zuhal had got off the gazebo and was looking at Fatma, fear pinching her face. 'Harun and Osman are in town!' she wailed. 'And Buket's with them.'

'Then we'll have to manage on our own. I'm going to get Nazla to call and report the fire. The fire service are permanently on standby at this time of year and they'll be here quickly. You need to gather the guests.'

Zuhal was running this way and that, flapping her arms and making little gasping noises.

'And try to stay calm,' said Fatma, striding off up the field.

# 31

Fatma's head was churning. She had spent the whole summer looking for ways to stop the retreat and now the perfect opportunity lay before her. All she had to do was leave with the others and the fire would race through the orchard. Despite what she had said to Zuhal, once they took hold these fires moved fast – there was already a plume of smoke above the trees – and by the time the fire fighters arrived it would be too late. Best of all, nobody would be able to blame her for it. Still she found herself hurrying up the field as fast as her heat-swollen feet could carry her.

Even if nobody else held her responsible, she could not live with herself if she walked away and let the place burn. Besides, if the retreat burned, Nazla's house would burn too, which would be even more awful given that they had only just taken proper ownership of it. She might not succeed in stopping the fire but Fatma knew she had to try.

Nazla was standing on the path at the front of the house.

'There's a fire beside the orchard. Call the forest fire service and Galip Bey too while you're at it. Then get the girls out of the house. Quick!'

Nazla stared at her in horror. 'The girls are at Mother's. Oh Fatma, are we going to lose the house?'

'Not without a fight! Now go and make those calls!'

Fatma went back down to the retreat where Zuhal and Barish had gathered the guests together.

'Take them to the Kismet,' she said to Zuhal. 'Melek will look after you all. Barish can stay here. We need his help.'

Zuhal looked as though she was going to protest.

'I'll be fine, Mum, don't worry.'

'I'll take care of your son, Zuhal,' said Fatma.

The boy gave his mother a hug and she stood on tiptoe to kiss his cheek and run a hand through his hair. Then she turned and led the group of guests out of the retreat and off up the lane. Some were carrying rucksacks, others were struggling with cases. They were talking loudly and gripping each other in panic.

A haze of smoke was starting to drift over the field.

'Come on, young man.' Fatma was already heading back up the orchard. 'We can't put out the fire but we can make it harder for it to take hold. We'll start with Osman and Nazla's house.'

Nazla was already at the side of the house priming the artesian well with a tin bucket. She pumped the handle until water poured from the wide spout, then plugged in the electric cable and directed the jet of water at the wood shed.

'You take the hose,' Fatma instructed Barish. 'Soak the walls and roof and all the trees that you can reach.

Then do the same with the house.'

He took the hose from Nazla and started spraying the water over the small hut. Nazla and Fatma filled buckets from the outside tap and hurled the water at the trees and bushes on the other side of the house beyond the reach of the hose. They went back and filled the buckets time after time, while Barish moved onto the house.

The ground became slippery and Fatma's feet squelched in her plastic sandals. Her trousers and top were soaked and her eyes were smarting. When she paused for a rest she saw a thick column of smoke rising straight up from the forest. The fire could now be heard too, even above the whirr of the electric pump.

'This hose won't reach far into the orchard. Do you have a longer one?' Fatma shouted to Nazla.

'No, but there's another artesian well somewhere down there. It hasn't been used for years and I don't know if we can get it working—'

'We have to try!'

Fatma showed Barish how to detach the hose and left him to fight with the screws while she and Nazla went to look for the well. The corner of the field was a tangle of blackberry bushes which Osman had tried to get rid of but which grew back each time with a vengeance. Nazla used a rake to pull at the brambles and after a few unsuccessful forages metal connected with metal and she pulled the briars away to reveal a rusted old well head.

Fatma pushed through, ignoring the prickles that caught at her clothes and scratched her hands and feet. She sloshed water from her bucket into the top of the well and Nazla pumped on the curved metal handle. There was a dry screech and the water Fatma had poured in came gushing out, coloured dark brown with rust.

'Keep going!' Fatma urged, emptying half the contents of Nazla's bucket into the top of the pump. Barish arrived dragging the hose pipe and took over from Nazla. The rusty metal groaned again and from deep in the earth came a few sucking noises but still no water. Nazla tipped in the last of the water from her bucket and Barish pumped harder and faster and suddenly the handle whipped from his grasp and a dark, muddy stream of water flowed from the spout.

'Now attach the hose!' instructed Fatma. 'There's no electricity nearby so you'll have to pump!'

Barish fed the hose onto the nozzle of the pump and tightened the screws in the metal clip. His hands were shaking.

The column of smoke had spread into a dark cloud that hung above the forest. Small motes of ash were floating in the air.

Barish grabbed the handle and started to pump – up, down, up, down. Fatma took the end of the hose and Nazla, a bucket in each hand, followed her towards the top corner of the field, to the area nearest the fire.

The air was even hotter there and felt dry and brittle. The fire hissed and crackled as though taunting them.

'It's burning uphill at the moment!' shouted Fatma. 'That's good!'

She pointed the jet of water at a large mulberry tree on the edge of the field. Nazla filled the buckets and hurled water at the first chalet – Harun and Zuhal's home. The wood was dry and at first the water ran off. It took some time but eventually it started to drink in the water and turn a darker colour.

They had just moved on to the second chalet when they heard a clanging siren and saw three fire trucks pass in front of the gate, followed by several minibuses filled with fire fighters. Fatma waved at Barish and pointed to the road, hoping he would understand that help was on the way. She thought he gave a nod of acknowledgement but it was hard to see through all the smoke and drifting ash.

Fatma took off her headscarf, wetted it and tied it over her nose and mouth. They moved through the field, wetting the wooden bungalows and the ground and trees between. Barish was tiring and the water was coming in erratic bursts. Fatma's eyes were watering so much she could not see clearly and her arms were aching from holding the hosepipe up. Nazla was coughing from the smoke.

The fire was clearly visible through the trees. It had turned and was burning across the slope, heading for the retreat. Fatma could hear the shouts of the men as they fought the flames but the fire was powerful. A pine tree on the edge of the forest exploded like a huge fire cracker and sparks rained down on both sides of the fence. There was nothing more they could do except wait to see if their efforts had been successful. She let the hose pipe fall to the ground and waved to Barish to stop pumping. Her hands were blistered. She and Nazla stumbled down the field, away from the heat. Nazla still clung tightly to her buckets.

Once it entered the orchard the fire took little time to dry out the water they had sprayed and start consuming the roof of the first chalet. The fire fighters had their large hoses trained on it, gushing water, but it carried on and crossed to the next chalet. A second patch of flames was playing around the trunk of the big mulberry tree.

The second chalet was soon, like the first, a blackened ruin and the fire was heading uphill again towards the house. Nazla let out a shout and Fatma had to stop her from running up there.

'It'll be alright. The men are winning,' she assured her friend.

Two huge hoses poured a deluge of water onto the fire. Where it had passed men were beating out sparks and raking the hot ground to stop any further breakouts and block off the route to the forest. The fire was cornered and after a final flare up in which it consumed most of a cherry tree, it turned from a roaring blaze to a gentle bonfire. The men moved in and beat at that and soon there were no flames, just heavy grey smoke that hid the sky and a dreadful smell in the air.

\*

Fatma was still standing with Nazla when the pick-up truck pulled in through the gate. Harun and Osman jumped out and stood looking around. She could imagine the shock they felt. They had left the retreat in good order and returned after a few hours to a scene of devastation.

Harun looked round frantically and saw Barish lying on the ground by the pump where he had collapsed in exhaustion. He ran over and knelt beside his son and Fatma saw the boy sit up and bury his soot-stained face in his father's shirt. Osman ran to Nazla, took her hand and looked enquiringly at her. She finally dropped her buckets and leaned against him.

'The house is fine,' she said, her voice muffled by his shirt.

'Are you two alright?' asked Osman, looking at Fatma.

'Just tired and dirty,' she said.

'And thirsty,' added Nazla. 'I'm going to put some tea on!'

The couple went off to check their home and Fatma was left alone. She rubbed her stinging eyes with her headscarf but it only made them worse. The firemen were raking the burnt grass and beating the hot earth. She caught sight of Mehmet, Galip and Communist Ali helping them. She thought she even saw Chetin wielding a spade. Sometimes, she thought, it took an emergency to get people to put aside their differences and work together.

Harun came over, one arm clamped round his son's shoulder. Barish had rubbed his face with his shirt but had only succeeded in spreading the soot in thick streaks across his cheeks. He was holding his arms stiffly out from his sides.

'I hear I have you to thank, Fatma Abla, for saving

this place and keeping everyone safe,' said Harun.

'I couldn't have done it alone,' said Fatma, nodding to Barish. 'And I'm afraid we didn't manage to save everything.'

'Pff!' Harun waved a hand to show how little it mattered. 'We can replace a few chalets. What's important is that nobody was hurt. I'm sorry I wasn't here.'

'You couldn't have known something was going to happen,' said Fatma. 'Now, I think I'll go to the pension and check on my family.'

## 32

Harun looked around at the mess. Over the last few months he had dreamed of building the retreat, seen the place take shape and made it a success. Now the fire had destroyed two chalets, damaged one more and turned the top corner of the orchard into a charred wasteland. The rest of the place was covered in greasy black soot. It would have been quite understandable if he had been feeling glum again.

In fact, he was in remarkably good spirits. The insurance assessor had been out to check the damage and, though he knew he would have to fight for it and they would do everything they could to reduce the amount, he hoped to get a payout fairly swiftly.

He, Zuhal and Barish had lost clothes and some small items but nothing that wasn't replaceable and Osman and Nazla had once more opened their house to them. Barish had spent the night on the cushions in one of the arbours, with a sheet to stop the mosquitoes feasting on him.

There were seven chalets remaining which were enough as two couples had left immediately, traumatised by the fire. Seven were sufficient for the bookings he had for the rest of the summer too and the other chalets could be replaced in the winter.

The head of the forest fire team had told him they had not identified the cause of the fire. He thought it was most likely to have been started by either a shard of glass hidden in the grass or a carelessly discarded cigarette. Sadly, he said, they could not even rule out foul play. He made it clear he did not usually approve of untrained people putting themselves in danger but he acknowledged that the efforts of Fatma, Nazla and Barish had saved the retreat from being completely destroyed, and possibly saved the fire spreading to other homes.

Harun had told his son repeatedly how proud he was of him and asked Zuhal to think of a suitable present for Nazla to thank her for her actions. He couldn't, however, shake a niggling suspicion about Fatma's role in the whole thing.

'Don't you think it was a bit of a coincidence that the fire broke out while she was here?' he asked Zuhal.

'You can't be suggesting Fatma started it herself, Harun? She was with me when the fire was discovered and anyway why would she have put herself in danger trying to put it out if she had started it?'

'I know, it does sound crazy. Given how she feels about the place I don't know why she tried to stop it at all. She could have just let it burn.'

'Perhaps she's finally accepted us.'

'Or perhaps she was feeling guilty.'

At night, back in Osman's daughter's narrow bed,

he had lain and thought about it for some time. In the end he had decided he had to forget his suspicions and hope that Zuhal was right and Fatma's efforts to save the retreat represented a sort of olive branch.

As soon as the insurance assessor had left, everyone had started clearing up. Osman was cutting down burned trees and pruning charred branches and Barish was raking up blackened grass. Buket and Zuhal were washing down windows and tables with buckets of soapy water that turned black as soon as they dipped the cloth back in. Even one of the guests, a young man a little older than Barish, was gathering the burned wood and making a pile at one side of the field. Zuhal had chosen a radio station playing lively pop music and turned it up so there was a sort of party atmosphere. Harun would have joined in himself but there was something important he needed to do.

As he walked along the lane he looked down at the valley. The first time he had seen, it he had been stunned by the magnificent view and by the lush greenness of it. Now, the verdant citrus groves stood out against fields of golden wheat and corn. Women in brightly-coloured clothes swarmed through the fields picking vegetables.

At the Kismet Pension Harun went round to the back and found Fatma sitting alone with a cup of coffee. Melek was clearing away breakfast dishes and Ahmet was putting cushions on the sun beds by the pool.

'Good morning, Fatma Hanum! I hope you slept well after yesterday's drama.'

'I slept very well, thank you, Harun Bey. And

Ahmet and Melek are not letting me do anything today. Shall I ask Melek to make you a coffee?'

'That would be nice. Make it sweet, please.'

In the pool some young people were having a game of volleyball with a piece of string tied to two umbrellas as a makeshift net. They were diving at shots with as much determination as if they had been competing in a national tournament, though there was a lot more yelling and laughter than would have been allowed in a real game.

Harun watched them. 'Your guests look happy.'

'They're a nice family. They stayed here two years ago and came back yesterday,' said Fatma.

Melek arrived with Harun's coffee and a glass of water. He left the coffee to cool and took a sip of the water.

'I want to thank you again for what you did, Fatma Hanum. The firemen said the damage would have been much worse, the retreat could even have been destroyed, if you hadn't acted so quickly. I'm very grateful.'

Fatma looked embarrassed and made a noise that sounded like 'tssk'. 'When there's a fire, everyone has to work together or it can destroy the whole village.'

'I've seen them on the news before but I've never been in the midst of one. Not that I saw much this time – it was all under control when I got back.'

'How's the clearing up going?'

'I've left the others at it. I came here to ask you for another favour,' said Harun. 'Though I realise that might seem a bit much after what you did yesterday. This one's not exactly for me, though.'

Fatma raised one eyebrow.

'You probably know Buket's father is a little unwell…'

'I know Mumtaz Uncle has dug his own grave and goes to sit in it!'

'Apparently he's desperate to see his grandsons circumcised.'

'And how can I help with that?'

'Well you see, I promised Buket we would sort it out. The boys had the thing done yesterday – it's why we were in town. We were supposed to be having the celebration at Kado's Garden the day after tomorrow.'

'And now you're busy cleaning!'

'Yes. And the retreat isn't looking its best. I know you're busy too but I thought perhaps you could hold the party here?'

Fatma sighed and shook her head. For a moment he thought she was going to refuse. 'Harun Bey, I couldn't say no even if I wanted to. My mother is good friends with Buket's mother and would never speak to me again if I didn't help the family. In fact, I'm surprised she hasn't mentioned it already.'

*

After Harun had left, Fatma sat for a while thinking of how suddenly everything had changed. Her body ached with the efforts of the previous day and her eyes were still sore and red but she felt calmer than she had for a while.

The previous evening Melek had told her how proud she was of her and hugged her in a way she had not done for some time. Fatma, her throat scratchy from the smoke, had managed to croak that she was proud of Melek too and it was true; whatever mistakes her daughter had made, she was still a lovely girl. Fatma had given her permission to see Barish on the condition that they would not sneak around anymore. The boy was not all that bad and anyway, she thought, the holiday would soon be over and he would be returning to the city.

Mehmet had returned from the coffee shop where the fire was the only topic of conversation.

'Everyone is talking about how brave you were,' he told her. 'Personally I've always known that,' he said with a cheeky wink and leant over to give her a peck on the cheek.

'Yeah, Mum, my friends were impressed too,' Ahmet added.

Fatma had smiled shyly. She was not used to receiving praise but she quite enjoyed the warm glow it gave her.

She saved the news of Harun's visit and the upcoming party for the evening, when they had finished eating grilled trout with pilau rice and tomato and cucumber salad. Melek cleared the plates and brought out the semolina helva Derya had made, knowing it was Fatma's favourite. She served it onto plates and started to pour tea.

'I hope you're ready for some hard work,' she said, licking the dusting of icing sugar from her fingers. 'We're hosting a sunnet party for Buket's boys the day after tomorrow!'

'That's a bit sudden, isn't it?' asked Ahmet.

'It was supposed to be at the retreat,' said Melek.

Then looked nervous and started picking the golden pine nuts from her plate of helva.

'Yes it was,' said Fatma. 'But given what's happened there, Harun Bey thinks it would be better if we held it here.'

'Latife said he paid for the operation and the boys' outfits,' said Melahat, shaking her head at Harun Bey's generosity. 'But she'll be happy to hear the party will be here. You're very good at organising these things,' she said and Fatma almost choked on her helva.

\*

The next day Melek went to the retreat. She walked along the lane with her head held high, no guilt or nerves to spoil her excitement. It was the first time she had been there since the fire. The bitter smell of charred wood hung in the air and the burnt-out chalets looked stark but the rest of the orchard was just as it had been before. They had done a good job of cleaning up.

Harun and Zuhal were sitting in one of the arbours, talking to Claudia.

'Hello, Melek,' called Zuhal. 'It's nice to see you!'

'Hello Melek, do come and join us,' said Claudia. 'We were talking about what a hero your mother is!' She shuffled along the cushions and patted the space beside her.

'She doesn't want to sit with us!' said Zuhal, smiling. 'He's just up there, still cleaning up,' she said, pointing up the field.

Melek followed her directions and found Barish raking scorched grass and ash behind one of the chalets. His face was shiny and his hair was damp with sweat. Melek thought he had never looked more handsome.

'Hello!' He reached out and touched her arm. 'I would kiss you but I'm a bit dirty!' He leaned his rake against the chalet and led Melek to the arbour furthest from where his parents were sitting. He went into the kitchen and came out with a bottle of water and two glasses. He'd washed his hands and face and he pushed wet fingers through his hair so it stood up. Melek had to stop herself from reaching out and smoothing it down.

'Is your Mum alright about you coming here?' he asked.

'Yes. She seems to have finally accepted your dad.'

'And me?'

'You too. I'm allowed to see you, as long as there are other people around.'

'Was it my fire fighting skills that impressed her?'

'It must have been. They impressed me too,' said Melek, giggling. 'What's going to happen to the retreat? Is your Dad going to get new chalets?'

'He says he might build stone cottages for next year.'

'So he's going to carry on?'

'Oh yes. He loves it here.'

'And,' Melek fiddled with the edge of the table cloth, 'will you be back?'

'Of course. We'll keep in touch by phone and email and see each other again next year. I'll miss you though, Melek.'

Melek felt her heart lurch. 'I'll miss you too.'

\*

The day before the party the little red car refused to start. Fatma watched Mehmet poking dispiritedly at the engine.

'It's no good, Fatma,' he said, 'You'll have to find someone else to do the shopping. I have to wait for Abdi to come up from the garage and fix this.'

Fatma rang Harun and explained that they had car trouble.

'I have to stay here today, Fatma Hanum; the insurance assessor is coming again. You're welcome to take the truck though. Ahmet can drive, can't he?'

Ahmet was thrilled with the chance to drive the big, shiny truck. Fatma was less thrilled. She made him promise to drive slowly and as he set off with Melek and Barish she said a prayer for their safety – and that of the smart, black truck. She was helping Derya change sheets when she heard the sound of the engine and looked out to see them returning.

The three youngsters tumbled out of the cabin. Barish jumped onto the back of the truck and started hefting the bags of shopping and crates of drink to where Ahmet and Melek could reach them. They were laughing together and Fatma thought how good it was to see her daughter happy again.

When they had finished making the bed, Fatma and Derya went down to the kitchen and found Melek sorting the shopping. The three of them spent the afternoon making food for the party. They boiled fava beans and mashed them with dill and plenty of seasoning; grated boiled beetroot into thick, creamy yogurt, turning it lurid pink; charred aubergine and peppers; mixed shredded chicken with breadcrumbs, walnuts and plenty of garlic for Circassian chicken. They left the liver for the following day when it would be chopped into pieces, floured and fried in the Albanian way. Harun had insisted on paying for the party even if he could not host it and he had provided a generous budget.

The kitchen was hot and when they had finished Fatma was glad to step outside. The sun had slipped behind the mountain and the shadows were stretching across the valley. The air was not exactly cool but it was pleasant. There had been no time to cook dinner for the guests so they served some of the meze they had prepared while Mehmet went down to the restaurant on the main road to get Turkish flatbread topped with spicy lamb and egg. The mechanic had managed to fix the red car but had said that with an engine that age and that had done that sort of service they were likely to have problems more and more frequently.

Over dinner, Ahmet raved about Harun's truck. 'You're so high up, you feel like the king of the road!' he said. 'And you don't have to jam it into gear – it slips from one to the other as easily as…a spoon through yogurt!' he said, helping himself to more beetroot tarator. 'Even the steering is light. You could steer with your little finger!'

'Well I hope you didn't!' Fatma snapped. But to herself she thought perhaps it was time to get a new vehicle – something a little grander and more fitting for the pension. They could manage with the little red car for now and look for something the following spring.

\*

Melek woke with a start. In her dream she and Barish were lying on the beach but this time as he kissed her his hand slid over her wet body. Even awake her skin tingled with his touch and there were stirrings in places she had never felt before.

She dressed and went round to the pension where her mother was fussing about whether the meze would be sufficient. The guests from both the pension and the retreat had been invited on top of all Buket's guests and Fatma estimated there would be close to a hundred and fifty people at the party. Melek reassured her mother that the things they had prepared would be sufficient since they were to be followed by a large quantity of lamb slow-roasted in the stone oven down at the restaurant and two large pans of rice that Derya, who was renowned for making the best pilau, would cook with pine nuts, tiny currants and plenty of cinammon.

A truck arrived with tables and chairs and Melek helped her father and Ahmet arrange them, with a long table on one side for the buffet and as many as could be squeezed into the space between the pool and the bar for the guests to sit at. They had borrowed plates and cutlery from the retreat and the beach restaurant and Melek set these out on the buffet table. She was going to find a cloth to protect them from the swallows but looking up she realised the nest was empty; the birds had left for their winter home.

*

The first to arrive was Buket with her parents and the two boys. The boys were not yet dressed in their finery.

'I know them too well!' Buket told Fatma. 'If I dress them now, by the time everyone arrives they'll have dirtied their trousers and torn their cloaks, not to mention broken their staffs using them as swords as I caught them doing yesterday. I'll get them ready when the guests start arriving.'

Mesut pulled up shortly after and Fatma followed Hilal into the house where she greeted Melahat and proceeded with a list of complaints that included the heat and her various aches and pains. Fatma changed into her party clothes – a pink top and a pair of trousers with pink and green flowers. The three women made their way round to the pension and Melahat and Hilal sat at a table with Latife.

The guests started to drift in and were greeted at the entrance by Buket and her parents flanked by the boys, who had been squeezed into shirts, trousers, fur-trimmed capes and jewel-studded hats. Hot and grumpy, they waved their staffs at each other and at the arrivals, desperate to be released to run around and play. Zuhal and Barish arrived with the guests from Kado's Garden. The Kismet guests came down from their rooms to join the party. Claudia looked particularly fine in a long, orange skirt and a sparkly silver top.

The days were getting shorter and lights were already twinkling down in the valley as Melek and her mother carried the meze from the kitchen and laid them out on the buffet table. The guests needed no encouragement and plates were heaped with food, glasses filled with cola and fanta. At the table in the corner where Mumtaz Baba was sitting there were several bottles of raki. He had told everyone who would listen how delighted he was to see his grandsons become men. The event had even had restorative powers since he appeared to have rallied and was no longer talking about dying.

Harun arrived accompanied by the irresistible smell of tender-cooked lamb and the guests forgot what was left of the meze and formed a queue at the table where Melek was dishing up the pilau and Fatma was serving the meat.

Once the important business of eating was over and the tables and chairs had been pushed to one side the band started up. A line of people formed holding hands, stepping in time and turning in a slow circle. Claudia was quick to join in, concentrating on counting the steps and on keeping up, laughing as freely as she had when she first arrived in the village. The circle turned faster and faster until the dancers were leaping and kicking and some of the older ones had to sit down and catch their breath.

Four Bulgarian boys who had been at the Kismet for a few days and were leaving the next morning to continue driving along the coast joined in with the halay dance, then insisted Ahmet put on some Bulgarian music so they could show their dancing skills. The other guests stood around clapping as the boys demonstrated a dance with intricate steps and a lot of energy.

Buket was sitting with her mother, her eyes shining with tears and her blouse shining with gold coins pinned there by the guests as gifts for her sons. The two boys were running round pretending to be superheroes, their capes flying behind them and their hats perched rakishly on their heads. Nazla's younger daughters had tried to join in their game but Fatma had heard them insisting only men could be superheroes. She had considered correcting them but it did not seem the time or the place.

Melek was at the bar deep in conversation with Barish. Leyla was sitting with her anxious mother who Fatma had made a point of welcoming and seating with Nazla. Demir dragged a protesting Dudu up to dance, appearing to have forgotten the humiliation of his last visit to the pension.

Fatma joined her mother and sister at the table. Her limbs still ached from the unaccustomed activity of hauling buckets of water and pumping water spigots, and the effort of preparing for the party had tired her further. Still, she felt happier than she had for some time. The Kismet Pension was still thriving and would continue to do so for many years if she had her way.

# Author's note

The Kismet Pension and the residents of Ortakoy have lived in my head for a long time and I am so happy to finally be able to send them out into the world. Thank you to all the people who encouraged me to keep writing and to get the book published.

I hope you enjoyed reading it. If you have a moment to spare, I would appreciate a short review on the page where you bought the book. Reviews help spread the word and enable new readers to find the book.

Watch out for the second book in the series, that follows another summer at the Kismet Pension and will be published later this year.

You can find more of my writing on my website www.melanieanngilbert.com where you can sign up for my newsletter and receive an exclusive short story.

You can also follow me here:
Facebook: Melanieanngilbertauthor
Instagram: @melanieanngilbert

*Melanie*

# About the author

Melanie grew up in England but has lived more than half her life in the Mediterranean region of Turkey. She loves the scenery, culture and history of her adopted country and sets most of her writing there.

She has run a hotel and taught English to locals and Turkish to expats. These days, she gets to spend more time writing. She also loves to go out hiking in the mountains and exploring ancient ruins. Luckily, there are plenty of these in Turkey!

Printed in Great Britain
by Amazon